UNDER SCRUTINY

"Harmless?" He glared at her. "I jumped in that ice water and could have broken my neck and you say. . . ." He seemed to lose the thought as his gaze stilled on her face. Then ever so slowly, moved to her breasts.

Looking down, Lyddie found her wet cotton camisole was transparent. Chilled, her nipples stood out like ripe raspberries.

Blushing furiously, she crossed her arms over her breasts. But her eyes were drawn to his body. His wet shirt was almost as transparent as her camisole and stretched across his wide shoulders, delineating the muscles of his chest. As her gaze lingered on him, Nick said, his voice low and husky, "You blushed when I did that."

Gasping, her gaze flew back to his face. His brown eyes darkened to ebony. A slow smile curved one side of his mouth as he took a half step nearer.

"No."

"No what?"

Nick placed a finger under Lyddie's chin, and she forgot about the bone-chilling water swirling around her thighs. She forgot all the reasons she should run to the bushes and get into her dress and petticoats. She felt paralyzed by the simple contact. And, lord help her, she liked the feeling. She liked it a lot.

Nick moved closer still, and she leaned toward him in silent acquiescence. His mouth came down, hot and hungry, on hers.

PRAISE FOR *GAMBLER'S GOLD*!

"Tori Light's unique characters will linger in your mind long after you've finished *Gambler's Gold.* This book will definitely put Ms. Light on your Automatic Buy list!"

—*Word Museum*

"Delightfully funny, with some of the most charming characters you've yet to meet. A true gem!"

—*Romance and Friends*

"This quirky cast of characters makes this book a definite must read. I laughed until my sides ached."

—*Word Weavers*

"*Gambler's Gold*—what a find! Tori Light's saucy, sexy style is irresistible from beginning to end!"

—Susan Grant, bestselling author of *The Star King*

"*Gambler's Gold* is a wonderful, hot Americana romance with charm and heart. The characters sparkle, and Tori Light's brand of humor is priceless. I'm still laughing!"

—Jillian Hart, author of *Montana Man*

"Tori Light has a wicked sense of humor and a deft hand with romance, so don't miss the wild and wonderful mix in *Gambler's Gold.*"

—Patricia Lucas White, award-winning author of *P.S. I've Taken a Lover*

GAMBLER'S GOLD

TORI LIGHT

LEISURE BOOKS NEW YORK CITY

There are some teachers for whom their job is not just a means to a paycheck, but a vocation. This book is dedicated to Nelda Sullivan Moore, who is such a teacher.

A LEISURE BOOK®

May 2001

Published by

Dorchester Publishing Co., Inc.
276 Fifth Avenue
New York, NY 10001

Cover Art by John Ennis
www.ennisart.com

ISBN 0-8439-4868-X

Printed in the United States of America.

GAMBLER'S GOLD

A LETTER TO MY READERS:

Hot dang! This was a fun book to write. I have been to many of the places I described, like the twins falls and the lazy clear-water creek. These still live fondly in my childhood memories. And the characters in *Gambler's Gold* seem to take on a life of their own—Bobbie June, by the way, is already scheming to get her own story.

I love to hear from readers. You'll find me on the web at my alter ego's site:
http//sites.netscape.net/victoriadark/homepage. Or you may write to me at:

Tori Light
P.O. Box 250
Neely, MS 39461

Chapter One

A gray squirrel chattered high in a pine tree, as though offended by the fumes rising from the big, black cast-iron pot. Squinting against the brightness of the day, Lydia Elizabeth Seaton looked up as the animal peeked around a limb. She didn't blame it. The noxious fumes offended her, too.

"Making soap isn't my idea of fun, either," she grumbled.

A spot between her shoulder blades ached from stirring and her lower back screamed from bending forward to keep her skirts away from the fire under the pot. But the mixture of red oak ashes, water, and lard was at last beginning to bubble and blend together. Soon, it would start to thicken and she could pour it into pans and leave it to cool. After it hardened she'd cut the soap into squares, and there'd be laundry and dish soap for Gentleman John's Hotel for another couple of months.

A pinecone bounced on the hard-packed path beside her, then rolled down the hill and into the spring bubbling from beneath the moss-covered bluff.

"Hey, watch out, will you." Lyddie looked up.

Whiskers twitching, the squirrel looked back at her.

"Who you talking to, Lye-Beth?" A tiny, silver-haired figure appeared between the wild mulberry shrubs at the top of the path.

"You know I hate that nickname, Gram." Lyddie took up her paddle and gave the pot's contents a hard swirl.

"That's why it gets your attention right fast," her grandmother chuckled, looking around. "Talking to yourself, eh? Not a good habit, that. Someone might think you're peculiar."

"Peculiar?" Lyddie stared at the old lady. "In our family? I'd have to stand on a washtub to even begin to stand out."

Gram made her way down the sandy path, using a walking stick fashioned from a gnarled limb of a huckleberry bush to hold holly branches and yaupons out of her way. Despite her seventy-odd years and patched dress, Gram moved with regal grace. "Point taken," the old lady conceded. "How's that soap coming?"

Gram stopped beside the big black washpot and fished her corncob pipe out of her apron pocket, then tapped it against her cane, knocking out the cold ashes.

"It will be ready soon." Lyddie brushed damp tendrils back from her forehead.

"You know, Lye-Beth, you ought to want to get married."

Though accustomed to her grandmother's abrupt changes of topic, Lyddie raised her brows, taken by surprise at this one. She focused on the witch's brew in the washpot and stirred energetically. "That's a fine idea.

Who should I leave in charge of the hotel when I do? Hortense, maybe?"

"Ack, I should say not. She'd run off with the first dry-goods drummer to come along."

"True." Lyddie rolled her head to ease the ache in her shoulders. "Molly, then. She's got a fine mind."

"No, not Molly. The girl's daft for doctoring. She'd never look up from her medical books if the whole place burned down around her ears."

"True, again." Lyddie nodded. "Well, that only leaves the twins. Bobbie June and Billy Fred are still a little young, but you have to admit they have a talent for turning a profit."

Eyeing Lyddie with a horrified expression, Gram crossed herself—though she'd turned Methodist more than fifty years before. "God, those two hellions would have the front parlor converted into a gaming den. Their Grandfather John's blood, God rest his soul, runs thick in their veins. And I guess you heard the sheriff asking them about that damage to the railroad tracks down below the creek where the Number Twenty-two derailed last week? Heaven only knows what that pair have been up to."

"Heaven, or slightly warmer regions." Lyddie stirred the pot. "And then there's the slight matter of me already having a husband." On record, she added silently.

"That might be a sticking point," Gram allowed thoughtfully.

"Might be."

"Funny, him disappearing like that." The old lady lifted a gray brow.

"Strange, one might say." Lyddie met her grandmother's gaze levelly. They had never spoken directly about what had befallen Lyddie's husband. Lyddie wasn't certain she wanted to know, and her husband, resting at the bottom of an abandoned well in the corner of the yard, didn't show much interest in how he came to be there.

Gram sucked on her empty pipe, then frowned at the cold bowl. "Anyway, you better run see to the gentleman. It's trouble he's bringing, I'm thinking, for all that he's the finest thing I've seen to look at in nigh' on twenty years."

Lyddie frowned. "What gentleman?"

"The gentleman waiting to check into the hotel, of course. You know I can't write where it can be read. I left him at the front desk while I came to find you. But Hortense is bound to have sniffed him out by now. She'll be right hard to keep away from this one."

"Why didn't you say so?" Lyddie thrust the paddle into Gram's hands. "Stir—it's almost done."

Catching up her worn skirts, Lyddie trudged up the shady path, through the hotel's back door, and into the kitchen. Jane, the cook, was busy chopping a carrot, her long knife clattering like a Gatling gun.

"You better rescue the poor man." The cook, a former slave, never looked up. Her knife didn't miss a whack. "He's the first paying customer we've seen this month."

Lyddie loosened her sunbonnet strings and used the cotton like a handkerchief, wiping the perspiration from her face as she headed for the lobby. But pushing through the door, she stopped short. For there on the Turkey carpet before the registration desk stood the most beautiful man in existence. An auburn-haired Adonis in a Sears and Roebuck suit, his flat-crowned hat resting on the desk.

Tall and broad-shouldered, he stood frowning as he gazed at the crossed cavalry sabers on the wall behind the desk—much to Hortense's irritation, Lyddie didn't doubt, as Hortense was propped on the registration desk in a way that made her neckline fall open, showing her ample charms.

He was downright noble, Lyddie decided, to work so hard at not looking.

As she spotted Lyddie, Hortense's face screwed up as though she'd bitten into a quince. Straightening her shoulders, she rang the desk bell imperiously. "There you are, girl. Come here."

Lyddie looked behind her to see who had come in. She then realized Hortense was summoning her. Oh, there would be retribution for this, she promised her sister silently.

"Mr. Brown—Nicholas . . ." Hortense caressed each syllable in the name. "After you sign the register I'll show you to our finest room. The girl will bring your bag."

Narrowing her gaze, Lyddie thrust her sunbonnet into the pocket of her apron and started forward. "Hortense, when you smile and bat your eyelashes like that, you look like a frog choking down a too-large dragonfly."

As Nick Brown turned away and coughed, Hortense's already mottled complexion achieved a full and glorious tomato hue. "Why, I . . . I never!"

Grasping the handle of the carpetbag, Lyddie murmured, "I kind of doubt that."

After another brief bout of coughing, Nicholas Brown signed his name with a flourish and slipped his room key into an inner pocket of his coat. "I'll get the bag," he told Lyddie. "But if you would send someone to the depot for my trunk, I would be grateful."

She was taken aback by the light of male interest in

his coffee brown eyes. His gaze slipped over her, warming where it touched.

"We'll take care of it," Hortense answered for her sister and flipped a hand at Lyddie in a shooing gesture. "Off with you, then. Go get Mr. Brown's trunk while I just show Nicholas to Gentleman John's suite." Looking at Nicholas, she did her frog impression again.

The twins appeared at the landing and bounced down the stairs, as always, reminding Lyddie of a pair of beagle pups. She'd seen them leave the hotel at daybreak, one carrying a pickax and the other a shovel. She wondered what they were up to. Then decided she really didn't want to know—as long as neither was hurt and no one's property was damaged.

"We heard and we'll get your trunk, mister," Billy Fred said, obviously scenting a tip.

"Sure thing!" Bobbie—Barbara June—dressed in the same type of loose shirt and rough overalls as her brother, followed on Billy Fred's heels as he dashed across the room and through the front door.

"No, don't trouble yourself to show Mr. Brown up to his room, Hortense. Seeing to the guests is my job," Lyddie said sweetly. "I wouldn't think of you leaving your post at the desk. Yesterday you did say Frank Worley is coming back today from his trip to Jackson. I'll just bet he was on this train."

Turning to the tall man at her side, Lyddie said, "Frank Worley is as big as a bull and extremely jealous, seeing as he and Hortense are practically engaged. If you'll follow me, please?"

She preceded him up the stairs, noticing as she rounded the first landing that Frank Worley was coming in the front door, as she'd predicted. Hortense, who had long mooned over the timber foreman, crossed her arms over her chest and gave the poor man a damning look.

"I take it that is Worley. And your mistress looks none too happy to see him."

Lyddie realized Nick Brown had mistaken her for the servant Hortense had pretended she was. She shook her head and started to correct the wrong impression. "I . . ."

The light of male interest was still in his eyes, and Lyddie clamped her mouth shut. Most men thought serving girls were fair game. Evidently Mr. Brown did, too, even though he'd avoided looking at Hortense's charms as steadfastly as Lot facing away from Sodom and Gomorrah.

And all she could think of was how long it had been since she felt a man's arms around her.

"You don't want to tell tales on your employers. I understand. I shouldn't have asked." He gave her another of those bone-melting smiles.

Lyddie looked away and marched briskly down the hall, unwilling to be swayed by his charm. She had learned a hard lesson in her short marriage, but she had learned it well—she couldn't trust her feelings where men were concerned.

Lyddie took a ring of keys from her apron pocket and unlocked the door, then preceded Nick Brown into the room. Going to the window, she spread open the drapes. Sunlight streamed into the room as she swung open the French-style windows and let in fresh air.

Crossroads' Main Street, lined by a half-dozen facaded shops, was visible just beyond the hotel's frontyard. At the edge of the tiny town were a livery stable and the train station. She saw Billy Fred and Bobbie June disappear into the depot building. It occurred to her that if Nick Brown wanted his trunk fetched, he was prepared to stay a while. Most people left their heavier luggage at the station if they were just waiting for a train out in a few hours, or even the next day.

The thought was an intriguing one. Why? Why would a man like Nicholas Brown be visiting Crossroads for an extended period of time? The hotel's main clientele was travelers simply staying the night before boarding another train. Or fortune hunters come to find Gentleman John's treasure. She hoped he didn't fit into the latter category. Men were undependable in general, but fortune hunters were the most untrustworthy of the lot.

Nick set his valise on the bed and opened it.

"I'll unpack that for you." Lyddie hurried to the bedside.

"I'll take care of it. Thank you, anyway." His coffee-brown eyes took her measure again. "Have you been here long?"

"Forever." Lyddie caught back a sigh.

"Did you know this Gentleman John?" He took a small cloth-bound book and pencil out of his bag.

"Not really." Lyddie had been only four when he died. "But Gram—Mrs. Moreland—was his wife. She would be glad to tell you about him, if you're interested." Gentleman John was quite a legend. A lot of folks were curious and wanted to hear the stories of his travels and the big card games he'd been in up and down the Mississippi.

As Nick opened the book, Lyddie saw with surprise that it was a book of blank paper, like the diary Hortense kept. As Nick made a note about his time of arrival at Crossroads, she looked on and wondered what the man was up to.

"Are you one of those magazine writers? We had one staying here last winter. Did a piece for the *Overland Review.*" The reporter had been supercilious, full of long-winded stories, and had waxed his mustache. Lyddie caught him trying to sneak into Hortense's room in the middle of the night.

"So, Gentleman John Moreland did build this hotel. He must have been quite a character, according to the stories I heard on the train." Looking into her eyes, Nick smiled again. Lyddie had the feeling he knew exactly what effect it had on her. "You know, you really are too pretty to be working as a maid."

Realizing just how close they were, and how Nick Brown seemed to purposefully initiate that closeness, she took a hasty step back. "I'll bring a pitcher of water for the basin." Lyddie hurried away.

What in the name of Sam Hill was wrong with her, anyway? she wondered as she escaped. She was acting as silly as Hortense!

The room door was open when she returned with the water. The twins had arrived with Nick's trunk, and Billy Fred was trying hard to ingratiate himself, offering to fetch this and that. Bobbie June wandered around the room, as though taking inventory of the gentleman's possessions.

Lyddie cocked an eyebrow at Bobbie June, who quickly stilled, an angelically innocent expression wreathing her lightly freckled face.

"Just leave any boots you need polished outside the door. I do the best spit polish south of the Mason-Dixon. And if you need to know where anything is in town, I'd be glad to show you," Billy Fred said.

"I was thinking of finding a barbershop."

"I'll show you. It's down Main Street, behind the mercantile. Old Jim does tooth-pulling, too. He ain't got much of a sign. You might walk right by it, if you don't let me take you there."

"Hasn't much of a sign," Lyddie corrected, setting the

pitcher of fresh water on the washstand. She hung the towel she'd brought on the bar. "Aren't you two supposed to help Jane in the kitchen about now?"

This remark earned her sour looks. "But Mr. Brown might need something, Lyddie," Billy Fred protested.

Nick turned from the window and quirked an amused brow at the boy. "You could tell me about Gentleman John's treasure."

Billy Fred exchanged a startled look with his twin, then rammed his hands deep in the pockets of his overalls. "Shucks, if you want to waste your time chasing that old gold, I got a sure-fire map I'll sell you."

"That wouldn't be right, Billy Fred," Bobbie June said. "You know there isn't any treasure, and that old map's so worthless, it's only good for the outhouse."

So that was it, Lyddie thought, disappointed. Nick Brown was just a treasure hunter. From the way he carried himself and the smooth way he spoke, she'd thought he must be more—a man of business perhaps, or a railroad official.

"Why don't you two tell Mr. Brown the real secret of Gentleman John's treasure?" Lyddie usually kept the truth to herself, to keep the treasure hunters at the hotel as long as possible. But disappointed that Nick was like the rest—like her husband—she didn't care if he stayed or left.

The twins slid a wary look at each other.

"Ain't—isn't any secret to the gold," Bobbie June said firmly.

Smoothing out a wrinkle in the bedspread, Lyddie shook her head. "The real gold is in the legend, you see. We have several treasure seekers stay with us every year. The mercantile sells a goodly amount of pickaxes, shovels, and compasses. And the newspaper prints maps and sells them through ads around the country."

Nick grinned and reached into his inside coat pocket, drawing a paper and unfolding it. "Like this map?"

Looking at it, Lyddie nodded. "So you came to town just to find Gentleman John's gold."

"I bought this from the train porter." He returned it to his pocket. "Actually, I'm with the Pinkerton Detective Agency. I'm here to investigate the recent acts of vandalism and sabotage to railroad property."

Chapter Two

Utter quiet followed this intelligence.

Lyddie stared at Nick Brown.

"A Pinkerton man," Billy Fred breathed reverently, breaking the silence. "I always wanted to meet me a real live Pinkerton man—*ugh!*"

Bobbie June cut her twin off with an elbow in his stomach.

"Ow! Whatcha do that—"

"You know, we'd better get down and help Jane." Grabbing Billy Fred's overall bib, Bobbie June yanked him toward the door.

"Wait."

The twins froze at Nick's one-word command. Slowly, they turned. Two faces dusted with freckles and framed by dark brown hair showed a mix of emotions, with trepidation at the forefront.

Lyddie studied each in turn and wondered what the

two had been up to now, though she wasn't at all certain she wanted to know.

"Here. Thanks for being careful with the trunk." Fishing in his vest pocket, Nick came out with coins and flipped one to each of them. They caught the money in midair.

"A two-bit piece!" Bobbie June gasped.

"Thanks!" Billy Fred pocketed his coin as they scampered out of the door.

"Nick Brown . . . Sounds like a made-up name to me. Why would a real Pinkerton man need a made-up name?" Sitting cross-legged on her bed, Bobbie June threw her thick, dark braid over her shoulder and glowered at her twin as if he should supply the answer.

"Sounds like just a common old name to me." Billy Fred shrugged.

Bobbie June paid this piece of unimaginative babble not the least bit of attention. She frowned, tapping her cheek thoughtfully. "Maybe he's really an outlaw, not a Pinkerton!" That was a much more exciting possibility.

Billy Fred shook his head. "Not likely. I saw him writing in a notebook, just like real Pinkertons do in the dime novels."

Sighing in disappointment, his twin said, "Well, anyway, if we can find out why he's got a made-up name, we can use that to bargain with if he finds out it was us that damaged the rails by Myers Creek."

"We didn't mean to derail that train," Billy Fred protested. "It was an accident. Number Twenty-two shouldn't a been ahead of schedule. We'd a had the spikes drove back in if it hadn't been ahead of schedule."

"Not meaning to won't count for spit in hell if Nick Brown finds out it was us that took the spikes out of the rails." She shook her head. "Of course, it wasn't a big derailing—just the engine run off the tracks in the dirt for a ways. Not like it went into the creek or anything. It had a full ten feet to go before it woulda run off the bluff." She took consolation in this fact.

"What I'm thinking is, a real Pinkerton man'll find the gold before we can." Billy Fred scratched his bare foot, then tapped the top sheet of several yellowed pieces of paper on the bed between them. The paper was covered in cryptic directions in their Grandfather John's handwriting. After finding the sheets in an old book in the study, the pair had decided it was directions to the hidden gold.

"I told you, I don't think Brown is a real Pinkerton man."

"But if he is," Billy Fred insisted, "if he is, our gold is as good as found."

As much as she hated to give her twin credit for any worthwhile thinking, Bobbie June nodded at the possible truth of this. She chewed a fingernail, then brightened. "Let's say that he is the real thing—for now. Better to overestimate your enemy than underestimate him. Did you see how old Pinkerton looked at Lye-Beth? She wasn't looking back—she's a lot smarter than Hortense. Well, Lye-Beth's gotten smarter since Bowler Hat ran off the night they got married. But if we could get Pinkerton to looking at Lye-Beth and her to looking back, they'd keep each other plum occupied and not have time to watch us too close. That way, we'd have a chance to decipher these maps and find the gold."

"I don't think it'll be easy to get her to look. I think she's still mooning for old Bowler Hat. That's why she didn't notice Pinkerton."

"Yeah, Bowler Hat sure did like to break Lye-Beth's heart clean in two, taking off right after she married him and all. I don't think she's laughed since," Bobbie June acknowledged. "But if we could get her and Pinkerton to start noticing each other . . . You know, Lye-Beth's always been the biggest obstacle to our looking for the gold. No matter where we begin to look, she's always watching us like a blue-darter hawk eyeing a brood of new biddies. She's always asking us what we're up to. Heck, you'd think she didn't trust us."

"I still say the gold's buried right in the lobby, under where the big chandelier hangs." Billy Fred tapped what looked like a chandelier drawn on the paper, amid tantalizing directions such as "25' l. by 35' w."

Bobbie June ignored her brother's lack of ability to grasp what was obviously a code and would take careful deciphering. She brought his attention back to the problem at hand. "Maybe it would be enough if we could just get them in the same place at the same time now and again. Then Lye-Beth might start to notice the Pinkerton man, like he notices her."

"Works with Hortense real easy," Billy Fred said.

"Like I said, Lye-Beth's a lot smarter than Hortense. But maybe . . ." Bobbie June smiled as the idea took root and she envisioned the pair staring raptly into each other's eyes—as she and Billy Fred had another go at deciphering their grandfather's instructions and digging up the gold.

Recognizing the far-off look on his twin's face, Billy Fred waited as Bobbie June made her plan. They were always real interesting and inventive plans, even if they usually got him in trouble up to his ears.

As Lyddie entered Bobbie June's attic bedroom a few minutes later, two determinedly innocent faces greeted her.

"Hi, Lye-Beth!" Bobbie June chirped, folding some papers.

"Hi, Sis," Billy Fred said. "You look pretty."

Lyddie looked down at her work-stained apron. "I'd ask what the two of you have been up to . . ." Looking from one lightly freckled face to the other, she paused, allowing time for a confession. None was forthcoming. "But if I knew, I probably wouldn't like it," she finished on a sigh.

"No need to get that sour-faced look. We aren't doing anything wrong, or illegal," Bobbie June assured her.

Lyddie wondered how *wrong* and *illegal* came to be separated in her sister's mind. "I know you never mean to, Bobbie June." And she knew it hadn't been easy for the twins, growing up without a mother or a father. It was little wonder they were always looking for something, she thought, feeling she'd failed them somehow.

She ran her fingers through Billy Fred's unruly curls. "It's time for supper. You two come on down. You have to help me protect Nick from Hortense."

"Nick, is it?" Bobbie June grinned.

"Mr. Brown, I mean." Lyddie's cheeks warmed.

"C'mon, Billy Fred, we have to protect Nick from Hortense." Bobbie June bounced out of the door. "So Lye-Beth can have him all to herself!" she called from the hallway.

Billy Fred laughed and ran to catch up.

"I don't . . ." Her protests falling on empty air, Lyddie shook her head and turned to the mirror over the bureau and checked her hair. Nick Brown was just another traveler, staying at the hotel. He planned to be gone in a week, Hortense had reported. And that would be that.

Lyddie pulled an unruly wisp forward and wound it around her finger, creating a side curl. Liking the effect, she made another on the other side. Then pulled off her soiled apron.

He'd be gone, so she wasn't worried about impressing him. She pinched her cheeks.

Downstairs in the family dining room, Lyddie sat on the other side of the table from Nick Brown. And was far too aware of the fact that he barely looked her way. Well, why on earth would she want him looking at her? Just because he was as attractive as sin and well-spoken?

Sipping her milk, she consoled herself with the fact that he was paying little attention to Hortense, either. Instead, he directed most of his conversation to Gram.

"Would you like more mashed potatoes, Mr. Brown? I declare, Jane does make the best mashed potatoes I've ever tasted." Leaning forward, Hortense held the bowl toward Nick, smiling sweetly.

"No. Thank you." Nick turned to Gram and gave the old woman one of his bone-melting smiles. "Would you care for more, Mrs. Moreland?"

"No, no. M'liver isn't as young as it was. Can't handle too much heavy food."

"Gram!" Hortense turned pink, her gaze flying to Nick's face. "One does not discuss one's . . . *organs* at the supper table. Particularly not when we're having . . . organs." She grew redder. "Calf's liver, that is."

Lyddie watched in silence. Nick Brown had seemed upset with her when they'd all arrived at the table and Gram had revealed that Lyddie was her granddaughter, not just a housemaid. It wasn't as though she had set out to deliberately mislead him. Still, maybe that was why he'd had little to say to her during the meal.

Well, that was just fine with her. Fine and jim-dandy. Lyddie stabbed a carrot with her fork. As far as the world was concerned, she had a husband, she reminded herself, noticing the strong line of Nick's jaw and the chiseled mouth.

"I'll take more potatoes." Billy Fred commandeered the bowl from Hortense and served himself.

"Pass it here after you finish," Bobbie June told her twin.

At Nick's other side, Molly looked up from the anatomy book she held propped on the edge of the table. "Calf liver looks very similar to human liver, but just a little larger and heavier, of course." Absently forking a piece of liver into her mouth, Molly sank back into her book.

With a horrified look at her younger sister, Hortense spluttered, "We do have a guest!"

Nick said, "If I've imposed by asking to eat with the family rather than dine by myself in the hotel dining room, forgive me. I didn't mean to intrude."

"Oh, no! I mean, why, it would have been plain inhospitable to make you dine there all alone." Hortense tried valiantly to regain her composure. "But I should have kept you company in the dining room. I fear my family is rather plainspoken and backward." This last with a scathing glance at Molly.

Lyddie rolled her eyes heavenward. It was a good thing Gram had the foresight to place herself between Hortense and Nick Brown.

Nick touched his napkin to his lips. "Not at all. I like this family atmosphere, not having one of my own. And yours is a very interesting family. Gentleman John must have been quite a character. I heard stories about him from when I stepped aboard the train at Memphis until I got off here at Crossroads."

"Stories about the gold, you mean." Gram cocked a gray brow, studying the man shrewdly.

"Yes, naturally. But though there are stories a plenty, no one, it seems, has a clue as to why he reportedly hid the gold. Five thousand dollars, wasn't it?"

Lyddie wasn't surprised by Nick's interest. Disappointed, yes. Surprised, no. Every man she'd ever met, except her father, was interested in the gold.

Gram tilted her head to one side and squinted through her half-lensed glasses. "Seems that you look some'ot familiar, young man. Have we met before?"

"No. I would remember such a regal lady as yourself. And I've never been to this town before. However, I have done a great deal of traveling in my job. Perhaps you saw me somewhere else?"

"I've not left Crossroads since I buried my John here twenty years ago."

"I'm sorry for your loss." Nick looked sincere.

"It must be ever so exciting, detecting crimes." Hortense touched his arm, drawing his attention back to her. She leaned toward Nick and scooped up his attention with her neckline.

"Actually, I detect clues that help to solve crimes."

"Silly me." Hortense giggled and batted her eyelashes in her best frog imitation. She had it about down pat, Lyddie decided.

Sipping her milk, Lyddie aimed a kick beneath the table at her sister. She felt the toe of her shoe connect satisfyingly with flesh and bone.

As Nick Brown jumped and looked around the table, Lyddie gasped, realizing her mistake. Damn, the man had long legs!

Her swallow of milk went down the wrong way. Coughing into her napkin, Lyddie struggled to draw breath. The twins looked on in consternation, but Molly came around the table at once and stoutly thumped her between the shoulders until the spasms passed.

Pressing her napkin to her mouth, her eyes watering, Lyddie looked up to find everyone's gaze focused on her. There was laughter in one pair of handsome coffee-brown eyes.

Ignoring Molly's concerned questions, Lyddie pushed back her chair and sought sanctuary in the kitchen.

No one came after her. Well, why should Nick Brown bother? He was just a guest at the hotel, and interested more in Gentleman John's gold than in her. And she had kicked him under the table.

After tying on an apron, Lyddie busied herself helping Agnes, their maid-of-all-work, wash the pots used to cook supper.

Later, after the maid and Lyddie finished the dishes and cut the soap she had made that morning into squares, she wandered out into the cool night air and sat in the porch swing. Looking up at the stars, she swung gently and wondered what her life would have been like if Gerald Seaton had been all the things she'd thought he was when she'd married him. They could have been in San Francisco, sitting together, holding hands. Or New Orleans . . .

Shaking her head, Lyddie put a foot down to stop the swing. Thinking about what ifs was a waste of time. Things were like they were and nothing was going to change them.

The night was pleasantly cool after the heat of the June day. The moist air held the soft scent of the roses blooming on the side fence. From somewhere in the dark grass a cricket shrilled. The twins' voices drifted out from within the hotel as they helped Molly with her studies, asking her questions from some medical text.

Lyddie sat there until, one by one, the lights went out in town and in the hotel, making the twinkling stars seem even brighter and nearer. And she felt as isolated as the bright points of light.

"May I join you?"

The deep timbre of Nick's voice flowed over her like the cool night breeze. Lyddie gazed into the shadows of the French windows, making out the tall male silhouette, and she pulled her shawl tighter across her chest.

"Certainly." Well, what else was she supposed to say? she wondered. After kicking him beneath the table, she didn't have the heart to treat him coolly.

To her surprise, he passed up the ladder-back rockers along the wall and sat on the swing beside her, his thigh almost touching hers.

She stared at it, imaging she could feel the heat emanating from it. Well, she had said he could join her, hadn't she? She just hadn't realized he meant to get this close.

He reminded her of just how long it had been since she'd been in a man's arms. Being with Gerald had been so sense-stealing; it had felt so wonderfully right.

But it had been wrong. A lie, all of it. A woman was weak that way. Easily deceived. She couldn't trust those kinds of feelings—wasn't that what she kept trying to get Hortense to understand?

Why then, Lyddie asked herself, was she thinking about how Nick's thigh would feel beneath her fingers . . . ?

"You seem lost in thought. I don't mean to intrude."

"Oh." Lyddie's cheeks warmed, and she dragged her gaze to the darkness beyond the porch. "I've just been looking at the stars. They seem so close. And you aren't intruding. A night this lovely should be shared."

Lyddie put her hand to her cheek and sat straighter. Goodness, where had that come from? That sounded like . . . like something Hortense would say!

"It's a night to inspire poets." Nick tilted his head back and stared past the edge of the veranda above them into the night sky, his features barely visible in the starlight.

"Yes." Quiet settled between them, and Lyddie began to relax.

"I must apologize again for mistaking you for a servant," he said at length.

"I told you earlier, it was an honest mistake. I was dressed as a housemaid. I was doing maid's work. And the fault is mine, for I could have corrected the misimpression my sister gave you." She smiled. "I didn't, because letting you assume me a maid seemed easier than apologizing for the rumpled, stained state of my clothing."

"Sometimes letting people assume is easier than explanations."

She found the deep tone of Nick's voice awash with mysteries. Lyddie looked at his profile. "I get the feeling you speak of something in particular."

He chuckled. "I'm suppose to be the detective—look!" He pointed to a falling star, blazing a bright trail across the night sky.

Seated on the inside of the swing, Lyddie leaned across Nick to see better. The star faded out just before touching the horizon, and she let out a pent-up breath. "Beautiful."

"Yes."

Lyddie jumped, surprised at how near him she was. Too near, her every instinct warned. She could make out the details of his face, the winged brows, the wide, well-sculpted mouth. Her gaze found his in the half light and something warm and, she didn't doubt, dangerous skittered through her as she read the male interest in his eyes.

"May I ask you something?" His voice was as rich as the chocolate sauce Jane made every Christmas.

He was going to kiss her. Lyddie swallowed. He was going to ask if he could kiss her, and she was going to let him.

"Yes. Ask me."

"Did you just paint this porch? I smell some harsh, chemical odor."

"Chemical . . . odor." Abruptly, Lyddie sat back, blessing the dark that hid her flaming cheeks.

"Yes. An acrid stench."

She rose, the scent of lye soap wafting around her. She'd been up to her elbows in it as she and Agnes cut the rather soft batch of soap into squares. "We haven't painted anything recently, though the hotel is in need of it. I have no idea what the scent might be. Good night, Mr. Brown."

Nick watched as Lyddie gracefully made her way through one of the tall French windows along the side porch. For an instant she paused on the other side, her silhouette etched there. Proud, high breasts stood out against the faint lamplight issuing from inside the hotel, emphasizing a narrow waist and rounded hips. She wore no restricting corset or cumbersome bustle, he noticed. Her soft curves were all her own.

He felt a warm surge in his groin.

That would never do, he decided. He was here for a reason—a reason beyond his job with the Pinkertons. He intended to find and take back what belonged to his family, the gold John Moreland had cheated his grandfather out of.

And he wouldn't let Lyddie Seaton's softly rounded breasts distract him.

Chapter Three

A lemony glow in the east, the sun slanted its first rays through the longleaf pines surrounding the town. As he buttoned his shirt, Nick stood at the open French windows, looking out on the morning. A farm wagon rumbled to a stop at the mercantile some distance down the street. Two gray-haired men sat on the bench before the store, giving the impression they were permanent fixtures, like the hitching rail.

Farther down still, the Shea twins meandered along, looking about as though they had no particular destination in mind. They disappeared behind the depot on the far edge of town, where the railroad tracks crossed the street. Just beyond the town, Nick knew from researching the area, the tracks split, with one line heading for the Gulf Coast of Mississippi, where longleaf pine was loaded onto ships. The other line went to Vicksburg.

People wanting to go on to New Orleans were obliged

to cross the Mississippi on a ferry and catch another train on the other side of the river.

Past the tracks, the spire and bell of Crossroads' schoolhouse was just visible along the tree-lined road. School was closed now for the summer.

Except for the arrival of a train, this seemed to be about as active as Crossroads ever got, Nick mused.

Small towns gave up their secrets easily. He would find the saboteurs—he hoped before they could strike again. When that freight train derailed no one was injured. Next time it could be a train filled with passengers, or a steam engine could explode, killing the engineer. Experience had taught him that this type of thing was probably the work of a disgruntled employee, or someone with a grudge against the railroad.

As he turned away, a movement caught his attention. Looking back, he saw Lyddie Seaton exiting the mercantile, a basket on her arm. She nodded to the older gentlemen on the bench; then, back straight, head high, she made her way down the street. Her sunbonnet dangled down between her shoulder blades by its strings, and wheat-colored hair was piled in curls atop her head. The early morning sun edged it with gold.

Nick wondered where her husband had disappeared to. The story Hortense had told him was that Lyddie and her husband had had a loud argument on their wedding night and the man had left the hotel, never to be seen again. A strange tale, considering Lyddie Elizabeth Shea Seaton was a beautiful woman. Comely enough to draw a man back after an argument—especially on his wedding night.

Watching her now, Nick felt raw male interest. That type of interest he could ignore. Far more dangerous, he admitted to himself, was the way she appealed to him on other levels. There was something about Lyddie Seaton that attracted him to the person she was inside. And that would never do.

Even if he didn't have other prizes in mind, after burying his wife, he hoped he'd learned not to trust a pretty face.

As Lyddie paused to speak with two older ladies, he tried to decide just what it was that set her apart. Perhaps it was the capable way she did things. Though he had only been here overnight, he could see she managed this hotel with little help from her siblings. Most of the women he knew were fluttery, helpless creatures, like his mother and wife had been. Practical Lyddie was something new to his experience.

Though his mother's limitations weren't really her fault, he added in mental apology to her memory. The daughter of a wealthy newspaper publisher, she had been brought up to privilege. After his family's financial ruin she'd never adjusted to her straitened circumstances—for twenty years she had bemoaned how Gentleman John had cheated her father-in-law at cards, luring him into betting the payroll gold meant for his two hundred factory workers. Though Nick's father had worked as foreman for the new owners of the carriage manufacturing firm, providing a living for his family, Nick's mother had died a bitter woman.

After Nick found the railroad saboteurs he'd find the gold and take it home. If it still existed. He suspected it did.

Though he'd been skeptical when he came here, believing Gentleman John had probably spent it or lost it gaming long ago, secrets thickened the air at Gentleman John's Hotel. The family was hiding something—especially Lyddie Seaton.

The object of his thoughts reached the gate to the hotel

and started down the brick walkway. Turning away from the window, Nick put his notebook in his pants pocket and made his way down to the hotel kitchen, where a slim woman of color was cutting up a chicken.

The cook offered to make him flapjacks, since he'd missed breakfast. He declined, but accepted the hot black coffee she poured into a blue cup.

Inhaling the rich aroma, he took a sip. "Mmmm. This is good. Tastes like N'awleans."

The cook said nothing as her blade found the chicken's hip joint and severed a leg quarter. Nick took another sip. It was his experience that servants generally knew everything going on in a household, and he'd purposefully waited until after breakfast before coming down, so he might find the cook alone.

"Have you worked for the Sheas a long time?"

Ignoring him, she lifted the chicken by the other leg and began slicing. Nick realized he had probably wasted his time.

Before he could try again, Lyddie Seaton entered the kitchen.

"Oh!" She drew up short.

"I didn't mean to startle you." Nick smiled.

"I missed you at breakfast." Her eyes widened. "I mean, you missed breakfast. Would you like something now?" She set her basket on the edge of the work table, out of the cook's way.

A faint blush stained her cheeks, and her full mouth was the most amazing shade of peach. Looking at her lips, Nick wondered how her kiss would taste. Like peaches . . . ?

He pushed the dangerous thought away. Spying bright red apples peeking from beneath a gingham cloth covering her basket, he reached in and pulled one out. "This will do fine."

Nick excused himself and left.

Staring at the back door after he'd disappeared through it, Lyddie tugged at the high collar of her dress, trying to let a little air in to cool her skin. "It's too danged hot for high collars and long, tight sleeves," she grumbled.

"I was wondering why you're all gussied up in your best dress. That is, until I saw the way you looked at that Pinkerton man." Jane arched a knowing brow as she picked up another chicken by the leg and began applying the knife.

"I don't know what you mean." Lifting her chin, Lyddie left the kitchen, going through the family dining room and down a short hall into the hotel lobby. It was empty, which suited her. So, she had worn her best dress. What of it? People had a right to wear their best dresses if they wanted.

After straightening the desk, she picked up the silver tray, on which guests left outgoing mail to be posted, and studied her hazy image. The side curls she'd patiently formed by her cheeks were wilted, the wisps across her forehead stuck damply to her flushed skin. She must look ridiculous.

The memory of looking into a hand mirror while the Widow Hatcher pinned the hem of this dress came to mind. It had been a present from Gram for her nineteenth birthday, and Lyddie had first worn it to the church social the night Sidney Carlyle proposed to her.

Lyddie sighed. He'd asked her where the gold was hidden in the same breath.

He'd been a smooth talker all right, telling her what a fine life they could have together if she'd just tell him where the treasure was.

Heaven help her, if she had known where any gold was hidden, she'd have told him. When he finally realized she didn't know, he'd disappeared—no doubt, just like he would have disappeared with the gold if he had found any.

And had she learned anything? Not at all. Not a year later, Gerald "Beau" Seaton had stepped off the train. From the big city of St. Louis, he had kept her fascinated with tales of all the places he'd been as a whiskey salesman, and the things he'd seen. He was soon courting her—though Gram had warned her that he wasn't to be trusted. She'd chosen not to listen.

Stuck in this small town all her life, Lyddie had waited for his visits to Crossroads each month to pitch his wares to the local saloon. She'd listened raptly to his tales of exotic places like Arizona and Duluth. The tales were as exciting as the possibility of escaping this sleepy backwater.

Lord, had she ever been that naive? Looking back, what the jackanapes had been after was painfully obvious. She couldn't believe she'd fallen for his lies.

It had been a hard lesson, but she'd learned it well. Never again would she believe smooth talk and lies.

"Well, look who's primping!"

Looking up as Hortense came down the stairs, Lyddie considered bashing the smirk off her sister's face with the small silver tray. She decided against it. The tray was somewhat valuable, and such an action was certain to leave a dent from her sister's hard head.

"I am not primping."

"Sure you're not. You're primping because Nick Brown is about the best-looking thing that every walked on two legs." Hortense joined her behind the desk and added pityingly, "He's just not the kind of man you can get serious about."

Lyddie stared at her sister. "I'm sure I don't know what you mean."

"But he sure is good to look at and fun to practice on," Hortense added with a sigh, paying Lyddie's protest not the least bit of attention. She plucked the silver tray from Lyddie's grasp and studied her own reflection, then pinched her cheeks to add color.

Lyddie picked up a duster made from the bound tail feathers of the wild turkey Frank Worley had given them last Thanksgiving and briskly applied it to the brass candlestick on the desk, the brass sconces on the wall, then moved on to her father's cavalry saber. But her strokes grew slower as she mulled over what Hortense said. Despite her better judgment, she just had to ask, "Why isn't he the kind to get serious about?"

Seeing the gleam in Hortense's eyes, Lyddie knew she'd made a mistake. "Not that I'm interested, mind you; just curious." Lyddie applied the duster furiously to the top of the pigeonholes where messages and room keys were placed. She added—to remind herself more than anything—"After all, I'm still a married woman." In the eyes of the world, at least. And, to protect her grandmother, that was something that could never be changed.

"That's right. You *are* married. So just leave Nick Brown to me."

"And you're almost engaged," Lyddie reminded her sister. The lumber foreman was a good catch—Lyddie didn't want Hortense to toss a good man like Frank Worley away on a whim.

"Am not," Hortense said. "Frank and me have just been keeping company. Since you're married and not interested, why are you wearing your best dress?"

"Because I'm afraid it's going to get too small if I just leave it hanging in the clothespress. It's tight now." Lyddie dragged a ladder-backed chair beneath the chandelier, which hung in the center of the lobby.

"Goes to show what you know. You think you'll impress a man like Nick Brown in a five-year-old dress. And you are putting on weight." Hortense smirked. "I guess that's to be expected in older women."

After climbing onto the chair, Lyddie applied the feather duster to the chandelier. Cut-glass prisms tinkled madly. Hortense was right for once. She did look a fool in this dress. It was too hot for summer, it was too old to impress anyone, and why the heck had she worn it when she wasn't even interested in Nick Brown?

Lyddie remembered the warm male interest in Nick's coffee-brown eyes yesterday when they were alone in his room, and the glass prisms tinkled louder.

"Lyddie!"

"What?" Lyddie snapped.

Smirking broadly, Hortense pointed at the door.

Whipping around, Lyddie discovered a well-dressed lady and gentleman standing just inside, their mouths agape. Their gazes were riveted to her exposed ankles.

Heat warming her cheeks, Lyddie scrambled down. "I am sorry!" She shot a fulminating glance at a chuckling Hortense. "I didn't hear you come in."

As Hortense laughed, Lyddie threw the duster down on the chair. "My sister will help you check in." Fists clenched in frustration, she brushed past the couple and out the front door.

But as she brushed past, she couldn't help noticing the woman's dove gray traveling suit and jaunty hat, with its stylish pheasant feather. Lyddie became even more aware of just how plain-looking and unfashionable even her best dress was. She bounded down the steps onto the walk and kicked a sweet gum ball in irritation.

The day was unseasonably warm, though it was still well before noon. Pausing beneath the big pecan tree at the side of the hotel, Lyddie ran her fingers across the rough gray bark. The old pecan tree had grown large by being cautious, putting on its leaves long after all the other trees were full and green. Long after all chance of a killing frost.

Tilting her head back, Lyddie looked up at the thick summer canopy and wondered when she would learn caution. How backward she must appear to a man like Nick. Nick Brown was from Chicago. He was used to women like the stylish guest in the gray suit, not awkward girls who ran railroad hotels. Women who smelled like lilac water, not lye soap.

It would be safest just to put him out of her mind. He'd soon be gone, after all.

The thought didn't make her happy.

Not stopping to examine why, Lyddie headed for her special place, where she'd always gone to sort out life's disappointments.

A train rumbled across the trestle bridge over Myers Creek on its way out of Crossroads. Kneeling on a bluff rising above the section of tracks that had been newly repaired, Nick ran his finger over the edge of a boot print.

There were two sets, made in soft mud, but as hard as brick now. On one set of prints the heel was run down on the outside. A different boot print showed a crack across the sole.

Setting back on his heels, Nick considered his findings. It hadn't rained since the night the train derailed. Two people had been standing up here in the dark, watching the accident. Now he just had to find these two pairs of boots and their owners and he would probably have his saboteurs. Flipping open his notebook, he jotted down his findings. He would come back this afternoon with plaster of paris and make imprints.

As the sound of the engine died away, Nick was struck by the tranquility of the area. Even though it was still early, the day was warm. The sun beamed down from between white cotton clouds. Bumblebees droned as they climbed over clumps of purple wildflowers. The sandy-banked creek gurgled as it splashed around the bridge supports. The air was clear and fresh. Unlike Chicago's gray pall of coal smoke, even in summer, the only trace of smoke was a faint and dissipating trail lingering where the train had passed. And surrounding it all, a tall forest of magnificent pines reached for the blue sky.

No wonder Gentleman John had chosen this place to settle and build his town. Maybe growing up in such natural beauty was the reason Lyddie Seaton seemed different than other women he'd known.

A distant, constant roaring peaked his curiosity. Listening, Nick stood and returned his notebook to his pocket. Deciding it was in the wrong direction to be a train, he climbed down the sloping bluff to the coarse white sand of the creek bank under the bridge and headed downstream to investigate.

The creek narrowed and deepened, forcing Nick to cut through the woods on what he assumed to be an animal trail. The growing roar told him it was a waterfall before he broke into the open. As he came out of the shadowed forest, a bowl of blue sky, sunlight, and surging white-water greeted him. The eight-foot-high falls created a lacy froth as water tumbled over the wide lip. On his other side there was a second falls where another, smaller stream merged with this one, both pouring into a pale tea-colored pool.

Transfixed, Nick drank in the raw power and beauty of the secluded spot as it filled his senses—the roar, the cool mist, the sunlight shimmering diamonds on the water. Then he saw Lyddie, lying on the far bank like a pagan goddess.

She had been swimming; her wheat-colored hair spread in wet ropes over the sugar-white sand. Her nipples pressed against her camisole, the distinct spots of color were revealed through the thin material. One shapely leg was bent, her toes half-buried in the sand. A dark triangle showed through her pantaloons at the apex of her thighs.

Desire, hot and sudden, slammed into his groin.

Then his attention was drawn to the long, dark shape slithering across the sand just above her. As if sensing Lyddie's presence, the snake paused, then coiled near her head.

Nick's throat went dry.

"Lyddie!"

The sound of the falls swallowed his shout. Lyddie remained unaware. The snake uncoiled and moved closer to her.

Panic curled in his stomach as Nick searched for a way across, a way to reach Lyddie before it was too late. The falls on either side of him offered none. The twenty-foot bluff on which he stood was a vertical drop into the creek.

Nick jerked off his coat, then his boots. After dropping his notebook into one of them, he went a few steps back up the path. With a running start, he launched himself into the air, leaping as far out over the wide basin of water as he could. The creek water closed over his head as he entered and sent icy shocks throughout his body.

Breaking the surface, he battled the undercurrent from the falls, an undercurrent that threatened to prevent him from reaching the shore. Pulling free of its grasp, he swam toward the bank.

"Don't move," Nick gasped as he reached the shallow water and tried to stand up, fighting to keep his balance as sandy bottom shifted underneath his feet.

Lyddie opened her eyes and screamed, sitting bolt upright as a man rose like Neptune from the water.

Nick grabbed her hand and jerked her to him, lifting her as easily as he might have a rag doll. Swinging her around, he shoved her behind his back.

"Nick?" Lyddie gasped, suddenly finding herself thigh deep in the cold water, her arms wrapped around Nick Brown's neck.

"Be still!" He pushed her away abruptly and reached for a dead limb lying nearby on the sand.

Lyddie flailed her arms but lost her battle for balance. Suddenly she sat neck deep in the creek.

"Damnation!" She bounced up, not liking the shock of the cold, spring-fed water against her sun-warmed skin.

Then she saw the snake and understood. But it was harmless!

As Nick raised the stick over his head, she caught it. "No!"

Nick looked at her incredulously.

The reptile lifted its head and flicked its tongue, as if shocked by what had been the man's intent. It then slithered up the sloping, leaf-littered bank, disappearing into the wild mulberry shrubs.

"Why did you stop me?" Nick gasped incredulously.

"It was a harmless black snake. Things shouldn't be

destroyed for no reason. Not even snakes."

"Harmless?" He glared at her. "I jumped in that ice water and could have broken my neck and you say . . ." He seemed to lose the thought as his gaze stilled on her face. Then, ever so slowly, moved to her breasts.

Looking down, Lyddie found her wet cotton camisole was transparent. Chilled, her nipples stood out like ripe raspberries.

Blushing furiously, she crossed her arms over her breasts. But her gaze was drawn to his body. His wet shirt was almost as transparent as her camisole and stretched across his wide shoulders, delineating the muscles of his chest. As her gaze lingered on him, Nick said, his voice low and husky, "You blushed when I did that."

Gasping, her gaze flew back to his face. His brown eyes darkened to ebony. A slow smile curved one side of his mouth as he took a half step nearer.

"No."

"No, what?"

Nick placed a finger under Lyddie's chin, and she forgot about the bone-chilling water swirling around her thighs. She forgot all the reasons she should run to the bushes and get into her dress and petticoats. She felt paralyzed by the simple contact. And, lord help her, she liked the feeling. She liked it a lot.

Nick moved closer still, and she leaned toward him in silent acquiescence. His mouth came down, hot and hungry, on hers.

Chapter Four

As his mouth molded against hers, warm sensations curled through her, rioting in her abdomen. Nick smelled of the sweet creek water, where swamp syrillas had dropped their blooms. His kiss deepened, and Lyddie drank in the heady scent, closing her eyes. The roaring of the falls grew fainter as a new roaring took its place, this one inside her head.

This was crazy . . . When she'd left the hotel, Lyddie wanted to escape thoughts of this man, disturbed at the way he preoccupied her mind. But after a swim in the cold water she had lain on the sun-drenched sand and it seemed to cradle her, warming her skin like a lover's caress.

Warm coffee-brown eyes and a flashing smile had slipped into her thoughts, no matter how hard she tried to think of other things. And she had imagined how it would feel to kiss Nick. To be in his arms. She thought it would be exciting.

Her imagination, she decided, was completely inadequate. Never could she have guessed kissing him would be like drowning. Like being tumbled helplessly along by strong, tingling currents, immersed in sensations, wonderful sensations, and very, very pleasantly drowning.

Winding her arms more tightly around his neck, Lyddie rose on her tiptoes, pressing against his length. She explored his broad shoulders through his wet shirt and moved against the hard thighs pressed against her own. Her breasts tingled madly where they flattened against him. Her skin was cold and hot. Chilled from her dip in the frigid water—water that lapped against her even now—but wherever his body pressed against hers, heat sizzled.

Lyddie clung to him like a cork life-ring in a storm-tossed sea; helpless to fight the sensations immersing her; content to let him take her as deep in this sublime pool as he would.

But even as she gave herself up to the pleasure of his arms and his kiss, in one small part of her mind a warning bell clanged. Far off and easily ignored, at first. What could be the danger? Never had she been possessed by such sweetness. True, Gerald had stirred her. But Gerald's kisses had never stirred such powerful need. Not even on their wedding night . . .

And she had been Gerald's fool. She hadn't seen that Gerald wanted to use her, that he had never really cared for her, until he showed his true colors.

The thought struggled to the surface of her mind, and she stilled. Lyddie became aware again of the bone-chilling water around her thighs and the way her wet pantaloons and camisole stuck to her skin uncomfortably. She pushed against Nick's chest until he broke his kiss.

"What's wrong?" Coffee-brown eyes blinked down at her.

"What's *wrong?"* Glancing down at her almost transparent underclothes, Lyddie felt heat rise in her cheeks and crossed her arms over her chest. "I . . . I think you should apologize."

Following her gaze, Nick smiled. "For what? You were enjoying it as much as I was."

"Oh!" Lyddie gasped. "You . . . you took advantage of me!"

"Took advantage?" He arched one dark auburn brow and touched her cheek, then trailed his finger along the line of her jaw. The look he gave her was not in the least contrite. "As I said, you were enjoying it as much as me." His finger stroked her lips.

Shivering from the new sensations left by his touch, Lyddie stepped back, and the cold water swirling around her legs steadied her resolve. "I certainly didn't . . ." She couldn't quite meet his gaze. "A lady doesn't expect . . . I mean, you caught me off guard!"

"Off guard?" Nick chuckled. "That's a new term for it."

Lyddie ground her teeth at his male arrogance. Oh, Nick Brown was no gentleman! How could she have ever thought him one? Imagined kissing him would be sweet . . .

Somewhere in the tall pines, a mockingbird sang a trilling song, the sound barely audible above the roar of the falls.

"Yes," Lyddie snapped. "You caught me *off guard.*" She gave him a hard shove.

"What—!" Flailing his arms, Nick stepped backward, trying to regain his balance. He sat down hard, landing up to his neck in the cold water. *"Damn!"*

"Looks like I just caught you *off guard.*"

Lyddie marched up the creek bank, ignoring the muttered imprecations behind her. Snatching her petticoat from the huckleberry bush where she had draped it, she fumed silently as she put it on and tied the string at the waist.

Nick was right; she had enjoyed his kisses. That made it all the worse. Was she as man-crazy as Hortense?

No, she decided. There had once been a time when she'd thought a man had appeared who would bring fulfillment and excitement to her life. Gerald Seaton should have been an education—enough to arm her against allowing any man to seduce her with kisses again. Lyddie sighed. Laughing, Gerald had told her on their wedding night that to a man, making love didn't mean anything but a moment's pleasure.

And that's all it would mean to Nick Brown.

Sniffling, Lyddie reached for her dress.

"Look," said Nick behind her, "I realize you are married, but—"

She whirled around. "Why did you follow me? Did you think, being a grass widow, I'd be willing to take a tumble in the hay? Well, you were wrong, so I'd appreciate it if you'd just apologize and leave."

"I didn't follow you." Nick stood in the sand, wet and dripping, a belligerent set to his jaw. *Sorry* wasn't in his eyes.

She snatched the dress over her head and thrust an arm through the sleeve. "I'd like some privacy, Mr. Brown." She tried to poke her other arm into its sleeve, but her damp skin refused to slide through the twisted cotton material.

Nick caught the sleeve and began to work it down onto her arm.

"I *said*—" As she took a step back, Lyddie's foot came down on a prickly holly leaf, which stuck into her tender instep. *"Ouch!"* She hopped on one foot, one arm still hopelessly trapped. Nick reached out, and she was obliged to catch his hand to keep from falling.

"I'd really like it if you would just leave!" Lyddie snapped after she had regained her balance.

"Hold on to me." Not waiting for compliance, he bent and caught her foot, lifting it, sole upward, and picked the sticker out. He then brushed off the sand and inspected the arch to see if there were any others. Finding none, he set her foot down once more.

Ignoring her stuttered protests, he then pulled her hand through the sleeve. After that, turning Lyddie around like a recalcitrant child, he started to fasten the row of tiny hooks that closed the dress.

"I can do that. Thank you!" Humiliated, Lyddie reached behind her, catching the bottom hook and fumbling for the eye on the other side.

"Fine."

He stopped trying to help. As she struggled with the fastenings, she sensed him moving away and wondered why she was disappointed. For once, he had done what she had asked.

"Is there some way out of here other than back through the water and up the falls?"

Without looking at him, she gestured at a path worn in the leaf litter between the trees. "The trail comes out behind the hotel."

Watching as Nick disappeared between the bushes on

the bank, Lyddie tried to rekindle her anger as she struggled with the hooks at her back. But her fingers trembled so badly, she couldn't do up the fastenings.

It was the gentle way he'd taken the sticker out of her foot that bothered her, she realized. And the softness in his eyes as he did so. Like he really wasn't a bad sort. And she knew in her heart he hadn't followed her. If he had, he would have come out on the path he'd just left on—the way she'd come.

And he'd jumped in to try to save her from a snakebite. Though it turned out it wasn't a biting kind of snake, Nick's heart had been in the right place. He hadn't plotted and planned to get her alone and kiss her until she was dizzy. It had just happened.

She sighed. Moreover, if she had pulled away when his lips first touched hers, he would have probably stopped then, but instead of breaking the kiss, she'd pressed closer.

So what was she really angry about? She chewed her bottom lip as she fumbled with the fastenings.

Because, she realized, she *was* a married woman in the eyes of the world, and she could never let the truth be known. Even if she was foolish enough to trust another man.

Her anger dissipated. There was no use railing against fate or whining that life was unfair. She had made her choice a long time ago, and if she had it to do over, she would make the same one. She had to protect Gram.

Nick picked his way through the winding path, past tall longleaf pines, magnolias, and spreading white oaks. After passing a spring and a great cauldron of a wash pot, he found himself at the back of the hotel.

Instead of going on in, he chose to clomp wetly down

Main Street in his stocking feet, drawing curious stares from the old men whittling and spitting tobacco as they sat on the bench in front of the mercantile. As he made his way back to the railroad bridge outside of town, where the noise of the falls had originally lured him like a Lorelei's song, he berated himself for ever giving in to the urge to kiss Lyddie Shea Seaton.

Solve the crimes against the railroad, see the guilty parties arrested, and leave with the gold that rightfully belonged to his family—that's what he'd come to Crossroads to do. There was no room in his plans for a dalliance with a married woman. No matter that he felt an empathy because her husband had, from all indications, abandoned her without a backward glance, much as his own wife had left him.

Lyddie was Gentleman John's granddaughter. He needed to remember that.

Making his way down the same narrow path he'd traveled earlier—a trail made by white-tailed deer and other animals, he decided—Nick found his coat and boots where he'd left them, though damp now from the mist rising from the falls. A glance at the other side of the pool showed Lyddie was gone. He could believe she was never there, except for footprints in the sand and the fact that his clothes were wet. And the memory of how soft her lips were.

The way she had looked up at him, in wonder and remorse, after she had pushed out of his arms, still puzzled him.

Maybe she felt guilty for having kissed him back when she was a married woman.

Bending, Nick plucked a thorny twig from the toe of his wet, filthy sock. Wriggling his toes, he decided against putting his boots on and reached for his coat.

Pausing, hand outstretched, he saw his notebook lay atop his jacket. He knew he had left it in his boot.

Picking up the notebook, he flipped through the pages, finding them all intact, and then thoughtfully looked up at the rainbow mist above the falls. So, he'd been wrong. More than animals used this trail.

Chapter Five

Shoes in hand, Lyddie closed the kitchen door behind her. She had sand in some very uncomfortable places, and her hair hung heavily around her face like clumps of wet rope. More sand was caked on her scalp, making it itch.

And she was mad at and disappointed in Nick Brown to the soles of her bare feet. For no real good reason, she admitted to herself as she moved to where Jane stirred a huge pot on the stove. As the broth simmered, enticing smells rose from it. Inhaling, Lyddie savored the aromas of roux, onions, and okra and realized she had missed dinner and was starving. Taking a stalk of celery from the worktable, she bit into it.

The cook paused, a winged brow rising high on her teak-colored forehead as she looked over Lyddie's dishabille. "What you been at, girl?"

"I just went in swimming." Lyddie glanced down at

her chest. Her wet camisole was spotting through her dress, which was only half done up, as the cool air sneaking in the open back reminded her. She hadn't been able to manage the tiny hooks. "That smells good. Chicken gumbo?" Lyddie asked, changing the subject from her swimming trip.

"Uh-huh." Jane gave the soup a final swirl, then cleaned off the wooden spoon by tapping it against the rim of the pot. "I was going to fry the chicken for supper, but two more guests signed into the hotel. Came into town by buckboard to catch the train to New Orleans in the morning. It's too warm to be serving gumbo, but we need to stretch those scrawny birds."

Placing her hands on the small of her back, Jane stretched as though her muscles ached. "I was planning to make buttermilk custard for desert, *if* I get the buttermilk in time. Milk's on the back porch, full curdled and ready to churn."

Lyddie frowned. A local farmer supplied the hotel with milk. It was the twins' chore to churn it and make butter and buttermilk. "Where are Bobbie June and Billy Fred?" she asked, taking a moment to lift the lid on a cast-iron pot setting on the worktable. She found it contained jambalaya left over from the noon-time meal, and her stomach rumbled louder. She closed the lid, deciding to get a serving after she got cleaned up.

"Those two was off like the devil was after them as soon as they chopped stove wood this morning." Jane picked up a butcher knife and began sharpening it on a stile. "Maybe he'll get 'em," she added enigmatically as she slid the blade up and down the long metal rod. It made a hissing sound as she worked it, honing the edge.

Lyddie didn't ask what Jane meant. She was afraid the cook might tell her. Shaking her head, Lyddie wondered when the pair would ever learn that chores came first. That the hotel was their bread and butter.

Never, probably. They let dreams of being rich and wild schemes push aside anything as mundane as making butter. "I'll get Molly to do it." Lyddie started for the back stairs in the corner of the kitchen.

"Molly's gone off with the doctor. Martha Vinton's having her baby. You know that Molly was off like a shot when she heard he wanted her help."

A hand on the newel post, Jane's words stopped her. Lyddie sighed. Couldn't she even take a few hours for herself without everything grinding to a halt? "Doesn't anyone around here have any sense of responsibility?"

"Just you." With another glance at Lyddie's state of dress, Jane commented, "And it looks like you went over Roaring Falls, instead of into the swimming hole." She inspected the honed knife edge critically, then wiped it with a cloth. "Funny thing, when I was throwing the vegetable trimmings out, I saw that Pinkerton man coming out of the woods on the path by the spring." Jane's black eyes gleamed. "He was looking like he'd been swimming, too. In his clothes."

Feeling heat surge in her cheeks, Lyddie turned wordlessly and headed up the stairs.

It was that evening before Lyddie saw Nick again, and it irritated her to realize she'd been watching for him. Place settings for the hotel guests had been laid in the guests' dining room and supper served in there, with Agnes attending the sideboard. But Nick Brown appeared in the family dining room, carrying his gumbo bowl and plate.

"I hope you won't mind if I join your family once more, Mrs. Moreland. I enjoyed our visit last evening and was hoping we could talk again." He smiled at Gram, a flash of even white teeth against his tanned skin. His dark rust hair was neatly combed and he wore a string tie and an embroidered vest.

Eyeing Nick shrewdly, Gram nodded. "My husband woulda said 'poppycock' to that pretty talk, but you're welcome at our table." She added, "Whatever your reasons."

"Thank you." If he was bothered by the backhanded invitation, he hid it behind another smooth smile.

Doing her frog impression, Hortense tittered, "Why, do sit down here by me." She patted the empty chair next to her.

As he settled himself at the table, Lyddie noted Nick didn't even glance her way. She stirred her gumbo to cool it, then took a bite of the spicy Cajun soup. It would be better if he never looked her way again, she decided. And best, if he hadn't looked at her in the first place. Sighing, Lyddie stirred the gumbo determinedly.

Smoothing a stray lock of her mouse-brown hair behind her ear, Hortense said, "Now, Gram, I think it quite wonderful that Nick so enjoys our company, he seeks us out. After all, Nick is from Chicago. He's been so many places and done so many exciting things working as a Pinkerton detective, I do declare, I'm just flattered he finds us worth talking to at all."

Gram snorted. " 'Spect he thinks he'll find out more in here about the tracks being torn up and the hole in the depot building than in there with people just passing through town on their way to somewhere else."

At the mention of the investigation, Billy Fred snorted buttermilk through his nose. Looking put out, his twin helpfully walloped him between the shoulders with enough force to send his face almost into his gumbo bowl. Then Bobbie June walloped him again as Billy

Fred tried to straighten up, sending him bowl-ward once again.

"Stop it, Bobbie June! I'm okay," he managed as she drew back for another blow. He glared at his twin. "You hit me hard enough to make my head fly off!"

"I was only trying to help you get your breath." Bobbie June blinked innocently.

Not deigning to answer, Billy Fred blew his nose into his napkin.

"I can certainly see the attraction of our company," Lyddie muttered.

Molly looked up from her book—a dissertation on the cause and effect bad "humors" had on the human body. "Lyddie got strangled last night, and now you, Billy Fred. I wonder if there could be some defective pathway in your throats, an inherited family thing?" Her eyes gleamed at the possibility. "I'll examine you both after supper."

"Will not. My throat is fine and jim-dandy." Looking militant, Billy Fred spooned gumbo in and swallowed it, as if to demonstrate that his throat worked well enough. He only choked a little this time.

"See!" Molly scooted back in her chair.

"It's fine!" He glowered at her, stilling her as she would have risen. "It's just that you were watching me, that's all."

"But—" Molly began.

"Now, children, don't quibble!" Hortense interjected, earning astonished looks from all her siblings.

Into the brief silence that followed, Gram mused, "Conscience could have some'ot to do with his swallowing problem, I reckon."

At this, Bobbie June seemed to find her steaming

gumbo all absorbing and stirred the bowl in imitation of Lyddie.

With a last reluctant glance at Billy Fred's throat, Molly lifted her book again and resumed eating and reading.

"Would you care for bread, Nick?" Hortense held the basket of freshly baked rolls out to him and eyed the twins askance when they half stood and reached across the table to snatch two, each.

"Thank you." Smiling, laughter lighting his coffee-brown eyes, Nick took a roll. Glancing at Lyddie, his smile died as he tore off a piece.

Lyddie looked back at her bowl and stirred.

"Why don't you tell us all about Chicago?" Hortense urged Nick. "Gram used to go there with our grandfather, when he was making the circuit of gambling houses. But I am just certain the town has changed a lot since then. Why, I heard there are four-storied buildings on Michigan Avenue."

"Yes, there are. And there are plans to build taller ones." Nick turned to Gram. "I'm sure you'd find it quite changed, Mrs. Moreland, since you were there last."

"It was a dirty, nasty place when I saw it, with poor throwed-away orphans running in the street." Gram sipped a spoonful of gumbo. "Lot like London was when I was young, for that matter."

"I'm afraid all big cities must seem much the same in that respect," Nick said.

Lyddie felt another glance—the back of her neck prickled, though she didn't look up again. She concentrated on her gumbo, completely aware of the man and disgusted with herself for being unable to control her physical reaction to his presence.

"I thought what set Chicago apart from all the other

towns John and I went to was the smell," Gram said. "It's a railhead, you know. The lines bring beef cattle in from the ranches in the west. Don't rightly know what smelled worse, stockyards or the slaughterhouses."

Lyddie sighed, her hunger battling against the unappetizing statement. "Gram . . ."

"Of course, the tanneries that processed all those cow hides into leather weren't too good-smelling, neither. Do you know how they get the hair to slip off?"

"Gram, *please!*" Lyddie banged her spoon down. In the quiet that followed she found Nick Brown looking in her direction. Along with all her siblings.

"I'm sorry, Gram, but I'd rather not talk about slaughterhouses while we eat. Maybe no one else is hungry, but after churning the buttermilk and helping Jane in the kitchen"—Lyddie frowned meaningfully at the twins and Molly—"I'd like to enjoy a pleasant meal."

Hortense said, "I did my chores—watched the front desk and did the ironing."

"I was helping Doc deliver Martha Vinton of her new boy," Molly said defensively. "It was a hard delivery. Doc had to cut her—" A look at Lyddie's dark features and Molly relented. "Never mind."

The twins exchanged a glance. "We was puttin' out bush lines down on Myers Creek," Billy Fred said. "We plumb forgot about the butter. I'm sorry, Lye-Beth."

"We are sorry. But those bush lines will get us some fresh fish. In fact, soon as we finish supper and see wood chopped to cook breakfast with, we're gonna go out and run 'em before dark. If the fish are biting, we might camp on the bank and run the lines several times tonight." Bobbie June turned to her grandmother. "I know how you love fried fish, Gram."

Arching a brow, Lyddie glanced from one twin to the

other. Something was up with the pair, that was certain. "You two may go check your lines after you wash the supper dishes."

"It'll be black-dark by then! Anyways, washing dishes ain't our job," Billy Fred protested.

"Churning butter *is.*" Lyddie arched an annoyed brow. "Pouring up the buttermilk afterward and putting it in the spring house *is.* I had to do your chores because you two were off fishing." She fixed her brother with a stern look. "So tonight, you two can pay me back by helping Agnes with the dishes in my place."

"Heck, you weren't doing nothing but lollygaging at the swim hole. We had important stuff to take care of," Billy Fred said, dipping his spoon into his gumbo.

"Now, Billy Fred, it wasn't that important." If looks could cut, the one Bobbie June aimed at her brother would have left him bleeding in buckets. "We can wash dishes before we go. Lyddie churned the butter. Fair's fair."

"But Bobbie—" He jumped, gasping, then frowned at his sister. *"What the . . ."*

"Fair's fair!" Bobbie June interrupted with a meaningful frown.

Looking from one twin to the other, Lyddie guessed Bobbie June had kicked Billy Fred underneath the table. Nick's raised brow showed he suspected as much, too.

Frowning, Lyddie asked, "How did you know I went swimming?" She hoped the two of them hadn't been watching as Nick held her and—Oh, lord!

The twins exchanged a look. Then Bobbie June blinked at Lyddie, an innocent-lamb expression on her deceptively angelic features. "We saw you when we were scouting out places to hang bush lines. You had been swimming and were just lying out on the sand in your underthings." She added primly, "I warned Billy Fred, so he didn't look."

At this information, Nick watched an apricot blush climb up Lyddie's neck. The heightened color made her glorious eyes sparkle with tawny lights.

His gaze moved to her lips, then skittered away. It would never do to start remembering the taste of them. He'd been foolish to give in to the desire to kiss her, but the sight of her lying in the warm sun on the creek bank had set a fire in his blood.

Shaking off the surging reaction the memory brought with it, Nick promised himself he wouldn't slip up again. He had come to Crossroads for two reasons: to uncover saboteurs and to find gold. He'd lost sight of that down by the creek this morning, but he wouldn't forget again.

Besides, if his investigation of the railroad sabotage led where he thought it was going, he and Lyddie would have another bone of contention between them.

Toying with his spoon, Nick asked, "Bobbie June, you two traveled down the creek itself?"

"Yes. Why?" Bobbie June blinked angel-innocent again.

Smiling, Nick decided she would have a great future if she went on the stage. "Oh, no reason." Picking up his roll, he tore off another piece. "Just looking down the creek from the railroad bridge with all the dead trees, log jams, and deep black holes in the water, I would have said it was impassable." He shrugged and bit into the bread.

"Why, it is impassable," Lyddie verified, frowning at Bobbie June suspiciously.

The younger girl looked nonplussed, but only for an instant. Throwing a thick dark braid over her shoulder, as though getting it out of the way to do battle, she focused on stirring her gumbo and said evenly, "Lyddie, you know when the water's low like now, you can wade down it." At the incredulous looks this drew from Hortense and Lyddie, even Billy Fred, Bobbie June insisted, "You *can.*"

An incredulous silence followed.

"Mostly, that is." Bobbie June relented in the face of such disbelief. "Some places we were obliged to get out on the bank just a little ways and go around deadfalls. But mostly you can keep to the creek."

Nick mused, "Being a Chicago boy, I've never been 'bush-lining.' It sounds like a lot of fun."

"Oh, it is!" Billy Fred sat forward, his eyes bright. "There's nothing to beat the feeling you get when you come to a line and a big ol' fish is bending the limb it's tied to!"

"I would like to try it. Maybe you would allow me to join you tonight?"

"Sure thing!" Billy Fred grinned. At this, it was Bobbie June who choked. She recovered quickly and glowered at her twin. He shrugged off her dark look and motioned at Nick's white shirt and embroidered vest. "You'll want to wear some old clothes, if you have 'em."

"Sure thing," Nick agreed. "Do I need shoes?"

"Old ones. It'll be nice having another man with us. Though you'll have to watch out for the soapstone. Slick as owl sh—" Glancing at Lyddie's frown, Billy Fred finished, "Dung. I'll show you the slick spots."

Hortense set her glass down hard, the rattle of china cutting off the rest of Billy Fred's words. "Nick, you're very nice, but you don't have to humor my . . . *uncultured* siblings. I had planned a musical evening. I'm going to entertain our guests on the pianoforte."

At this prospect, Lyddie muttered to no one in particular, "I want to go fishing, too."

Hortense shot her a scalding look.

Interrupting before any discussion of Hortense's musical talent—or the lack of it—could ensue, Gram pointed to Nick with her spoon. "Now I recollect who you remind me of. All this mention of Chicago finally jobbed it out of the back of my mind. You look like Michael Bennington. Or like he did twenty-five-odd years ago. 'Course, you got hair a might darker than that carrot red his was, and you're a bit taller, too. But you talk real cultured like he did, like you come from the same stock."

Nick took a sip of his gumbo, then asked in mild interest, "Really?"

Something in his reaction tickled between Lyddie's shoulder blades. She had the feeling underneath his casual facade, strong currents were stirring.

"You look a danged lot like Bennington, now that I consider it."

Nick said slowly, "There was a Bennington Carriage Works in Chicago at one time, I believe."

She nodded. "Aye, until Bennington gambled with my husband." Gram sighed and fiddled with her napkin, a frown puckering her forehead into lacy wrinkles. "It was an awful thing to see."

Unable to stop himself, Nick asked softly, "What was awful to see?"

"The fever that was on Bennington. Gambling fever. John saw it and tried to cry off after the third night Bennington lost big, but the man wouldn't have it. Arrogant, he was. Insulted John 'cause . . . well, never mind." A faraway look stole into her eyes. "John allus regretted letting hisself be goaded like that." Gram shook her head.

"Bennington regretted it, too, I'll be bound. For the next few hours, least ways. After that, he didn't mind so much."

"Why?" Nick asked. The one syllable was dry as sheets of parchment rubbed together as he fought to keep his emotions under control. This family was innocent of John Moreland's perfidy; he had to remember that. "Why didn't Bennington mind?"

" 'Cause after he lost the five thousand in gold, he put a gun to his head and blew his brains out." Gram returned her attention to her gumbo.

Watching Nick's reactions, Lyddie realized he didn't have to wait for the twins to go fishing, he was on a fishing trip right then. Fishing for information about the gold. That finished off her appetite.

As Lyddie rose from the table, she waved Nick back down when he started to rise, also. "No. Please stay seated. If everyone will excuse me . . . ?"

Frowning, Nick watched as Lyddie disappeared through the kitchen door.

"Wonder what's got into her?" Molly murmured to no one in particular.

Nick gave himself a mental shake. Why was he more interested in following Lyddie than in finding out everything he could about the gold from Mrs. Moreland, now that the subject had been broached?

" 'Spect she works too hard and worries about all these hellions too much," Gram answered Molly's question.

Deciding to follow Lyddie, Nick said, "Excuse me. Perhaps I should see what is the matter."

"Oh, you mustn't mind Lye-Beth." Hortense placed her hand on Nick's sleeve, preventing him from leaving the table. "She'll be fine. She's just a bit squeamish, and the talk might have made her queasy."

"Seeing you get all calf-eyed is enough to make anyone queasy." Bobbie June wrinkled her nose in distaste.

"I don't know what you could possibly mean!" Mottled color rose up Hortense's neck.

Billy Fred elbowed his twin. "Come on, Bobbie June. We'd better get finished eating if we're going to do the dishes in time to get down to the creek before black dark. I wanna show Nick the best holes."

"I'd like that," Nick said.

Growing thoughtful, Bobbie June was quiet for half a second; then a sly look narrowed her eyes. Nick noticed it was gone as she turned to him and blinked innocently. "I know why Lye-Beth—I mean, *Lydia Elizabeth*—took off like that. It wasn't that the talk made her queasy." Bobbie June looked abashed. "I don't know how we could have been *so* thoughtless. She said how much she wanted to go fishing, too. And we didn't even have the good manners to invite her. Shame on us."

Chapter Six

Nick's after the gold.

There was no doubt in Lyddie's mind. There was, however, a sick feeling in the pit of her stomach as she lifted the empty kettle from the back of the stove. Nick Brown might be a Pinkerton agent here to investigate the sabotage to the railroad, but it was the gold he was after, first and foremost. And he'd not learned about the legend of the gold first on the train, as he had implied.

Lyddie knew because she had been watching him when Gram said the name *Bennington.* He'd known the name, known who lost the gold. It had been there in his eyes. There was no surprise in Nick's gaze when Gram had related the tragedy of what happened to Michael Bennington. But there had been something . . . She mulled over his reaction for a moment but was unable to name the emotion behind it.

Well, it didn't matter what else was there. The important thing was, she had almost let herself be taken in. Again. Thank goodness she had learned the truth.

Sighing, Lyddie placed the kettle under the cast-iron pump on the kitchen worktable. The gold had been won and lost so long ago that the legend of it had grown and changed, as those things were prone to do. Now, instead of five thousand dollars in gold coins, the amount had swollen to twenty thousand. However, Nick had known the true amount.

The map Nick had, one of hundreds printed by the Crossroads newspaper every year, declared Gentleman John had won it from an English industrialist named Wainwright aboard the paddle wheeler *Sweet Sue.* Afterward, the Englishman had thrown himself into the Mississippi in despair. There was another story that it was a lost payroll from the Confederate Army, although that was ridiculous. Gentleman John won the gold long before the war broke out, and the Confederate Army paid its troops in useless Confederate dollars.

But most people didn't care a fig where the gold had really come from. Treasure hunters who came to Crossroads were only interested in where it might be hidden.

Lyddie frowned as she took a dipper of water from the bucket and poured it into the top of the pump, holding her hand in front of the spigot as she did so, to keep the water from running back out. She worked the handle up and down until the pump was primed and water sluiced into the dishpan beneath. Then she filled the kettle.

Nick Brown had known where the gold had come from, all right. And that, Lyddie decided as she hefted the kettle onto the stove to heat, meant he must have researched the whole matter before he'd ever gotten onboard that train. Before he ever bought that map from the porter.

And that brought her back to her original conclusion: He was here for the gold.

Lyddie remembered the scoundrel's kiss and her lips burned. She scrubbed the back of her hand across her mouth, angry that she had fallen for the ploy. No doubt he thought he could cozen her into telling him where the treasure was, just like Gerald had tried to do. Well, for a detective he wasn't thinking things through. Did he think the family would live like this, working this hard at running the hotel, if there *was* any gold?

Darn it, she had wanted Nick Brown to be different. To be as nice as his looks and as sweet as his talk. To be decent and honest. And she'd had no reason to assume he was any of those things. She alone was to blame for her feelings. It was no fun to fool oneself.

Bobbie June entered the kitchen and headed purposefully to the worktable. "You have the water heating? Good. Go up to my room and get into my other pair of overalls." She pushed up the sleeves of her flannel shirt as she spoke. Lyddie blinked at the younger girl, who grabbed a cake of lye soap from the saucer on the windowsill and started shaving slivers into the dishpan.

"Well, hurry, Lye-Beth," Billy Fred admonished as he carried a stack of bowls and silverware into the kitchen.

Bobbie June nodded at her brother as he placed the dishes into the pan. "You get on with the wood chopping. We'll be finished in here by the time you've stacked up enough for cooking breakfast."

Looking from one to the other, Lyddie asked, "And why do I need overalls?"

"Because we're going to the creek fishing as soon as we've finished the chores." Hortense entered with another stack of dishes. "I'm going to wear a pair of Father's old trousers beneath one of my skirts." She paused and held the door open with her hip, letting Nick enter. He carried the tureen that had held the gumbo and the bread basket, in which two rolls were left.

"Nick, I do hope you don't think I'm too improper, wearing breeches under my skirt." Hortense's lashes fluttered.

"You said fishing was *uncultured.*" Lyddie placed her hands on her hips and looked askance at Hortense. Though she felt Nick's gaze touch her like a warm spring breeze, she avoided looking at him.

"I changed my mind," Hortense said.

Lyddie persisted, "You were going to give the hotel guests a musical evening."

"I changed my mind about that, too." Hortense glared.

Shaking her head, Lyddie continued, "And who said I wanted to go fishing?"

"You did." Nick grinned.

Frowning, she pulled an annoying curl back behind her ear. "I never said any such thing."

Bobbie June shook her head, as if in sympathy. "Now, now, Lyddie, when Nick said he'd like to come fishing, we *all* heard you when you said you'd like to go, too. And then you looked all mad and left the table when no one offered you to come along. We didn't mean to hurt your feelings by not giving a special invite to you, sweet sister. So go on, now, and get my old overalls. Shoo, now. We'll wash up everything in here and leave Agnes to handle the main dining-room dishes when the hotel guests are finished."

Lyddie blinked, realizing she had been dismissed. *Sweet Sister . . . ? Sweet Lord.* What was Bobbie June up to now?

Throwing down the dishcloth she'd been holding, Lyddie started to leave the kitchen but paused at the base of the backstairs. She was reluctant to go before she found out just what her sister was scheming.

"Do you have an extra ax?" Nick asked Billy Fred.

"Sure do. Follow me." Billy Fred disappeared out the back door, with Nick rolling up the sleeves on his crisp, white shirt as he followed.

After Nick was gone, Hortense clutched a checkered dishcloth to her ample bosom. "Did you see those muscles on his forearms when he rolled up his sleeves?" Her eyes gleamed, her thin lashes fluttering. "Why, just thinking of those arms around me . . ." She grabbed a plate. "Let's hurry with the dishes. I want time to fix my hair before we go."

Instead of the sarcastic remark Lyddie expected, Bobbie June gave Hortense an encouraging smile. "I do think he likes you."

"I know." Hortense giggled.

What was going on? Lyddie folded her arms across her chest and leveled a serious look at Hortense. "I thought Frank Worley was about to come up to scratch and ask you to get married."

"He is." Hortense used a small pot to dip water out of the hot water well on the side of the stove and pour it into the dishpans.

"If he gets wind of how you're chasing after Nick Brown, he won't," Lyddie warned.

"I still intend to marry Frank. But what Frank doesn't know won't hurt him." As Hortense poured the hotter water from the now steaming kettle over the dishes in the pan, she winked at Bobbie June, who grinned.

"Don't encourage her, Bobbie June." Lyddie rolled her eyes heavenward and shook her head. Though Hortense had had her share of beaux—mostly after the gold, Lyddie was certain—the timber foreman was the only man to seriously court her.

And it looked like Hortense was going to throw away a good man over someone like Nick Brown, who'd be gone in a few days—sooner, if he discovered who the saboteur was and that there really was no dad-blamed gold to be had.

"What are you waiting for? Get on and get changed," Bobbie June admonished.

Picking up the hem of her skirt, Lyddie resolutely went up the stairs. No matter how much she'd like to avoid Nick's company, there was nothing for it but to go along on the fishing trip. Someone had to play chaperone, to keep Hortense from ruining her reputation and losing what might be her only chance to be properly married.

Holding her fishing pole in both hands, straw hat tilted back on her head, Lyddie sat on a log scrubbed to a smooth gray by sand and water and time, the shadows of the railroad bridge zigzagging over and around her.

Her siblings were farther down the sandbar, helping Nick rig his pole and arguing over the best fishing spot. Hortense was bravely showing Nick how to bait his hook. She screamed suddenly, throwing down the bait and rubbing her hand vigorously on her old black skirt.

"It wriggled!" she whined.

With a disgusted look, Billy Fred picked it up and baited Nick's hook, then spit on the worm to rid it of sand. "There. You fish while me and Bobbie June get more bush lines made up and ready to put out. With the way they're already biting, we'll have all we can carry home before we're done!"

"Do you want me to help?" Nick asked.

"No, thank you," Bobbie June said politely, and

pushed Billy Fred toward the trail up the bluff.

"Of course they don't." Hortense wound her arm through Nick's. "You are our guest. You just enjoy yourself, now." She guided him down to the edge of the water.

Lyddie noticed Nick's frown as he turned back and watched the twins scramble up the bluff to where they'd left the twine, weights, and hooks with which to rig more bush lines.

The two had already taken Nick down the creek toward the falls and run several lines they'd put out along that section. Nick had been almost boyish in his enthusiasm as he'd shown Lyddie and Hortense the rope stringer of catfish and small trout they'd taken from the hooks. The stringer was now staked in the edge of the water, where the fish would stay cool. The plan now was to go up past the railroad bridge and tie more lines onto limbs overhanging the water.

Lyddie wondered again what the twins were really up to—and from the look he'd just shot after them, she suspected Nick must be doing the same about now.

Drawing in a deep breath, Lyddie watched her line trailing in the current. Some minnow had probably stolen the worm she'd baited her hook with. No matter. The westering sun sat just above the tops of tall, long straw pines on the opposite bank, dappling the creek bank with light and shade. Dragonflies zipped this way and that, in and out of the shadows cast by the railroad bridge.

Listening to the water rushing around a half-submerged tree trunk and the more distant noise of the falls, Lyddie let the peace of the place seep into her, putting her worries and problems to the back of her mind.

A smooth male voice interrupted her tranquil mood.

"May we sit here?" To Lyddie's surprise, Nick was standing beside her.

Hortense, obviously vexed, gave Lyddie an unhappy look that clearly said sitting near Lyddie wasn't her idea.

"Nick, Lyddie looks all comfortable and I hate to disturb her. We could sit on that other log, over there. It's more in the shade."

"We won't disturb her." To Lyddie, he added with one of his melting smiles, "Will we?"

"Not at all." She wouldn't give him the pleasure of knowing that smile disturbed her like all heck. He was just a gold hunter, she reminded herself.

As Nick sat, Lyddie scooted farther along the log. To her consternation, he followed her, making room for Hortense on his other side.

"It is nice here. It has to be one of the most beautiful, peaceful places I've been. I could get used to it here." His gaze encompassed the tall pines and high bluff on the opposite side of the creek.

Lyddie was surprised. His tone seemed warm and genuine. Like his laugh, when a few seconds later his makeshift cork—a dried twig tied onto his line—went under and he pulled out a "red belly." He held it aloft and grinned.

Hortense babbled that it was a fine fish, ignoring the fact that it was barely four inches long.

"Maybe," Nick said, eyeing it judiciously. "But I think I'll throw it back to grow some more."

"I'm certain the fish would like that," Lyddie agreed.

As his gaze met hers, Nick's coffee-brown eyes lit with something besides the pride of success as an angler, and Lyddie felt like she'd swallowed a fish. Whole. And it was flopping around inside her.

Lyddie frowned. Oh, he wouldn't disturb her at all,

she thought darkly. Why couldn't she remember he was just after the gold?

Nick went to the edge of the water and squatted to release the fish. Hortense followed him, chattering all the while about how she thought the fish was worthy of frying.

Drawing in a deep breath, Lyddie looked up at a turkey buzzard soaring above the trees, winding circles in the air. The big bird was silhouetted against thunderheads rising in the distance. She took the sight as an omen. She had to get herself under control. Even if Nick Brown was good and honest and trustworthy—all the things he *wasn't*—she had no business being attracted to him. She was a married woman in the eyes of the world. And she had to stay that way, she reminded herself yet again.

"Hortense!" Bobbie June called from atop the bluff. "Please bring me that can of bait—it's by the first piling on the bridge."

Please? Lyddie felt her brows riding up and looked toward the apparition. It looked just like Bobbie June. But she had said "Please." And earlier, there was the "sweet sister" remark. An uneasy feeling wormed through Lyddie's middle.

"All right." Hortense moved to comply, treading carefully through inch-deep water toward the can. She suddenly windmilled her arms, looking like a circus tightrope walker that had lost his balance.

"This is soapstone," she said, when she'd regained her footing, an accusing tone to her voice. "Why'd you put the can where we'd have to walk across soapstone to get it?" She glared up at Bobbie June.

"I just put it there in the shallows to stay cool." Bobbie June climbed down the path worn into the clay bluff. "Never mind. If you *can't* manage to do me a little bitty favor, I'll come all the way down there and get it myself."

Raising her chin at the challenge, Hortense took a few more careful steps and picked up the can. Looking down into it, she wrinkled her nose. "What *is* this?"

"Chicken innards. Agnes saved them for us when she cleaned the chickens for supper." Sprinting barefoot across the slippery expanse of soapstone as though it was no more than the parlor rug, Bobbie June caught up with Hortense and took hold of the can. "Let me have it."

An instant later, Hortense was lying on her back in the muddy shallows, with various parts of a chicken's inner workings scattered over her blouse.

Lyddie blinked. She could have sworn . . . She dared a look at Nick. Dark auburn brows rode up on his forehead as he met her gaze. He looked like he'd seen the same thing.

"Now, look what you've done!" Bobbie June said.

"What I did?" Hortense gasped, propping up on her elbows. "You pushed me!"

"Don't be stupid. Hold still." Squatting, Bobbie June busily retrieved the pieces of bait from her sister's chest. "I wouldn't push you—this is all the bait we got!"

"All the bait . . ." Hortense awkwardly got to her feet, brushing off Bobbie June's helping hand. When she made it back to the dry sand, she snapped, "You did! You pushed me!" As she looked down in dismay at the nasty spots dotting her white blouse, her mouth trembled.

"Now, 'Tense, why would I do that?" Bobbie June said in conciliatory tones. "I'll go back to the hotel with you and we'll get you into another blouse and be back in a wink. Now, c'mon. I am sorry you fell, you know." Shifting the bait can into her other hand, Bobbie June linked her arm through Hortense's and helped the older girl up the bluff.

At the top, Bobbie June gave Billy Fred the bait can, then disappeared with Hortense, presumably on their way back to the hotel. Billy Fred sank out of sight, too.

"What do you make of that?" Nick asked.

Lyddie turned to find Nick studying her closely and shook her head, looking back at her line. "I really haven't a clue." But something smelled fishy besides the trout and catfish on the stringer.

Nick sat back beside her on the log, and suddenly she was again all too aware of the man. Lyddie gave her line more studious attention.

"If I was the suspicious sort," he mused, "I'd say Bobbie June just engineered that whole thing to leave us alone together."

"Why . . . ?" Lyddie stared at him. She *had* thought Bobbie June pushed Hortense. Was getting them together the reason? But why? "I hope you don't think I had anything to do with that!"

"I think Bobbie June has her own agenda," Nick said. "Maybe it's just keeping us occupied."

Lifting her hook out of the stream and watching it twirl above the water, Lyddie felt warm all over. "I don't know what she's up to. If anything."

"Funny, when I went with the twins to run the lines, I never found a place where I could see the sandbar you were on this morning."

"So?"

"Billy Fred said he saw you lying on the sand. 'Lollygagging,' I think was the term he used." Lyddie's ears turned pink, and Nick felt a little warm himself as he remembered how Lyddie had looked. Then, when he'd kissed her, her body had been incredibly soft and warm.

Nick picked up a stick of driftwood and threw it into the creek. "Only he couldn't have seen you while they were putting out lines, like he said. There are too many bends in the creek."

Her ears grew redder. "Which means what?"

"He saw you from the same vantage point I did, from atop the bluff between the two falls—when I mistakenly thought you were about to be bitten by that snake."

"He saw me *before* you came along and tried to rescue me from the snake?" she said hopefully, staring into the swirling eddies in the creek.

"He saw you after I jumped into the water, but before I made it back around to collect my things." Nick thought about telling her that his notebook had been disturbed but decided against it. He didn't believe Lyddie was involved with the twins in whatever they were up to.

And the way her cheeks were going red as she watched the water was fascinating. It meant she was thinking about his kiss, about being in his arms. And she was damn well as affected by the memory of it as he was.

He sighed; remembering that didn't change the fact that she was married, and she was John Moreland's granddaughter. And her brother and sister were in serious trouble, from all his instincts were telling him.

Nick touched her shoulder, drawing Lyddie's attention back to him. He noticed how delicate her bones were—thought of how much weight those shoulders carried. It wasn't his choice to add to her troubles, but the truth had to come out.

"Do you have any idea what the twins are up to?" he asked gently.

Lyddie started to deny they were up to anything, sighed and shook her head. She'd known even before Nick showed up that they were embroiled in some scheme. Nothing serious, she was certain. Some of their usual shenanigans. But something.

His hand felt nice—warm and comforting. Without thinking, she placed her own hand over it. "I've no idea."

Her face, upturned as she studied his, was caught by a shaft of late afternoon sun that had slipped between the boughs of the stately pines.

She surprised him by saying, "But you know, don't you?"

"Not really." He shrugged. "I haven't got all the pieces of the puzzle fit together yet."

"But . . . ?" she persisted.

"But . . ." Nick drew in a deep breath, hating to add to Lyddie's burden: "I think it was Bobbie June and Billy Fred who derailed the train."

Chapter Seven

Lyddie brushed Nick's hand from her shoulder. "I don't believe you."

His look was filled with kindness and understanding. "I don't want to believe it, either. I like them, Lyddie. The twins don't seem the kind to play malicious pranks. But someone on that train could have been seriously hurt. Maybe killed." He glanced at the geometrically arranged timbers of the bridge rising above them. "The train might have fallen into the creek, if it hadn't been slowing down as it approached the depot."

"The twins wouldn't derail a train. Why would they?" She scooted farther away on the log. No, what he was saying was preposterous. The twins never did anything without a reason. And their reason was always money. There was no profit that she could see in tearing a hole into the side of the depot building, or in derailing a train—and the twins would have never placed people in danger like that.

"I'm waiting," she demanded, sensing by his expression that he was unsure of their motive. "Why would they do those things?"

Why was a sticking point, Nick admitted to himself. In his detective work he'd been trained that discovering three things were necessary to solving any crime and then proving the perpetrator's guilt: establishing motive, method, and opportunity.

Motive was key. Though he had little doubt the twins were guilty, he still had no idea why they had pulled the spikes out of the rails. Or why they knocked holes into the depot wall. If they had a grudge against the railroad, he'd yet to discover what it could be.

He shook his head. "Maybe you could talk with them, find out what's going on."

Lyddie glowered at him. He looked so sincere and honest. And more handsome than anything that had ever gotten off the train in Crossroads before. It was an act, she reminded herself. Nick Brown, she decided, wanted convenient suspects. Maybe he wanted to get the twins into trouble, just to have leverage to pry information about the gold out of her.

"I might try. If I believed for one second that they were involved."

"Lyddie, you just acknowledged that they were up to something."

She gritted her teeth. "They are *always* up to something. Some scheme to make money. But they wouldn't derail the train, or smash up the depot. How could they get any money for that?"

"Maybe someone with a grudge against the railroad paid them."

She glowered at him. "That's ridiculous! Maybe you should look for someone with a grudge against the railroad and investigate *that* person and leave the twins alone. They didn't do anything!"

"Lyddie," Nick said quietly, in case Billy Fred was listening from atop the bluff, "I have proof."

His words hung in the warm evening air, the muted roar of the falls and the babbling creek unable to drown them out. Suddenly the sun edged behind a pine top, and shadows pooled around them. A distant whistle at the depot shrilled a warning of a train about to depart. A slow chugging and another whistle followed.

Dear lord, could the twins really be responsible? No, she couldn't believe it.

"What is your proof?" she demanded.

The look in the wide eyes she turned to him made him want to gather her close and tell her not to worry. She had no doubt done far more worrying than she should have as she held her odd family together and ran the hotel.

But he couldn't save her from this added burden. It was something Lyddie had to accept and deal with. Or rather, let the twins deal with.

Still, Nick considered how much he should tell her. Really, he shouldn't discuss his investigation with her, especially not until he had enough to level charges. He shook his head. "I don't want to reveal what I've found. Not yet. But it does implicate them."

Her expression hardened. "I see." She turned her attention to her pole and began rolling it, winding her line up along it. "I guess they do make perfect scapegoats. You won't have to spend a great deal of energy on this *investigation*, now that you've found someone to blame."

"I'm not making them—*hell!*" Nick caught her wrist and tugged her to her feet.

"What are you doing?" Lyddie demanded.

Taking her pole from her hand, he tossed it to the sand. "Showing you what you don't want to see." He pulled her along, compelling her to follow him toward the path up the bluff. "It ties in with the lie about seeing you at the swim hole while they were putting out lines in the creek, when they couldn't possibly have seen you from there."

Lyddie made no comment, but shook off his hand and scrambled up the bluff in front of Nick. She had asked to see proof, hadn't she? She could hardly refuse to look at what he was going to show her. But there was a knot of dread in her stomach. What if he was right? What if they were responsible?

As Nick followed close behind her, he reached for a root to steady himself and glanced up. Lyddie's derriere, the rounded curves revealed to perfection in the old denim overalls, was before him. Her behind wriggled with her efforts as she climbed the steep path, catching handholds to help her up. Desire, hot and hard, slammed into him.

Damn, he'd already decided wanting her was a bad idea. Why did that idea just keep on occurring to him? Reminding himself again that she was a married woman, Nick paused and let her go on up the path.

If he could just stop remembering their kiss that morning, it would be a lot easier, he decided. Lyddie wasn't a woman of easy virtue, though she had responded with passion. She'd also been embarrassed by her response—it was obvious she hadn't been aroused in a very long time.

And that was all it had been for her—being alone had made her vulnerable. Nick realized the hunger he had tasted as she'd kissed him had been an eruption of long-denied need. A need to feel arms around her. To be desired. To be held. The natural needs of any woman.

But she didn't need him. Not really. He had just been the one to bring her hunger to the surface.

Nick drew in a deep breath at the thought.

Her husband, Nick decided, was the biggest fool in creation to walk away from a woman like Lyddie. Just why the man had left was a mystery that begged to be solved.

Nick decided that before he left town he would find out the answer to that mystery, too.

Topping the bluff, Nick joined Lyddie at the spot where the engine had derailed. The wounds gouged in the earth where steel wheels had left the tracks were still raw and deep. A ball of fishing twine and the can of bait sat on an old stump. Billy Fred was nowhere to be seen.

Lyddie glanced in the direction of town as the chugging grew steadily faster and louder. "The train will be here shortly." There was a vibration trembling through the ground as a train approached. "Whatever you want to show me will have to wait. We can't stay here. It's too close to the rails."

"C'mon up here," Billy Fred called, peeping over the edge of the second bluff, which rose up like the top tier on a wedding cake.

"What I want to show you is up there anyway." Nick motioned for her to precede him and scrambled up after her, carefully keeping his eyes diverted from the dangerous sight of her bottom in the overalls.

Lyddie and Nick made it to the top of the second bluff just as the train appeared on the other side of the creek and started across the bridge. Noise and smoke boiled into the air, making communication impossible. As the train passed, the engineer smiled and waved from his window, then drew down on the cord, shrilly sounding the steam whistle again.

After the eight cars and caboose had passed, Billy Fred waved a hand in front of his face, dissipating the lingering smoke. "I got the lines rigged. You going with me, Nick?" He held up a piece of board with the hooks neatly sunk into the edge. Twine lines were securely wrapped around it.

"No. You go ahead. I need to show Lyddie these footprints I found earlier."

"Footprints?" Lyddie frowned. "What footprints?" She looked down at the red clay beneath her old shoes. It was dry and as hard as rock.

As though reading her thoughts, Nick said, "It rained the day the train was derailed." He led Lyddie over the back side of the narrow ledge, just before briars and persimmon shrubs marked the edge of the woods.

Billy Fred followed, looking wary.

"The night these prints were made, this area would have been covered in soft red mud. Two people stood up here, hidden, and watched the whole thing. It hasn't rained since that night, so I think it likely these prints were made by whoever sabotaged the rails."

On the weather-beaten ground, pieces of white chalky substance were scattered over the impressions in the red clay. "That's odd." Kneeling on one knee, Nick stroked his chin, looking thoughtful.

Billy Fred thrust his hands into his pockets. "What's odd?"

"Looks like someone went to a lot of trouble to destroy the casts," Nick said.

"What casts?" Lyddie had the feeling Nick was play-acting now.

"Casts? You mean that white chalky stuff?" Billy Fred's gaze shifted uneasily between Nick and Lyddie.

Studying her brother, Lyddie felt the knot in her stomach tighten.

"Yes. I poured plaster of paris into footprints here and here." Nick pointed to where he meant. Broken shards of white were all that remained. "The casts have been shattered." He sat back on his heels. "This evidence is useless."

"Ah, shucks, Nick, I'm sure enough sorry it got broke." Billy Fred pushed his hands deeper into his pockets and kicked a stray piece of plaster with his bare foot. "Me and Bobbie June found those big white spots on the ground and we didn't know what they was, so we broke 'em up, trying to figure it out. So I guess we're to blame." His gaze met Nick's and skittered away. "I shore am sorry."

Kneeling, Nick moved all the chunks from the area where he'd poured the plaster. It wasn't simply that the plaster was broken. The footprints he'd tried to cast had been gouged and scratched until they were destroyed, too. Looking up, he met Lyddie's distressed gaze—she was no one's fool. Her expression told him she recognized the truth and wasn't happy.

"Well, I guess if you didn't know what it was, I can't hold a grudge," he told Billy Fred.

He brightened. "That's awful good of you, Nick."

"Sure. You'll know what it is, if you ever find more, won't you? So you'll be real careful about leaving it alone?"

"Yep."

"And I know you'd be honest and truthful, and if you

could help me find out the truth about what happened that night, a fine young man like you would do it." Nick paused, then added, "Wouldn't you?"

Billy Fred's bright expression faded, the corners of his mouth drooping. He nodded, looking at his dusty toes.

"Tell you what, it'll be dark soon. You go ahead and start putting out the lines. We'll wait here for Bobbie June and Hortense to get back, then I'll go on back to the hotel. I have a few things to do tonight."

Billy Fred scrambled down the bluff and, after collecting the bait can from the stump, disappeared down the path toward the creek.

As Lyddie watched him go, she kicked a shard of plaster. "How does this tie in with the twins seeing me on the sandbar this morning?"

"You believe me when I say they were involved?" Nick looked at her levelly.

Feeling warm under his gaze, she thrust her hands into her pockets in imitation of Billy Fred. "I told you, I believe there is something going on with those two. I'm still not convinced they maliciously damaged the rails." Lyddie just couldn't believe they would do that.

"I've pointed out that there isn't any way they could have seen you on the sandbar except from the bluff between the falls." Nick added softly, "And when they saw you, they saw us."

"Oh, no." She put her hands to her cheeks. That was too embarrassing to contemplate.

His expression softened, his gaze moving to her lips. "Yes." Blinking, he shook his head, as though trying to collect his thoughts. Taking a notebook from his pocket, he flipped through the pages. Finding what he wanted, he stepped closer and showed her where he'd made a note about finding the boot prints.

"So?" Lyddie wanted to step away. She was all too aware of the open neck of his shirt, the strong column of his throat and the tanned skin on his chest visible in the exposed vee. He smelled faintly of shaving soap.

"I left this in my boot when I jumped into the creek and swam over to save you from the snake."

His smile was self-deprecating and oh so endearing. Lyddie tried hard not to notice the one dimple on the right side of his mouth when his lips curved upward. Or how well sculpted his mouth was—she remembered all too well how his lips felt on hers.

Get a hold of yourself! Lyddie kicked another piece of plaster. She cleared her throat. "But what has leaving your notebook in your boot—*oh!*" Lyddie gasped as the truth hit her.

"It had been tampered with when I went to retrieve my things," he confirmed.

It all fell into place. The twins were at the top of the falls when they saw her—no, her and Nick; they found out about the prints from the notebook; then they destroyed the evidence.

Lyddie felt she had been dunked under Roaring Falls as she realized the ramifications. The twins could really be involved. *They could end up in jail. . . .*

She had heard of the horrors of life in the state penitentiary. Strong men often didn't survive. What would happen to a boy like Billy Fred? And women's prison, she'd heard, was just as bad. How would Bobbie June survive?

"I can't believe they're guilty. There must be another explanation!"

Looking down into her frightened eyes, Nick hated having to be the one to make her face the fact that her brother and sister were in serious trouble. "I haven't gathered definitive proof. You and I see how it must have happened, but I can hardly bring that to court." Unable to help himself, Nick gathered her to him and stroked her shoulders and back.

Lyddie sighed and pressed against him. Oh, but it felt so good to lean into his strength, to feel his hard chest beneath her cheek. His touch was comforting, soothing, as his strong fingers trailed circles on her back.

Then she remembered Nick Brown was really after the gold. He couldn't be trusted.

Lyddie pushed out of his embrace. "*Definitive proof*..." She clenched her hands into fists. "I know what you're really after, Nick Brown. If you solve this case too soon, you won't have a chance to look for Gentleman John's gold, will you?"

Frowning, Nick watched as Lyddie scrambled down the bluff and headed back toward the hotel, passing Bobbie June on the way.

"Hey, where are you . . . *hey!*" Bobbie June stared at Lyddie as she disappeared between the low shrubs lining the path.

Bobbie climbed up next to Nick and looked in the direction Lyddie had gone. "What bee got up her nose?"

"I think she's worried." Nick watched as Bobbie June's gaze darted to the broken pieces of his mold, then back to his face.

"About what, do you suppose?" Bobbie June swung an old Confederate infantry soldier's knapsack from her shoulder.

Shrugging, Nick said, "I think Lyddie worries about a lot of things, like keeping the family business open. If bad things happen and can be connected with the hotel, the railroad might withdraw its support and endorse another hotel on down the line."

"It wouldn't!" Bobbie June paled.

"It might. If someone connected with the hotel caused the damage to the depot or derailed that train . . ." Nick shrugged and changed the subject. "I think Lyddie worries about taking care of everyone. Your grandmother seems to live in the past much of the time."

"Gram just likes to remember. She's not senile or anything."

"Not at all," Nick agreed. "But she doesn't seem to take an active part in the running of the hotel."

Bobbie June shrugged. "I guess she sees we're all grown and can do things for ourselves."

"Yes, that should be true. But when Molly's not busy teaching school she's totally focused on medicine. Then there's Hortense—where is Hortense, by the way?"

"Frank Worley was waiting at the hotel when we got back," Bobbie June said.

Nick guessed that the young girl had something to do with the lumber foreman's appearance at the hotel. Why was she trying to keep Hortense busy? Or was it Lyddie she wanted to keep busy—Lyddie and himself? He suspected it was the latter.

"Well, anyway, you and Billy Fred seem bent on your own adventures and might not notice, but Lyddie seems to be the lynchpin that holds the family together." Nick turned away, ignoring Bobbie June's mutinous expression at this remark.

"We do our part!"

She followed him as he moved to a clump of pine straw on the backside of the open area, half-hidden beneath low-hanging huckleberry bushes.

"But she has to be the one always organizing, seeing that things are taken care of." As he knelt down and brushed the pine straw aside, revealing more plaster casts, he sensed Bobbie June's alarm. "I need something to carry these back in, before something happens to them, too." He motioned at the canvas bag. "Could you lend me that knapsack?"

Chapter Eight

"What are we gonna do?" Billy Fred asked. He used pliers to catch hold of the tough hide on the small catfish. It was suspended from a hook attached to a limb of the old china ball tree behind the hotel, where they always hung up their catfish to skin them. The fish, quite dead, made no protest as Billy Fred stripped a section of tough skin away.

"Well?" As he chewed a straw stuck into the corner of his mouth, he slung the remains off his pliers into an oaken bucket. One of the waiting neighborhood cats grabbed the delicacy and made off with it across the backyard.

Billy Fred chewed the straw back to the other side of his mouth and watched the cat's progress as the silence from his usually opinionated sister continued. At length, he asked, "Think we should tell Lye-Beth?"

The news that they hadn't destroyed all the prints had

come as a nasty shock. Just thinking about it made his stomach feel funny. The smell of dead fish wasn't helping. He hadn't even been able to enjoy their night camping out on the creek. Billy Fred had felt an empathy for every fish he'd taken off a line, feeling well and thoroughly hooked himself.

Bobbie June and her big ideas! Sometimes he could just smack her a good one.

"Well?" He glowered at her as her silence continued.

"I'm thinking." Straddling the bench, her overalls rolled up to expose her legs and bare feet, Bobbie June held their grandfather's indecipherable sketches spread out in front of her as she waved felines and flies away from the enamel dishpan of cleaned fish in front of her.

For once, his sister looked stumped. Billy Fred frowned, not liking that impression at all. "Hey, you better come up with something. It was your idea that landed us in this mess. I said the gold wasn't anywhere near the creek—Gentleman John wouldn't have taken a chance on the bluff wastin' away in some spring flood. He was too darn smart for that." He returned his attention to the fish.

Bobbie June sighed. "If Number Twenty-two had been on time instead of ahead of schedule—"

"Yeah, we been over that. Truth is, it was jus' plain stupid on our part. We shouldn't a taken a chance with the rails. Not even if a ton of gold was under 'em. Which none *was*. Someone could have been hurt."

Arching a superior brow, Bobbie June returned her attention to the yellowed velum. "Why did Gentleman John have to make this so darned cryptic?" she sighed.

"You don't think I know what *cryptic* means, do you? Well, you're wrong. He made it cryptic so not just any ol' body could find the gold."

"Ssssh! Not so loud. Pinkerton is likely to be lurking around. I noticed he lurks a lot."

"Don't *ssssh* me! It wasn't me who knocked the holes in the depot wall."

"Well, that sledgehammer was heavy and I missed the crowbar. And anyway, the railroad should thank us for finding out that wall was eat up with wood lice before the whole darn place had to be tore down."

"Twice. You missed twice," Billy Fred reminded her ruthlessly. He'd been holding the crowbar in question and thanked quick reflexes for his escape without injury. "What I want to know is, how are we going to throw ol' Pinkerton off our scent now that he has . . ." He quickly glanced around the backyard, making certain they were alone. "Well, what we gonna do now?"

"Am I suppose to know *everything?"* Bobbie June eyed her brother askance.

Shaking his head, Billy Fred broke the catfish's backbone and cut the body off the head, then placed the freshly cleaned fish into the enamel pan on the bench. "Fine time for you to run out of ideas."

"I haven't run out of ideas. I've already tied our boots to a rope and hung them in the old well. Pinkerton can't compare the soles to his casts if he can't find the boots." Bobbie June covered the pan with cheesecloth again, keeping the cleaned fish from the houseflies buzzing about.

"That's good. With all the black widow spiders in the well, nobody will fool around there." Billy Fred tossed the fish head into the scrap bucket. A large calico, obviously a nursing mother, grabbed the treat and ran beneath the hotel.

"That must be where she has her kittens hid," Bobbie June mused.

"We'll have fleas coming up through the floor," Billy Fred predicted.

"You two have plenty of hot lime left over from that stupid get-rid-of-your-fleas business," Molly said, rounding the corner. "You'd better crawl under the hotel and sprinkle some around."

Grabbing the papers reflexively, Bobbie June clutched them to her chest. "Molly!" She rolled her eyes heavenward. "You scared the wits outta me."

"Why?" Molly's tone was at once suspicious. "What have you got there?"

"Our flea business was not stupid. We performed a needed service and made lots of money at it," Billy Fred protested vigorously, trying to divert Molly's attention. "People were grateful for us to crawl around under their houses and spread the lime."

"Yes, until they found out it was you two who were putting the fleas under their houses to start with." Not to be sidetracked, Molly casually snatched the papers from her sister's grasp as Bobbie June tried to stuff them into the bib of her overalls.

"Give those back!" Bobbie June rose.

Paying the protest no attention at all, Molly sat on the end of the bench and spread the sheets out on her lap. "Why, this is the hotel."

"The hotel?" Bobbie June frowned. "No. It can't be."

"Sure it is." Molly smoothed the top sheet, then turned it. "You had it upside down."

"That's what *I* said." Billy Fred shot his twin an I-told-you-so look. He'd long maintained they should concentrate their efforts in looking for the gold in and around the hotel. That way, if something went awry, at least they wouldn't be as likely to get investigated by the Pinkerton.

"Yes. Look, this is the railing of the landing behind

the front desk." Molly pointed at ill-drawn vertical lines—lines that distinctly had the word *rail* written above them.

"It can't be! Why does it say 'ten feet'?" Bobbie June frowned, moving nearer to peer at the paper.

"The ceiling in the lobby is about ten feet high, I'd say, until it opens into the air well at the stairs."

"That couldn't be it. If it's the lobby, what does this *X* mark?" Bobbie June protested, stabbing at a series of crossed lines sketched just below the railing.

Frowning, Molly twisted the drawing this way and that. "It's the chandelier in the lobby."

"She's right." Billy Fred edged nearer, a sinking feeling roiling his stomach. In all their many interpretations—whether the sketch was of the tracks, which just happened to be exactly ten feet from the depot building, or the tracks on the bluff above Myers Creek—they had always agreed that the *X* marked the gold. *X* always marked the gold on treasure maps—everyone knew that. He'd thought it had only been a matter of reading the map correctly to find it.

Now, to discover the *X* was just a dumb chandelier. . . .

"That can't be right," Bobbie June said, but her tone was less certain than before.

"Of course I'm right. I'm a schoolteacher, after all," Molly said. "This is Grandpa's handwriting, isn't it? It looks the same as the family names he wrote in the Bible, so it must be his. These must be the sketches Gentleman John drew up for the carpenters when he had the hotel built."

Molly shifted the pages and smoothed out another drawing. "That has to be it. Look, this is the front of the hotel."

Bobbie June frowned at the wavering lines. "I thought

those lines were Roaring Falls. How can you tell it's the hotel?"

"Here's the veranda. Here's the widow's walk on the roof." Molly jabbed the paper with a finger, pointing to various features. "The front steps. But I don't know what this oblong thing is in the corner."

"The old well," Billy Fred supplied.

"You're right. I had forgotten about it being there," Molly said, rising, still holding the sketches and ignoring Bobbie June's outstretched hand. "I came out to tell you that Jane is ready for the fish. Hurry up and get them to her." She started away, shifting through the sheets.

"Hey, those are mine," Bobbie June declared. At Molly's inquisitive look, she added, "I found them, and I was looking at them first."

"I'll give them back. I'm just going to show Nick. He's really interested in the hotel and is always asking me questions about how it was built."

"No!" The twins protested in unison as Molly disappeared around the corner.

Complete silence reigned for an instant.

"Think Molly's smitten with ol' Pinkerton, too?" Bobbie June asked.

"No, she's in love with doctoring. But Pinkerton is going to get an eyeful of our treasure maps."

"Yes," Bobbie June agreed dourly. "Nick's smart. It was real sneaky of him to hide those other boot prints while he made casts of 'em."

"Then to put the casts in the depot safe," Billy Fred added, then brightened. "But, you know, Gentleman John was pretty smart, too. It was real smart to put an *X* for the chandelier—kinda like he wanted to throw people off from the real mark."

His sister looked at him, hope rekindling in her gaze.

"That's it. A *fake X*! The real mark won't be so obvious."

"The key to the treasure is still in those dang drawings, if we can just figure it out before Nick does." But with Nick getting an eyeful of the plans, Billy Fred reckoned they hadn't a shot in blazes of finding the treasure before the Pinkerton agent did.

"I'll take these fish to Jane so she can start, then go get our maps back." Bobbie June left with the pan, a determined spring to her stride.

After shooing the cats away, Billy Fred lifted the board covering the fish bucket and took out the last one. Hanging it on the hook, he sent up a silent hope that Bobbie June would be able to get the drawings back without casting more suspicion their way. Maybe she could.

And maybe, a little voice warned, it was already too late to avoid suspicion. Why else would Nick have let them know he had those casts?

How could she keep Bobbie June and Billy Fred out of prison? Lyddie dipped her rag into the pail of vinegar water and gave the window a vigorous wipe, cutting a clean swath through the mildew clouding the pane. She was on the inside of the roof cupola, looking out on the town. The day was already shaping up to be a scorcher. Heat rose from within the hotel, finding its way up through the air well. Sweat beaded her forehead and trickled between Lyddie's breasts.

Determined to finish quickly, she rinsed her rag again and moved on to the next pane. As she did, she searched for an answer to her silent query. There had to be an answer!

It wasn't likely they were innocent. Despite her protest to Nick, she'd felt their guilt in her bones long before he had pointed out that the twins' story about seeing her while putting out lines didn't hold water.

She had to believe they hadn't meant any harm. But lord only knew what they thought they were doing. Now it was just a matter of time before Nick had the evidence he needed to go to the sheriff. If he didn't already.

Then what was she going to do?

Lyddie rinsed her rag and cleaned the next pane without an answer presenting itself.

Through the high windows, she had a view down Main Street, all the way to the depot building, where Nick Brown had disappeared earlier. With its engine puffing black smoke, a train pulled forward, then backed up every few minutes as it hitched to flat cars filled with long pine logs. The short toots from its steam whistle warning of each change of direction grated on Lyddie's nerves.

There was the usual foot traffic along the street and an occasional horse and wagon. A man Lyddie had spotted earlier as a treasure hunter came out of the store carrying a shiny new shovel. He headed off in the direction of the trestle bridge over the creek, casting a quick glance over his shoulder, as if afraid of being followed.

Lyddie was almost finished with the windows when Nick reappeared. Closing the depot door, he started back along the boardwalk toward the hotel. The two men who always sat on a bench in front of the mercantile nodded amiably as he passed, and Nick returned their nod.

Lyddie could imagine the pair's curiosity over how the investigation was going—there were no secrets in a small town. That morning, Ned Jones, the farmer who sold them milk, had asked her about the plaster casts of the boot prints that Nick had placed in the depot safe. She'd seen only the shattered ones—it was the first she had heard that any casts had survived. And the news had made her breakfast feel like lead in her stomach.

Well, there was one secret in this small town, Lyddie amended, remembering that Gerald Seaton rested in the old well. And that one secret must be kept at all costs.

"What on earth are you doing up here?" Hortense blew a wisp of lank brown hair from her forehead as she ascended the stairs into the cupola.

"Cleaning. Thank you for volunteering to help." Lyddie raised the window she'd just finished and wiped the sill. "You can start on the outside." She motioned at the widow's walk surrounding the air well.

"No, thank you." Hortense peered over her sister's shoulder as the couple who had checked in the day before made their way down the front walk, passing Nick Brown at the gate. "They're going out for a stroll before lunch. They'll be catching the afternoon train to New Orleans to visit their son. He's a banker."

Hortense leaned closer to Lyddie's shoulder. Lyddie doubted it was to get a better view of the strolling couple.

"Don't let him catch you staring." As she spoke, Lyddie tore her rag into two pieces and thrust one into her sister's hands. "Here. If he looks up, he'll see you washing windows instead of just gaping at him."

Rinsing the cloth out, Hortense said, "I could have bashed Frank Worley over his half-bald head for showing up unannounced last evening, what with Nick waiting for me down by the creek." Smiling, she applied the cloth to glass Lyddie had already cleaned. "But what could I do? The poor man is smitten—he brought me a dozen yellow roses all the way from Jackson."

Having heard about the yellow roses every time she'd seen Hortense that morning, or having them thrust beneath her nose to smell every time she'd passed through the lobby, Lyddie rolled her eyes heavenward—and spotted a dirt dauber nest on the ceiling, which would have to be removed.

At least the appearance of Nick Brown hadn't totally swept the lumber foreman from Hortense's mind. Feeling compelled to nurture that seedling, Lyddie said, "Frank is a fine catch." Pulling the next window down, she rinsed her cloth as she prepared to start washing, but was stilled by the sight of Molly rushing up to Nick and showing him some sort of papers.

"I'll likely accept when he proposes." Hortense sighed. "If he ever gets around to doing it proper. That is, unless Nick gives me a sign that he's truly interested. What do you think that's all about?" She gestured at Nick and Molly, both of whom were giving rapt attention to the papers. Looking thoroughly irritated, Bobbie June joined the two.

"Wish I could hear what they're saying," Hortense murmured.

"Just look busy," Lyddie advised as she raised the window she'd been about to wash. However, because of the train's rumbling and tooting as it hitched to cars, she still couldn't understand what Nick and Molly were saying.

Lifting her skirt, Lyddie stepped over the windowsill onto the widow's walk and made a show of cleaning the outside pane. "This side has to be washed too, doesn't it?"

"Sure does," agreed Hortense, passing the bucket to Lyddie and following her out.

As Nick and Molly bent their heads over the papers in deep discussion, Bobbie June casually took the sheets. Molly pulled them from her grasp and gave them back to Nick.

"Must be mighty interesting, whatever it is," Hortense

mused. She grabbed a rag from the bucket and began wiping the glass as the trio looked toward the hotel.

Pausing to wipe the sweat from her brow, Lyddie watched as Nick bent his head near Molly. And she didn't like how close he was to her sister, or the rapt interest he pretended in whatever she was saying.

Stop it! You are not jealous of Molly! Lyddie told herself firmly.

"I can't tell what they're talking about. Knowing Molly, she's asking something personal about his digestive tract." Hortense shook her head pityingly, giving up all pretense of washing the window. "She'll never find a beau or get married, you know."

Lyddie thought about telling Hortense there were other things in life besides getting married but decided to save her breath. Besides, she was much more interested in what Molly and Nick were discussing. Leaning back against the railing surrounding the widow's walk, she tried to listen.

"You'll get paint flakes all over you, Lyddie," Hortense warned.

"Sssh!" Clutching the railing, Lyddie listened as Molly pointed into the azalea bushes surrounding the old well, then took Nick's arm, leading him toward it. Bobbie June took off her straw hat and threw it down on the grass.

Lyddie felt her mouth go dry. They were going to the well. Why on earth was Molly taking him there? Leaning as far as she could over the weathered railing, Lyddie tried to hear what was being said. Snatches of the conversation came to her over the pounding of her own heart. Molly explained that the well was abandoned because, when their grandfather had built the hotel he'd put a pump down inside the kitchen.

Then Nick said, "Gerald." Or Lyddie thought he said, "Gerald." Holding her breath, she leaned out farther, trying to hear more.

"That railing don't look too good. I wouldn't lean on it like—" Hortense began.

The rail snapped. Lyddie pitched headfirst down the steeply angled roof.

Frantically spreading her hands on the wooden shingles, she slowed her progress.

"Lyddie! Lyddie! Oh, no! Oh, no, *Lyddie!*"

Lyddie wanted to tell Hortense to shut up before she drew Nick's attention—but it was too late. As Nick looked up, then rushed forward, she was acutely aware that her skirt had fallen up over her thighs, showing her bloomers. *Well, it's not as if he hasn't seen my bloomers before. . . .* The incongruous thought faded completely as she gained speed.

Instinct took over. Spreading her legs, unmindful of the unladylike view she was giving anyone whose attention was drawn by Hortense's wails, Lyddie dragged the toes of her shoes against the split cypress shingles. Gradually, she slowed. Then she stopped, her outstretched hands just inches from the edge.

Sighing with relief, she rested her cheek against the sun-warmed wood.

Her relief was short-lived, however, as it occurred to her that, should she start sliding again, she would fall in a heartbeat. She eyed the gutter attached to the roof. She might make a grab for it to stabilize herself. But the metal was rusted badly; it didn't look likely to hold her weight.

"Just stay still!" Nick yelled.

"Yeah, be still!" Hortense echoed.

"Of all the stupid advice!" Lyddie barked, then groaned as she slid forward another inch. Pressing down harder with her toes, she stopped herself again.

Behind her, Hortense was wailing like a banshee. Lyddie wanted to tell her to shut up but didn't dare risk it. Telling anyone anything seemed to put axle grease under her.

Staring at her fingers splayed on the shingles, she watched as her hands slid forward a fraction of an inch, then slid again. To her horror, she slipped a tiny bit each time she breathed.

Chapter Nine

Looking up at the roof, Nick caught Molly's shoulders. "Hurry, get a rope."

"There's one in the shed." Molly turned to go.

"It's not there." Bobbie June grabbed her sister's sleeve, stopping her.

"What do you mean?" Molly demanded, the forgotten drawings crumpled tightly in her hand.

"That it's not there!" Frowning, Bobbie June plucked the papers from her sister's grasp and stuffed them into the pocket on the bib of her overalls. What could she say, with Pinkerton listening? How had hiding their boots in the well led to this? "I mean, I didn't see it there when I was looking for it earlier. It's . . ." Oh, she had to tell them the truth, she had to tell them where the rope was. Even if it did mean going to jail, it was the only way to save Lye-Beth. "It, ah, it, it . . ." She tried to force the confession out past stiff lips.

"We need something, now," Nick interrupted. To Molly, he said, "We'll tie sheets together to make a rope."

"Leave tying the sheets to me. You go see if you can do anything to help Lyddie right now." Molly darted a glance at her sister on the roof. "Maybe there's something you can do."

"Okay," Nick agreed. Sprinting across the yard, he leapt up the steps and across the porch, disappearing into the hotel with Molly on his heels.

Drawn by the raised voices, Billy Fred ran to where Bobbie June stood. "How the heck did Lye-Beth get up there?" he asked, shading his eyes to look up at the roof.

Catching his wrist and eyeing the skinning knife he was holding, Bobbie June said, "Never mind. Come on! We got to get the rope out of the well."

A few moments later they had plowed their way through the thick azalea bushes, and Billy Fred tossed aside one of the old oaken planks covering the top. Leaning over the edge of the crumbling sandstone and mortar at the spot Bobbie June directed, he felt along the inside wall until he found the rope tied to a root, which stuck out about four feet down.

He had to hand it to Bobbie June, he thought as he fought to saw the damp hemp in two with his knife; no one would have found her hiding place.

As he hauled their old boots up by the rope, a brown cobweb spider ran up his arm. Yelping, he almost dropped the prize back into the well.

"Watch out!" Bobbie June caught the rope as he let go completely and beat at the spider, which fell into the grass and disappeared. She finished hauling the boots out. "Hurry! Cut them off the end."

With a final wary glance at his sleeve, Billy Fred

grabbed the hemp and sawed against the knot holding the boots. The footwear fell free.

"Okay, what now?"

"Darn, I hate to do this. These were the best wearing boots I had in years." Bobbie June grimaced and heaved the boots back into the well. They made a distant splash.

"Bobbie June! What the heck did you do—"

"Shush! We can't let Pinkerton find 'em and match 'em to the prints." Bobbie June grabbed the rope and pushed through the bushes. "And we have to get this to Lye-Beth now, before it's too late!"

From out of nowhere, the yard had filled with people, all gaping and pointing at Lye-Beth splayed on the roof, red-faced. More people were rushing down the street, exclaiming as they converged on the spectacle.

Running, Bobbie June dodged through the gathering crowd, hoping they'd been too busy gawking to wonder what she and Billy Fred had been up to by the old well.

But if Lye-Beth fell because the rope wasn't in the shed when it was needed . . . The thought was too horrible to finish. Bobbie June knew she wouldn't care who knew what they'd been up to if any thing happened to Lye-Beth.

A sob caught in her throat as she pushed past Old Ben, who was usually to be found sitting in front of the mercantile, watching all the goings-on in Crossroads. "There now, Bobbie June. No need to fret." Seeing how distressed she was, he caught her shoulder with a gnarled hand. "I reckon that Pinkerton man'll find a way to help Lyddie."

Swallowing down a lump, Bobbie June snapped, "If you'll let me get this rope to him, he might!"

"Sure." The old man released her and she rushed inside.

* * *

It hadn't taken Nick long to reach the landing that circled the inside of the air well. There was a strong smell of vinegar still in the air, and a bucket and rags were on the widow's walk beside the broken railing, showing what Lyddie had been doing when she fell.

This is bad. Through the window, the roof seemed even steeper, and the time-polished wooden shingles looked damned slick. From this viewpoint, Lyddie's position on the edge of the roof appeared even more precarious. Hampered by her long skirt, he didn't know how she was managing to stay on at all. The ground was a long way down. If she slipped . . .

His heart thumped painfully. "How are you doing, Lyddie?" he called softly.

"Just enjoying the sun," she retorted without turning to look at him.

He was drawn to smile, in spite of his fear for her. She had pluck, did Lyddie Shea Seaton.

"Thank *goodness* you're here!" Catching Nick off guard, Hortense hurled herself through the open window from the widow's walk. He barely managed to catch her without being knocked over the railing and down the air well.

"Oh, whatever are we going to do?" she wailed.

Forcefully unwinding her arms, Nick told her, "Go get a good blanket and several of those men in the yard to stretch it beneath the edge of the roof, in case she falls."

"But—"

"Now!" He turned her toward the stairs.

As Hortense descended, sniffling, Nick leaned over the stair railing and saw sheets flying out of a second-floor bedroom. "We'll need at least four," he called to Molly, calculating the distance to the edge of the roof. Five would be better, but he didn't want to take the time to tie five together. Every second Lyddie stayed out on the roof was a second too long. Taking them three at a time, he started down the stairs, intending to help speed things up. Lyddie couldn't hang there indefinitely.

"Forget the sheets," Bobbie June called as she pounded up the stairway, a rope coiled over her shoulder. She almost overset Hortense as they passed on the second-floor landing. She took the last flight two steps at a time.

Nick took the rope from her shoulder. "Where did this come from?" Not waiting for an answer, he dropped it down the roof and felt hope surge as it went well past Lyddie and dropped into the gutter.

"I—found it." Still gasping for breath, Bobbie June took the end from him and secured it around the casement between two of the windows, tying it in a strong square knot.

Nick tested the knot, then nodded and stepped through the window onto the widow's walk. After wrapping the rope around his arm, he passed it behind him, where it could slip through his hands as he lowered himself.

"Hold still, Lyddie. I'll have you in a moment."

"Hold *still?*" Her muffled voice was indignant, her wheat-blond curls trembling. "I thought I might get up and dance a jig on the edge of the rain gutter—of course I'll hold still! Would you please hurry?"

"I'm on my way." Nick grasped the rope hand over hand, lowering himself as he made his way past the broken railing and started down the roof. The rope, he noticed, was old, the hemp damp and slimy, deteriorating in places. It would have to hold, he decided. It was all they had. Besides, Lyddie couldn't weigh more than a hundred pounds soaking wet.

Unbidden came the memory of Lyddie rising from the

creek water, her nipples taut points against her transparent camisole. A hundred pounds, but in all the right places . . .

He pushed the image aside as he maneuvered himself beside Lyddie on the edge of the roof.

She looked up at him. "Glad you made it." Her light tone gave no hint of her distress, although there was a shadow of fear in her eyes. Yes, she was quite a woman, this Lyddie Shea Seaton.

"Me, too." Glancing at the sheer drop to the hard ground below, he sat beside her on the roof and propped his heel against the gutter. When Nick was certain he wouldn't slide, he said, "Push up, if you can, Lyddie, and I'll run the rope under your arms."

Billy Fred joined his sister at the window. "Just get the rope around Lye-Beth and we'll help haul her up," he called to Nick.

Nick asked Lyddie, "Can you do it?"

"I don't have a lot of choice, do I?" Palms moist against the slick wooden shingles, Lyddie carefully raised herself a couple of inches. As he slid the rope beneath her, she sucked in a sharp breath as the back of Nick's hand brushed her breasts. A riot of tingling sensations surged through her.

It sure wasn't the time to be thinking about that! she scolded herself. Or to be remembering how it had felt to be in his arms, her breasts flat against his hard chest, or how his mouth tasted, for that matter. Well, it did beat thinking about how it would feel to hit the ground, which was all she'd been thinking about for the last few minutes.

Looking up into darkening eyes, she guessed he was thinking about things he shouldn't be, also.

"Tighten it up and keep the slack out," Nick told the

twins. Billy Fred and Bobbie June pulled the extra rope around the windowsill for leverage and then pulled it taut.

To Lyddie, Nick said, his voice softening, "There. Now you can't fall."

"You can." She wet her lips, eyeing his shoe propped against the rusty gutter. "That looks like a poor prop."

He smiled. "I won't fall. That would hurt too much." Glancing over the edge, he added, "Besides, they have a blanket stretched below us now."

"That's reassuring, considering it's at least thirty feet down." Despite the dry comment, Lyddie dared to relax a little. "So, what do we do now?"

Good question, Nick thought, examing the rope once more. Old, wet, and slimy, its condition wasn't reassuring. He only hoped it wasn't rotten, as well.

Stroking her back reassuringly, he said, "Now, you're going to have to trust me."

Lyddie blew at a curl that was tickling her nose and eyed Nick askance. The last time a man had asked her to trust him, she'd ended up married to Gerald Seaton. *"Trust me. I'm not interested in any mythical gold. Your love is much more valuable to me."*

"To do what?" Lyddie asked.

A roguish smile lit his coffee-brown eyes, but he made no reposte to her parry. Instead, Nick called down to the crowd below, "Has anyone got a ladder long enough to reach up here?"

A ripple ran through the onlookers. Someone called, "The railroad has one, but it won't do. It ain't long enough." As the crowd below called up various suggestions, Nick looked up at the twins, gauging the determination on their features, and decided on a course of action. The only one, really.

Glancing back at Lyddie, he smiled. "Have you decided to trust me yet?"

"That sun has to be about a hundred degrees. If you don't do something soon, Pinkerton, you'll have to haul my body off of here without any help from me. I'll have fainted from heatstroke."

"Eh, Lye-Beth? Whatcha doing on that roof?" Gram appeared on the lawn at the edge of the crowd, shading her eyes as she looked up.

"Just enjoying the view, Gram," Lyddie huffed. Chuckles ran through the crowd.

Nick grinned. His wife would have been in a dead faint long before now. But then, his wife would never have been up there washing windows. She would have just bemoaned the lack of servants to do it.

His smile died as he remembered the accident that had claimed her life. If he'd been able to give her the life she wanted, she would never have been running away. With a man he had thought was his friend.

Turning back to the twins, he instructed them to haul on the rope at his command, and to feed the loop of slack created as they drew Lyddie up, back through the other open window, explaining that he'd catch it and use his body as a counterweight.

Joined now by Molly, all nodded their understanding as they prepared to pull.

Touching Lyddie's face, Nick said, "You have to relax and roll over onto your back. Then the twins can pull on the rope and turn you so that your head is pointed upward. You can better move up the roof in that position. Your skirt will help you slide."

"I can't. I'll fall."

"You can. Catch the rope when you roll over. I'll be

holding you as well as the rope. Only your legs will go over the edge, and just for a moment before we get you hauled up to the widow's walk."

He stroked her cheek again, and Lyddie wet her lips, suddenly willing to do anything to escape the sensations he was creating inside her. One thing was certain: He sure knew how to take her mind off her predicament!

"Okay, say when." She swallowed hard.

"When." Nick nodded at the twins, who started pulling her up, hand-over-hand, the rope rasping on the window casement providing leverage.

Lyddie rolled over, comforted by Nick's strong hand grasping her arm. Grabbing hold of the rope as it bit under her arms, she clenched her teeth as her body was swung around and her legs fell over the edge of the roof, dangling into space. Lyddie felt her face flame as everyone in the yard was treated to a view of her bloomers. Her old ones, with the torn hem.

Nick reached over and twitched her skirts down.

"Thank you." That was all she had time for before another pull from the trio above took her higher. Slowly, a foot at a time, the twins and Molly moved her upward. His hand under her foot, Nick pushed her from below, aiding her progress until she was out of his reach. Then Lyddie saw Nick catch the slack in the rope that the twins and Molly had fed through the window. Thank goodness he had something to hang on to!

With Nick's help as a counterweight, Lyddie was quickly maneuvered up the roof and through the broken railing onto the widow's walk. A cheer went up from the crowd.

Nick watched as Lyddie pulled the rope from around her chest and disappeared through the window. Then he hooked the toe of his shoe in the rain gutter and wrapped the rope around his hand, ready to start his own climb back up.

Suddenly, metal shrieked and the gutter gave way.

Chapter Ten

As Nick disappeared beneath the edge of the roof, the rope popped taut.

"Nick!" Her heart in her throat, Lyddie gripped the windowsill. She watched, horrified, as one strand of rope snapped apart and spun off the main line at the edge of the roof. Then another strand came unraveled. The rope wasn't strong enough. It wasn't going to hold. . . .

Suddenly, the rope went slack as a collective gasp rose from the crowd below. Lyddie screamed, then stifled another cry with her hand. *No! He couldn't have fallen! He couldn't!*

"He's gone." Looking green beneath his summer tan, Billy Fred turned to Molly, his eyes wide. "We'd better go see if we can do anything. He's sure to need doctoring."

"No, I heard something hit the second-floor balcony." Molly caught Billy Fred's arm. "He must have jumped!"

"He landed on the veranda?" Like a shot, Lyddie was running down the stairs, calculating onto which room's balcony Nick might have landed. Taking a guess, she rushed to the bedroom closest to the stairwell.

As she threw open the door she saw Nick rising from the porch floor and rushed to meet him. Cramming her knuckles against her mouth, Lyddie drank in the sight of him as he brushed dust from his shirtsleeve.

The crowd cheered wildly for the second time in the drama.

"You're really okay? You jumped to the balcony?" Finally finding her voice, Lyddie felt tears on her cheeks. She didn't care. Glancing from the still-dangling rope, then back to Nick, she touched his arm, savoring the feel of muscle and bone, hard and vital, beneath her fingers. He was really okay.

His grin was a little lopsided. "I guess I did." He put a hand to his head. "But I don't know where my hat went."

Lyddie smiled and wiped at her wet cheek. "I think I stepped on it on the stairs."

"Not my new bowler hat?" Nick looked at her in mock horror.

Smiling and sniffling at the same time, Lyddie nodded. "It didn't become you anyway, you know."

Nick gazed into her watery blue eyes. Seeing the emotions she was fighting to contain, he wanted to take her in his arms, to tell her to cry it out. But the whole town of Crossroads was watching. And listening. He brushed at his pant legs. "Madam, you skewer my ego," he proclaimed dramatically.

"The hat still didn't become you." She sniffed again. "You saved me. You're a hero. You should wear a wide-brimmed hat, like those adventuring men depicted on woodcuts in the *Overland Review* magazine." *And an open collar*, she added to herself, *and a flowing cravat.*

Their audience below laughed and applauded in appreciation.

Remembering suddenly that they were being watched, Lyddie stepped away from Nick.

"Hey, *Nick! Nicholas!*" The voice came out of the crowd below.

Frowning, Nick looked down as a heavyset man in a white suit and a planter's hat stepped forward, a jovial smile wreathing his face.

"Hey, Nick Be—"

"Gus!" Nick shouted abruptly. "Gus, you old dog, stay right there! Don't say another word! I'll be right down."

Nick turned back to Lyddie, his expression unreadable. "He's an old friend—and the last person I expected to find in Crossroads. I have to go say hello."

Was it her imagination, Lyddie wondered, or had Nick deliberately cut off whatever that man had been about to say? She dismissed the notion. Why ever would Nick have done that?

"Certainly." Lyddie straighten her shoulders, regaining control over her emotions.

He paused in the French windows. "You're certain you're okay?"

"Certainly. Go on."

Nodding, Nick disappeared inside. The twins and Molly, standing at the window, parted and let him pass. The crowd began to applaud as he disappeared.

Blushing, Lyddie hurried inside also. To her mortification, the applause picked up again.

"You're a success, Lyddie," Bobbie June said.

"I'll never be able to show my face in town again," Lyddie muttered. Hurrying past her siblings, she left the bedroom, closing the door behind her. After all she'd been through, she just wanted to be alone.

After Lyddie left, Bobbie June nudged her brother. "Just look at all those people."

"Yep." Billy Fred nodded. "They sure got a show," he snorted. "Lye-Beth didn't like being the center of attention."

"This was better than that vaudeville show we went to Jackson and saw last summer," Molly said, moving closer. "And we had to pay a nickel each for that," she added indignantly. She'd been disappointed in the performances and had bitterly regretted having spent any of her small hoard of cash on the trip. She was saving for medical school—if she ever found one that would accept a woman.

"This *was* better than that woman on the fake balcony." Bobbie June clasped her hands before her dramatically, batting her eyelashes. "*Romeo, Romeo!*"

Molly and Billy Fred laughed.

"Hey . . ." Bobbie June's voice trailed away and she turned to her brother, an expression he was all too familiar with lighting her eyes. "*We* could have charged a nickel, just like they did in Jackson!"

"And they would have paid," Billy Fred agreed, awed once more by his twin's calculating mind. He frowned thoughtfully. "I don't suppose we could talk Lyddie into hanging on the edge of the roof any more? She was blushing like fire when she left here."

"We won't have to," Bobbie June told him with a slow grin. "Anybody can be the one hanging off the roof." She paused. "But it *is* better if it's a woman, I suppose. It's the heroine who always has to be rescued in the dime novels. We could work up an act. . . ."

"Will you two ever learn?" Molly shook her head in

exasperation. "There's no such thing as easy money."

"Just some that's easier than others," Bobbie June said with conviction. "Anyways, seems like you'd be interested in helping, since you could make cash enough to pay for going to that medical school you're always talking about," she added slyly.

"What are you thinking about doing?" Molly asked, her brows rising in interest.

"Mr. Brown, I'm sure I speak for everyone when I say I'm happy you were here to save poor Lyddie." Hal Williams, the stationmaster, beamed and clapped Nick on the shoulder.

"That's for sure," the sheriff agreed, shaking Nick's hand. "I'm afraid I'm just too old to have got out there and done what you did."

"Anyone would have done the same," Nick said. Before he could move away, several other people surrounded him, all wanting to shake his hand or pat his back. The attention made him aware that when he'd come to town, helping the Moreland-Shea family had been the last thing on his mind.

Uncomfortable with the effusive praise, Nick excused himself and looked through the lingering people for Gus Elverston, an old friend of his grandfather's. Spotting him on the fringe of the crowd, Nick made his way to join him.

"Gus! Good to see you. How are you?" Nick smiled as he pumped the older man's hand.

"Fine, fine. Say, Nick—"

"Care to walk?" Nick cut him off before Gus had time to say more. Putting an arm around the gray-haired man's shoulders, Nick guided him away from the hotel. The cook, Jane, was headed toward the corner of the hotel, most likely going back to the kitchen. She'd been standing by Gus, Nick had noticed, when he'd first spotted him. However, nothing in her smile or manner as she paused to speak with Lyddie's grandmother gave Nick cause for alarm. Maybe she hadn't heard, after all.

"Sorry I interrupted you before, Gus," Nick said, lowering his voice as they put distance between them and the crowd. "I'm here on an assignment for the agency and I'm going by the name 'Nick Brown.' "

"So that's it. I was about to yank the cat out of the bag." There was keen intelligence in the gaze that met Nick's. Gus's financial acumen and mentoring had helped Nick invest in ways that had set him on his way to financial independence. Nick only regretted it had come too late to save his marriage.

Gus added, "Hope I didn't give the game away."

The crowd was rapidly breaking up into groups of two or three. Others moved away, talking among themselves as they strolled back toward town and whatever tasks they'd dropped to come watch the rescue.

Nick smiled. "No harm done."

"The last time we spoke, you said you were ready to leave the agency," Gus continued offhandedly as they gained the corner of the yard. "You were only waiting for the right business opportunity to come along."

Thrusting his hands into his pockets, Nick raised his brows. It was a question without being a question. But he had no desire to discuss his business here with Gus. Especially when he was no longer certain just what his business was. "I took on one last assignment. Then I'm resigning." He changed the subject. "So, tell me—what is the richest financier in Chicago doing in Crossroads?"

* * *

"You going to hurt that poor girl." Jane brought the cleaver down, cleanly cutting the fish on the board into two pieces. She tossed both pieces into a bowl of cornmeal; then, straightening her shoulders, she glared at Nick. The lantern hanging from the ceiling behind her cast a glow around her red bandana, making her appear like some dark angel.

Taken aback, he paused just inside the kitchen and carefully closed the door. So, she had heard, and she knew exactly who he was. There seemed little point in denying his identity. Worse, Jane had just echoed what he had been thinking and trying hard to deny.

Shaking his head, Nick said, "I wouldn't do that."

"No way you won't end up hurting her." Jane cleaved another fish into two pieces, then met Nick's gaze. "You came here pretending to be somebody you're not. When she finds out the truth, it can't be good. Too many people have lied to her before."

"I regret, now, that I wasn't straightforward from the start."

"Regret don't butter no bread."

"Before I knew the Shea children and Mrs. Moreland, it seemed the best way to get their cooperation in certain matters." Nick thrust his hands into his pockets.

"You're after the gold." It was a statement, flat with disgust. She took a pinch of salt from a salt cellar and sprinkled it over another fish, then followed it with cayenne pepper. "Thought you'd just find and take back what you think belongs to you and yours." She wielded the cleaver again.

"That's what I thought when I came here, yes." Nick found he respected the cook too much not to answer her charge. "I grew up being told how Lyddie's grandfather cheated my grandfather at cards, ruining him. Causing his death." He was quiet a moment, then met her direct gaze again. "But being here, I see that the gold is a myth, just like Lyddie said. It was probably spent long ago, building this hotel. Lyddie and all of the Shea family would hardly work so hard if they had a treasure at their disposal. And even if it wasn't a myth, I'm not certain any longer it would rightfully be mine to take."

"Gentleman John never cheated. That's why everyone called him 'Gentleman.' He had his code." She speared Nick with another dark glare. "And you *are* going to hurt Lyddie. All her life, that girl has broke her heart believing in the wrong men. First, her no-account father left to go to Jackson to buy a horse. He was supposed to be back in the next couple of days. He wrote two months later from the Black Hills, where he went to prospect. Later, the family got a letter from some sheriff up there, saying he'd been killed.

"Then that drummer came along with his fancy tales of this place and that and pure swept her off her feet, she wanted to get away from here so bad and see something of the world. But he was really after the gold. I could tell it right off from the questions he was always asking me. Guess he figured marrying Lyddie would get her to tell him.

"When it didn't, I heard he got drunk and started in on Lyddie, slapping her around. Mrs. Moreland had to set him straight about how he should treat her granddaughter by laying her walking stick across his hard head." Jane salted another fish, then picked up her cleaver again. "I guess he decided there really wasn't any gold, 'cause he took off in the night."

Nick had heard the story from more than one source during his investigation. He knew from his own wife's desertion how painful such a betrayal of trust was, and he could guess how much Lyddie had suffered.

And Jane was right, when Lyddie found out the truth, she would be hurt. There was no help for it.

The only thing to do was tell her himself.

Nick asked, "Do you know where she is?"

"Most likely her special place, down by the falls. It's where she usually goes to lick her wounds."

As Jane watched the backdoor close behind him, Gram came in from the family dining room. "He's going to tell her, you think?"

"You were listening?" Jane frowned. "How long have you known who he was?"

Gram shrugged. "I'm old, but I can still see as deep in the rock as the man what pecked the hole. He looks a great deal like his grandpa, but more handsome." She shook her head. "I think he's got more character than his grandfather, too. I hope so, leastways." She fished her corncob pipe from her apron pocket and considered the empty bowl for a second. "I think he'll do the right thing."

"So do I," Jane agreed. "As far as he can," she added. There were sparks aplenty between Nick and Lyddie, but she was still a married woman. Maybe Lyddie wasn't going to be the only one hurt.

Gram raised gray brows, her eyes sparkling. "You know, you weren't completely honest, I reckon. I know of one time Gentleman John cheated at cards."

Jane nodded, her eyes misting even as a smile curved her lips. "I know."

Gentleman John had been playing cards in a New Orleans "gentlemen's" club when a young slave was brought in wearing a whore's dress and lip rouge. She was thirteen and scared to death; she had been bought off the auction block the day before. John had told the young girl not to worry, she wouldn't spend another night there. And she hadn't; he won the girl in a winner-take-all pot. Gentleman John had signed papers giving the girl her freedom the next day.

Jane said, "When Gentleman John wrapped his coat around me as he took me out of that place, I found two aces in his pocket. But that was special. That was to save me. He wouldn't have cheated for his own sake."

"No," Gram agreed. "You know, Jane, Nick reminds me of my John, somewhat," she said thoughtfully. "I think he's got honor, underneath it all." She stuck the unlit pipe into her mouth. "Think I'll go fetch some green onions from the garden plot to put into the hushpuppies."

Her arms propped on her knees, Lyddie wriggled her toes, burying her feet deeper in the warm, sugar-white sand. The roar of the waterfall on the other side of the swimming hole was soothing to her frayed nerves. The froth sparkled like diamonds in the midday sun. A squirrel scurried down a wild pecan tree on the far bank, pausing every few feet to study her and bark, as if questioning what she was doing there, intruding on his domain.

Lyddie sighed. How had she ended up dangling on the edge of the roof, showing the whole town her bloomers? That would take some living down. If she ever could.

Well, she'd lived down embarrassing stuff before, she told herself, remembering the pitying looks she'd gotten when everyone thought her husband had run off in the night. That had been worse.

Lyddie threw a stick into the water. It bobbed in the froth from the falls and started its long way downstream.

"Penny for your thoughts," said a smooth male voice behind her.

Looking over her shoulder, she found Nick standing

at the edge of the path. *Who else could it be?* she asked herself. Who did she least want to see right now?

And most want to see, if she was honest with herself.

Well, nobody said she had to be honest with herself!

His white shirtsleeves were rolled up to his elbows and the shirt was open at his collar. It was stained in spots with slime from the rope, and dust from where he'd slid down the shingles and off the roof. His deep auburn hair was still tousled from his exertions.

But, as he moved to where she was, it was the look in his coffee-brown eyes that caught at her heart.

Without waiting for her approval, Nick sat down in the sand beside her.

Forcing her gaze back to the sparkling creek water, tinted tea-colored by fallen leaves, Lyddie flung another stick.

"It is beautiful here," Nick said, gazing at the falls.

"Yes," Lyddie agreed. She found she couldn't say more. She was all too aware of him. Prickles ran through her, radiating outward from where his shoulder brushed hers. She started to scoot away, then sighed and settled back, wriggling her bare toes deeper into the sand.

Was it so wrong to enjoy Nick's company? To feel these feelings? It had been so long since she let herself feel like a woman, always aware she had to maintain the charade of the abandoned bride. Nick would be going back to Chicago soon, and her life would go on as it had. If she found a little joy in his company before he left, who would it hurt?

Nick took her hand, brushing the sand from her fingers as he studied it. Lyddie blushed and tried to pull it away. "Don't. My hands are ugly." They were red and work-worn. A lady's hand should be soft and white. The ladies he knew in Chicago wouldn't have rough, red hands.

"Your hands are lovely. Strong and capable," Nick murmured, gently winding his fingers through hers. "You work hard to keep your family together and bread on the table. And I suspect you sacrifice a great deal, too."

She was uncomfortable with his praise and looked away, but left her fingers entwined with his. Surely it couldn't be so very wrong to enjoy this little pleasure.

"I have to tell you something." His tone was low, sincere. Nick looked out at the falls.

Instinctively, Lyddie knew what he had to say was something she didn't want to hear. Not now. She tugged her hand free of his. This time, he let her pull it away. "I came here to be alone," she said.

"Because you are upset. And what I have to tell you will be more upsetting, still."

Alarm washed a cold path through her. The twins. He had to be talking about the twins. Nick had found the evidence he needed against them, and he'd come there to tell her that they would be arrested.

And once he'd said what he was going to say, the thrilling warmth and joy she felt when she was near him would disappear. Things couldn't stay the same after he charged the twins.

"Not now," she whispered.

"But, Lyddie—"

"Not now," she insisted, drawing a deep breath, looking up at the rainbow etched in the mist over the falls. A rainbow stood for hope, didn't it?

Relenting, Nick followed the direction of her gaze. A large bird with black and white markings sailed across the clearing, disappearing into the pine forest on the other side of the creek. "Beautiful bird."

"A pileated woodpecker," Lyddie supplied, glad that he had changed the subject. "There is a pair that live in the area. See." She pointed at another bird that looked much the same. "There is his mate." She watched the bird disappear in the direction the other had gone, then went on pensively, "After Dad came home from the war, he used to spend a great deal of time here. He'd studied biology in college and he loved birds. One time, I came here and found him, and he pointed out the different birds and animals and told me about them. After that, we would often come here together to watch the birds."

Lyddie hugged her knees. Remembering was bittersweet. "I barely remember him before the war—I was only four when he left—but Gram said he'd been changed by what he'd been through.

"Young as I was, I knew something was wrong. I'd heard Gram and my mother whispering. I knew they were concerned, too. He had bad dreams, you see, about the war. He said he never wanted to be responsible again for the death of another living thing."

She paused and drew in a deep breath, then let it out slowly. "Then Mom died when the twins were born, and Dad just left."

"I'm sorry. Your father shouldn't have left, leaving just you and your grandmother to bring up the younger children. It's forgivable if you're angry." His tone was sincere, reaching deep inside her, balming a place that had been hurt far too long.

She met his gaze. "I don't want to be angry with my father. He loved her so much—he seemed to die with her. I understand now that I'm older. Dad felt he caused her death and he just couldn't stay here."

"But it still hurts, doesn't it?" Nick pulled her to him and gently stroked her shoulders.

Lyddie stiffened, resisting. She had kept her feelings hidden for so long, it seemed wrong to be sharing them this way. Disloyal to the memory of her father.

But she *was* angry that her father had deserted them when she had needed him. It was a relief to say it to someone. And Nick seemed to understand.

He was a special man. He'd risked his own life to rescue her from the roof, without giving it a second thought. Lyddie drew in a deep breath and relaxed, placing her head on his strong shoulder, accepting the comfort he offered.

She wished it was only comfort she wanted from him. . . .

As if he sensed her thoughts, the energy between them changed. As Nick lightly stroked her back and rested his cheek against her hair, his touch became more sensual. His warm, masculine scent filled her nostrils and she breathed deeply, drinking it in, along with the smells of clean, damp air and decaying pine needles.

Warmth began in the pit of her stomach and she closed her eyes, not knowing whether to push away from him and end this sweet madness or to savor it.

She realized, to her surprise, that she never really had a choice at all. She wanted this time with Nick, to feel desirable and feminine, and she would take whatever these moments offered. These were memories she could take out later, when he had gone back to Chicago and his life there and she was making lye soap to scrub the hotel floors with.

He lifted his head. "Lyddie, I need to tell you something. What I came here to tell you—"

"Ssssh!" She placed her fingers against his lips. At the contact with his warm mouth, a thrill chased up her arm.

His eyes darkening, he caught her fingers and kissed them, and more thrills chased through her breasts.

"Lyddie." There was a note of pain in his voice. "I don't want you to hate me later."

She searched his eyes, seeing the sincerity of his feelings plainly written there. "I could never do that. You risked your life to save me on the roof. How could I hate you?"

Nick sighed. "You will—"

Not letting him say more, she wrapped her arms about his neck and pressed her lips to his.

Chapter Eleven

Lyddie pressed closer. It was as if she had been waiting all her life for this man, brave and smart and kind and heroic. Hadn't he risked his life without hesitation to rescue her? Nick was a man a woman could count on.

A man a woman could fall in love with.

Any woman but her, she reminded herself. Her ardor cooled a little, despite his warm lips teasing hers. There could be no forever for her. Not with Nick. Not with anyone.

The thought was bitter. Until Nick cupped her face between his warm palms and deepened the kiss, probing the soft places in her mouth with his tongue. She wouldn't have forever, but she had now, she realized, melting against him again.

They had now.

It would be enough.

All will to resist disappeared, as if blown away by the

soft southern breeze. The ferns and the dead leaves behind them on the creek bank rustled softly. Somewhere in the tall forest the woodpecker they had just seen gave its haunting call.

Why should she want to resist? Lyddie asked herself. It wasn't as if she was making a commitment. And this would be her last chance to taste what love *should* be like—her experience with Gerald couldn't be all there was to passion between a woman and a man. Not when one look from Nick made her ache as Gerald never had.

The rioting feelings just Nick's kisses engendered inside her took her breath. A shaft of sheer desire pierced through her, leaving liquid heat in its wake.

Before she had time to think, to consider what folly it might be, Lyddie pulled back from Nick's embrace and got to her feet. Taking his hand, she urged him to stand also. When he did, she wrapped her arms around his neck and pressed her body against his length. She didn't really know how to seduce a man, but this seemed like a good start.

"Kiss me again," she whispered as he frowned questioningly down at her.

He did. His lips were quick and light as they pressed hers, drawing a little mew of protest from within her that the contact wasn't deeper. This wasn't at all the kiss she wanted.

Nick lifted his head, his eyes almost black with desire. And something more. Something like regret. "This isn't a good idea, Lyddie."

"Why?" Her confusion stabbed at his heart.

"I told you, you'll be hurt." Nick caught Lyddie's waist, marveling as his fingers almost met behind her. She was filled with such strength, such character and courage—how could such a slender package contain so much heart?

Lyddie brushed her wildly tousled curls back from her cheek. Her eyes were dark gold beneath her thick lashes as she studied him, her lips moist and parted, tempting him to taste them once more. "How could you hurt me? Didn't you risk your life to get me off the roof? You didn't have to. You could have stood back and let others try to help. But you didn't hesitate—and you were almost hurt badly because of it."

"And I don't want you to be vulnerable because you are grateful. If I hadn't helped you, someone else would have. I just happened to be there." His voice was a harsh rasp. It was taking almost more will than he had to resist laying her back on the sand and making love to her. He wanted to. God, how he wanted to.

She wanted to tell him that if he hadn't helped her, she'd probably still be there.

"I'm a grown woman," Lyddie said at length, her voice husky with emotion. She brushed sand from her skirt. "You won't be staying—I know that. There's no such thing as happily ever after for me. I don't expect anything from you. I don't want promises."

"There *should* be promises. And a happily ever after for you," Nick said softly. "You give so much to those around you, you deserve it, Lyddie." He caressed her cheek. Her skin was petal soft, her cheeks tinted peach from the sun. With her wild, wheat-gold curls, she was beautiful—but her beauty was more than skin deep. After all the helpless, needful women in his life, Lyddie was a breath of sweet summer air.

Nick drew her to him, unable to resist. Stroking his hands up and down her back, he marveled at her warmth and softness. Her curves fit against him as if they had been made for each other, when nothing could be more impossible. "You are a hard woman to resist," he rasped.

"Then don't." Lyddie tilted her head back and he kissed her. She sighed into his mouth as his hands worked their magic, stroking her back, fitting her between his long legs, pressing her more firmly against his arousal. He smelled of clean sweat and man, scents mixed with the tangy aroma of pines and the fresh, damp mist of the falls. The roaring of the waterfall was no louder than the roaring inside her head.

To Lyddie's infinite disappointment, Nick pulled back. Wrapping her in his arms, he tucked her head beneath his chin and held her. Her breath came in ragged gasps—as did his.

"You test a man's will," he sighed. "I've never wanted a woman so much."

"Then why . . . ?" Suddenly shy, she couldn't form the rest of the question. If he wanted her as she wanted him, why was he stopping?

With his finger beneath her chin, Nick tilted her head up until she was forced to meet his gaze. "Because if we make love, you *will* hate me."

"No, I could never—"

He put his fingers against her soft lips, bruised from the kisses they had shared. "Yes, you will," he said with conviction. "There are things you don't know. I haven't been honest, and you deserve that much. I tried to tell you when I found you here."

Her face was upturned, an errant breeze playing with a curl by her cheek. Confusion and longing warred in her golden eyes as she blinked up at him.

With a sigh, Nick turned and left the way he'd come.

* * *

Hortense strummed an ominous chord on her Autoharp and looked to her brother and sister, who were posed on the front porch of the hotel. Lanterns had been strategically placed along the railing to create the effect of a stage, and sheets hung as a backdrop.

Bobbie June nodded and Hortense began to play the introduction. " *'Camp Town ladies, sing dis song, doo-da, doo-da,'* " Billy Fred sang as he crossed the porch in a rhythmic strut, his thumbs hooked in his red "Sunday" suspenders.

" *'Camp Town racetrack five mile long!'* " Bobbie June sang out. Garbed in a calico dress, she twirled her umbrella between daintily gloved hands as she crossed Billy Fred's path. Leaning together, both sang, ' *"Oh, de-doo-da-day!'* "

As the performance went on, Lyddie sighed and drew her shawl about her shoulders against the damp night air. There were seven people standing in the front yard who had been persuaded to part with a nickel each for the privilege of watching the show. Lyddie noticed Frank Worley was front and center, Sunday suit on and hair slicked back, though Hortense contrived not to notice him. She smiled instead at the new telegraph operator, and Lyddie groaned inwardly as the burly timber foreman shot the stick-slender young man a menacing look.

Standing between the two, Gram obliviously tapped her cane in time with the music.

When the song ended all clapped enthusiastically, and there were even a few whistles. Billy Fred and Bobbie June beamed and took their bows.

Lyddie frowned. Such encouragement was bound to lead to future performances.

She'd done her best to talk them out of this scheme.

When would they learn there was no such thing as easy money and no substitute for hard work?

At least Molly had ended the twins' plan to reenact the scene on the roof by refusing to dangle from a rope while they rescued her.

Shaking her head as the pair began another Stephen Foster selection, Lyddie started for the side porch, but she paused as Nick Brown stepped into the lantern light spilling from the makeshift stage. The sheriff was at his side.

Lyddie had managed to avoid him for the last few days, after she'd humiliated herself by the creek. But Hortense had informed her this evening that Nick had asked that his bill be ready in the morning.

That meant he was leaving.

And life would go on much as it had for the last four years. Well, that was what she wanted, wasn't it? Lyddie asked herself. That was the way it had to be—so why was it such a disheartening thought?

Sinking into the shadows, Lyddie watched the way the lantern light danced on Nick's dark auburn hair and showed the strong angles and planes of his face in relief. She would have her memories when he was gone.

Piquing her curiosity, Nick pulled a short length of red ribbon from his coat pocket and handed it to Sheriff Woods, who examined it critically.

As she watched the two men, Bobbie June warbled to a halt, looking like she'd been turned to stone. Billy Fred nudged her with his elbow and sang louder. Gradually, she started singing again and got back into the performance.

Seeing her sister's reaction, a sense of foreboding danced along Lyddie's spine. She'd tried to talk with the twins, to get them to admit if they were in any trouble.

But they had sidestepped her efforts, and, Lyddie admitted to herself, she had wanted to believe they were innocent of damaging the rail lines. After all, Nick hadn't been able to prove the boot prints were theirs.

But that ribbon looked like the one Bobbie June used to wear on the end of her braid, and Nick had to be showing it to the sheriff for a reason. Her trepidation growing, Lyddie wondered if it was somehow the "proof" Nick had been looking for.

Chapter Twelve

As she listened to Nick and the sheriff, Lyddie remembered that Bobbie June had been wearing a string to tie her braid lately. She hadn't worn her red ribbon for the last couple of weeks . . . since about the time the depot building had been damaged.

When Bobbie June faltered again as she sang, the truth written on her face, Lyddie drew in a sharp breath. She shook her head, wanting to continue to deny her sister's involvement. But she couldn't. Not when she added up all the other evidence against her: the plaster casts that Bobbie June and Billy Fred had destroyed; the twins' missing everyday boots, which weren't available to be compared to the new casts; the twins furtiveness lately.

Oh, Bobbie June, what have you done now?

Candle flies—tiny silver moths—swarmed madly about the lanterns, beating their wings against the glass. Casting huge shadows against the sheets hung as a backdrop, the insects danced a macabre ballet. The twins were no different than those crazed moths, drawn irrepressibly to the glow of gold.

When would they learn?

"You're the oldest, Lyddie," her mother had whispered after giving birth to the twins. "I know you will watch after the little ones and take care of them." Smiling, her mother had touched her hair. Then the doctor, looking grim, had shooed Lyddie from the room.

I tried, Mama, Lyddie said silently. *I tried. It's just too big a job.*

Meeting Nick's sympathetic gaze, Lyddie became aware that she'd been staring at him—as if she hadn't embarrassed herself enough already, practically throwing herself at him down by the falls. Now he was feeling sorry for her.

Feeling her cheeks flame, Lyddie turned on her heel and headed inside the hotel.

As Bobbie June had faltered, Billy Fred's elbow dug into her side, and she found her place again, pushing all thoughts of her ribbon and the pesky Pinkerton man to the back of her mind. He was just trying to rattle her. She lifted her chin a notch. It would take more than a piece of ribbon! she thought.

As they began the final chorus, Hortense bungled a couple of chords. The reason, Bobbie June saw, was that her sister was too busy smiling at the new telegraph operator, Willard Turlow, to pay attention to what she was playing. Turlow, a scrawny young man with a prominent Adam's apple, was grinning back like a mule eating briars—blissfully unaware that Frank Worley was glaring at him. No doubt the timber foreman thought he had proprietorial rights to Hortense, since she certainly had done nothing to dissuade him from thinking so.

As the song ended, Bobbie June frowned mightily at her sister. She'd be darned if she would have their premiere performance ruined by Hortense's lack of good judgment where anything in trousers was concerned!

Hortense paid her not the least attention. "We shall take a small intermission before the finale." Hortense put the Autoharp aside, propping it against her chair, and managed to bend and display her cleavage as she did so.

The telegraph operator was at Hortense's side in an instant, blushing and Adam's apple bobbing. However, Hortense had barely had time to bat her lashes at the fellow before the timber foreman took hold of the young man's collar. Lifting him off his feet, Frank Worley removed the upstart from the porch in one smooth motion, depositing him in the yard.

Frank followed the startled young man, pushing up his sleeves as he did so. Bobbie June ran down the porch steps and stomped Frank's booted foot.

"Stop it this instant," she demanded. "I'll not have you ruin our show!"

"And I'll not have this upstart ogling the woman I'm walkin' out with," Frank declared, glaring at the telegraph operator, who took a quick step backward.

"Miss Shea is right, I reckon," said Sheriff Woods, stepping between the foreman and the frightened young man.

"I, uh, I-I didn't mean no disrespect to the lady." Turlow's Adam's apple bobbed.

The people who'd paid a nickel to watch the show seemed to take this byplay as an interesting bonus and pressed closer.

"I guess you should get back to the telegraph office, Mr. Turlow," the sheriff suggested.

"Yes, sir, I shore should." The young man dared a quick glance at Hortense and nodded.

Frank growled and the telegraph operator fled through the onlookers.

"Come on, Hortense. Let's keep the audience happy." Bobbie June took up her parasol again. The rest of the show went off without a hitch, but after nearly seeing fisticuffs, the crowd seemed harder to please and drifted away during the last song.

Taking her final bows to a near-empty yard, Bobbie June sighed. It wasn't exactly an unqualified success.

It would certainly have been better if certain people wouldn't have diverted attention from their act! She glared at Hortense, who, arms akimbo, was telling Frank Worley that he didn't own her as he'd not bothered to make a formal proposal for her hand, and she'd just as soon she never saw him again.

Frank turned his hat in his hands and looked abashed at his lack of sensitivity and proper feeling, as detailed by the object of his affections, before that object stamped her foot and fled inside the hotel.

The sheriff clapped a friendly hand on Frank's shoulder, and the two ambled back toward Main Street. In the sudden silence Bobbie June chewed her under lip and started helping Billy Fred take the sheets they'd used as a backdrop down from the clothesline they'd strung across the porch.

Later, after the stage settings had been cleared away, Bobbie June went into the lobby, holding her skirts and scratchy petticoats up before her like a bundle of washing.

"That's not very ladylike." Hortense smirked from behind the desk as she folded a paper. "Half the people who showed up tonight just paid to see you in a dress."

Bobbie June bristled. "If it's ladylike to have to wear these horsehair petticoats, then I'll never be a lady." She paused, then said meaningfully, "And neither will a girl who lets herself get a reputation for being fickle."

The salvo hit home, and Hortense stiffened. Bobbie June went on, "Frank Worley would be a great catch for you, but you're batting your lashes at that skinny telegraph man."

Hortense stuffed the paper into an envelope. "If you had any feminine wiles at all, you'd understand I'm trying to bring Mr. Worley up to scratch by making him jealous. He's had plenty of opportunities to ask for my hand." She spilled wax from a candle across the flap of the envelope and went on thoughtfully, "Beside, Mr. Turlow is from an old Vicksburg family, very rich—before the war changed their fortunes. I'm sure he's going places with the telegraph company. Cream rises to the top, you know."

Bobbie June rolled her eyes but resisted a retort as she started for the stairs.

"Wait." Hortense held out the envelope and lowered her voice. "Take this to Mr. Turlow at the telegraph office. He's on duty until midnight."

Taking it gingerly, Bobbie June eyed her sister askance. "You can't be serious!"

"Sssh!" Looking about, as if to make sure they weren't overheard, Hortense said, "It's just an apology. I feel I owe him that."

"At the least, since you nearly got his eye blacked for him. But you can take it yourself. I'm hot. I'm going to my room."

"It wouldn't be proper for me to," Hortense said, looking affronted that her sister would suggest such a thing. "Not if people saw me," she amended.

Bobbie June thrust the note back at her sister.

"I'll give you a nickel." Hortense fished a coin from the evening's take from her pocket, and Bobbie June sighed, eyeing it a moment.

"Okay. But just this once." Taking the nickel and the letter, Bobbie June turned to go.

"And wait for an answer," Hortense hissed to her.

An answer, to an apology? Bobbie June shoved the possibilities from her mind as she went out the door.

Lyddie lay awake long after the singing and applause outside had ended and the hotel had settled into quiet for the night. What goaded her was that she was thinking more about Nick leaving than how to get the twins out of the mess into which they'd landed themselves.

A light appeared under her door and a soft knock sounded. "Lye-Beth, it's me," Bobbie June called. "I have to talk to you. It's important."

Sighing, Lyddie sat on the edge of the bed. "Come in." She needed to talk to Bobbie June, too. Only she wasn't quite certain what to say.

Bobbie June closed the door behind her. The candlestick she carried showed her winged brows were drawn together in a frown.

"I watched part of the show and heard the rest. You and Billy Fred did a very nice job. Molly said you were better than the show you all saw in Jackson," Lyddie said.

"Thank you. That was sweet of Molly." After setting the candlestick down on Lyddie's bedside table, Bobbie June sat down beside her. "You weren't in the yard when Frank Worley took exception to the way the new telegraph operator was making calf eyes at Hortense, were you?"

"No. I was listening from here. I heard it when, in between some of the songs, some men started talking angrily. I wondered what was happening. So you came to tell me about it?" Lyddie felt disappointed that Bobbie June wasn't ready to make a clean breast of her problems.

"Well, yes and no." Bobbie June fidgeted with the sash tie of her dressing robe. "After the show, I took a note from Hortense to the telegraph office. She said she was apologizing," she defended before Lyddie could object to her helping Hortense in some ploy. "Willard Turlow was beside himself. Seems he didn't come to the hotel to watch the performance—though he said he was right taken with it when he found it in progress and didn't mind paying his nickel when Molly asked him for it." She made a new knot in the sash.

Lyddie frowned, trying to pinpoint where the speech had derailed, losing whatever point her sister had been aiming for. "So, this Turlow fellow had come to see Hortense?"

"Oh, no. Anyway, I think he's much too shy to have gotten up the gumption to do that." Bobbie June untied the knot, then met her sister's gaze. "He came to deliver a telegram to Nick and got sidetracked watching the show and Hortense. When Frank Worley snatched him up by the collar, he kinda forgot why he'd come in the first place, until he was safely back in the telegraph office. Needless to say, he didn't want to come back and chance meeting Frank again."

"I can understand that," Lyddie said. She didn't blame him. The timber foreman was massive.

"So he was right glad to see me and gave this to me

to give to Nick." Bobbie June pulled a crumpled page out of her dressing gown pocket.

Taking it, Lyddie frowned. "Why didn't you give it to him?"

Bobbie June rose and eyed her sister sadly. "I've seen how you look at Nick when you think no one is watching. I know you're getting sweet on him, so I thought you needed to give it to him."

Lyddie looked down at the telegram in her hands. It was addressed to Mr. Nicholas Bennington.

Chapter Thirteen

A thunderhead lay on the eastern horizon. Lightning, flashing within its confines, outlined it against the night-black sky. Thunder was a distant murmuring. Somewhere in the woods behind the hotel, a whippoorwill's calls echoed. As Lyddie listened, she remembered an old saying that when a whippoorwill called, it wouldn't rain.

She rubbed her chilled arms and looked up at the clouds sailing across the moon. The saying didn't seem as if it would prove true this time.

She stood on the balcony outside Nick's room. The French windows were open and the breeze played with the sheer curtains, floating them out, then whipping them in, as if trying to draw her inside. Thinking of Nick lying on the bed in the hot, dark night was powerfully compelling. She wanted to go inside.

At the same time, she wanted to quietly turn and rush back to her own room.

But if she did that, some part of her knew that she'd always regret it. She'd never know what it would be like to be with Nick.

Drawing in a deep breath, she knocked lightly on a pane of the open window.

"I've been wondering if you were going to stand there all night or come inside," said a deep, soft voice within the darkness.

A Lucifer match flared, and Nick's face was cast in dark and light as he touched the match to the wick of his bedside lamp. Shaking the flame out, he lowered the globe and adjusted the height of the wick.

Lyddie stepped tentatively into the bedroom. As her eyes adjusted to the lamplight, she saw Nick was sitting on the bed, his chest bare. And to her shock, so were his well-muscled legs. A thin line of rusty-colored hair ran from his navel downward, disappearing beneath the sheet, which was carelessly draped across his loins.

Fanning herself with the telegram she held, she cleared her throat. "It's warm tonight."

A slow smile curved one side of his mouth. The golden lamp flame danced as it was reflected in his eyes. "I know. I've been too hot to sleep myself." His voice was soft gravel.

Lyddie felt heat rush to her cheeks. Suddenly, her dressing gown seemed unbearably heavy and hot. Her feet leaden. Nonetheless, she resolutely moved nearer, stopping inches away from the bed. "I know now why you turned away from me down by the falls, Nick."

"You do?"

"Yes, I do. Nick Bennington." Watching his frown deepen, she gave him the telegram. "Willard Turlow was bringing you this tonight, but before he delivered it, he ran afoul of Frank Worley."

After glancing to see to whom it was addressed, he put it on the bedside table, unread. "I went to the creek to tell you everything, but I ended up kissing you instead. Then, you wouldn't let me tell you, and I couldn't . . ." He drew a deep breath and released it in a sigh. "I'm not usually so honorable. But if we had made love, you would have been hurt when you found out the truth."

Gingerly, she sat on the bed beside him and took his hand, twining her fingers through his. Lyddie squeezed his fingers, enjoying the feel of their firm strength. "You came here after the gold, didn't you, Bennington?" she asked softly.

"Yes," he admitted. "But it didn't take me long to realize the gold wasn't real. Just a legend, like you told me the first day I was here." The look in her eyes was warm, her lush peach lips were slightly parted. "You aren't angry," he realized. He lifted her hand and kissed the soft skin on the back.

Her breath caught in her throat as shivers ran from the point where his lips touched her skin up her arm and shimmied through her chest. "*Sssh,* don't tell anyone the truth. The town needs the business the story brings in."

"The fools look for gold." His eyes were dark. Serious. Gently, he touched her cheek. "But I've found the only treasure here."

"Nick . . ." As she waited, her heart pounded in her ears, drowning out the distant rumbling of thunder. Then his mouth touched hers and she felt the lightning flashing in the night sky could hold no more power than his lips as they tasted hers, savoring, possessing. Promising.

He broke the kiss. "Ah, Lyddie," he breathed against her mouth. Standing, he drew her up also. The sheet fell away. He was completely, gloriously naked.

She could no more not look at him than she could stop

her next breath. Wide shoulders beckoned her to twine her arms about them and test their strength. A smooth, well-muscled chest invited her to touch, explore the texture of his skin, as did his lean hips and strong legs. But it was his male member, standing proud from rusty-colored curls that held her attention. She wanted to touch him there most of all.

Feeling a blush heat her cheeks at such brazen thoughts, she whispered, "I've never really looked at a naked man before."

Her husband had scarcely taken time to undo his pants as he'd tumbled her back on the bed on their wedding night. What had followed had been over quickly, leaving her unsatisfied and feeling she should have experienced more. Then he'd started ranting at her to tell him where the gold was hidden, and she'd realized what a terrible mistake her marriage had been.

With Nick, everything would be different.

Reverently, Nick smoothed her dressing gown from her shoulders and let it fall, puddling on the floor. He tugged open the buttons on her gown. She tried to help him, her fingers trembling too badly to do much, until he gently brushed her hands aside. As he unbuttoned the nightgown, he bent and kissed each area of her skin exposed, from the base of her throat downward, between her breasts, then the mounds on each side of the cleft. Going down on one knee, he pulled her to him and pressed warm kisses down her torso.

Her head falling back, Lyddie held his shoulders and trembled as he moved lower, laving his tongue into her naval. It was such an intimate gesture. Her knees growing weak, she felt she was melting. A core of liquid heat simmered low in her belly.

Standing, Nick pulled her to him, pressing her against

his naked length, skin to skin. Wrapping her arms around him, she explored the ropy muscles of his back and shoulders as she lifted her mouth for his kiss. His eyes, heavy-lidded and dark with passion, still held a reverence and tenderness as he lowered his mouth to hers.

The kiss was a possession, pure and complete. As his tongue twined with hers in an age-old dance, Lyddie knew what it was to lose all will, all sense of self. And she didn't care.

Cupping her head, he splayed his fingers into her hair, while his other hand stroked the length of her back and lowered, cupping her bottom and pulling her against his arousal. As she pressed still harder against him, he groaned deep in his throat.

"Witch. You've bewitched me," he murmured against her throat. "I've thought of little else but being with you since I saw you that first day."

"Me?" She clung helpless to his shoulders. "And what are you doing to me? I've never felt quite this way, quite so out of control!"

"Never?"

"Never. I can't even stand," she whispered.

Hooking his arm behind her knees, he scooped her up. "You don't have to." His voice rumbled deep in his chest, vibrating where her hand pressed against it. He laid her gently on the bed, blew the lamp out, then joined her, pulling her close.

The lightning was growing closer, the flashes lighting up the inside of the room through the open French windows. The murmur of thunder, though still distant, was growing louder.

Wanting to slow things down, to savor each moment, Nick pulled Lyddie half across him, fanning the sweet silk of her hair across his chest, combing his fingers through the glorious waves. The faint scent of lavender drifted from it and he smiled. "You are so beautiful."

"Do you mean that? You don't have to say pretty things you don't mean, you know." Pushing up onto her elbows, Lyddie looked down at him, her eyes luminous in the lightning flashes.

"You are beautiful. Beautiful in body and beautiful in spirit and strength."

She said shyly, "When you look at me like that, you make me feel beautiful. You make me want you."

Need surged within him as she admitted his power over her. Never had he wanted a woman more. But he didn't just want her body. He wanted her. All of her.

But right now his physical need demanded attention. He was intensely aware of her breasts, round and firm, as she looked down at him. One crest touched his male nipple, making it tighten pebble hard. She was exquisite.

Wrapping his hands around her torso, he lifted her above him, so that her breasts brushed across his chest. As she caught her breath, her eyes widening in wonder, he lifted her higher and tasted the sweet peaks, suckling them and laving them with his tongue. He wanted to give her pleasure, more pleasure than she'd ever known with another man.

Lyddie moaned, her fingers curling into his shoulders, and he felt triumphant. "Ah, Lyddie, touch me."

Her eyes opened and she looked at him uncertainly. "I've never . . ." He shifted her weight until she was lying beside him. She rose on one elbow, and tentatively, her finger sought his manhood. As she touched it, it jumped beneath her hand. Looking down at his hard length in wonder, she closed her fingers around it and caressed him.

"Yes, Lyddie, yes. Like that. Just like that." He kissed

her as she stroked him, and his need to sink into her grew almost unbearable.

Sifting through the nest of silky curls at the apex of her thighs, he murmured unintelligible love words as he found her hot, wet center. As he kissed her again and inserted a finger into her warmth, Lyddie gasped into his mouth, her body arching with need, her hand tightening as she stroked him.

That was all he could endure.

Nick rose above her, and Lyddie instinctively opened her legs, wanting more, wanting all of him. He moaned against her neck as he entered her with one quick thrust. She wrapped her legs around him in wonder. Nothing had ever felt like this before. Nothing could feel better.

Then he began to move, thrusting hard and quick, filling her completely and drawing nearly out before filling her again, and she knew she'd been wrong. Lightning, which had grown close, flashed again and again, starkly lighting the room. A cool wind swirled through, tugging at the sheer curtains on the French window. Thunder boomed, then boomed again, vibrating the glass panes. Rain suddenly slashed down on the veranda outside the room.

Holding Nick's shoulders, feeling the muscles ripple beneath her fingers, Lyddie melted into a puddle of pure sensation, helplessly carried along on a different kind of storm. Melding with him in a rush of liquid heat, conscious thought flew away as the shattering pleasure became too intense to bear. As she felt his release, she spun upward into the dark night sky and exploded among the stars.

Nick kissed Lyddie's neck and nuzzled her ear. He had been watching her sleep for some time, loving the sight of her. Her hair was in wild disarray, her lashes sable fans against her cream-beige complexion, and one fist was curled beside her cheek like a child. He hated to wake her, but the sky in the east was showing the pearly gray of predawn.

"It's almost morning," he whispered against her cheek, before planting light kisses where his breath had touched.

Stirring, Lyddie rolled toward him, and her tawny eyes opened and blinked. And widened. She snatched up the covers, letting cool air race over his skin where it was pressed to her warm, bare body, then snatched it back down. Roses bloomed in her cheeks.

Nick grinned. "Good morning."

"Morning!" She sat up, scooting against the carved mahogany headboard, clutching the covers to her breasts. She pushed her hair out of her eyes and looked toward the French windows. Seeing it was still early, she relaxed. "Oh."

"It will be morning soon. I thought you might want to get up before the rest of the household." Nick propped a pillow against the headboard and scooted up until he sat beside her, his shoulder pressing hers.

"Yes. Of course." Lyddie found she had trouble meeting his gaze and stared at the peak her toes made under the sheet.

The feel of his warm lips on her bare shoulder snapped her head around. She sucked in a sharp breath as tingles of pleasure ricocheted around inside her. With the tingles came memories and warm echoes of the beauty and pleasure she had experienced last night. It had been more wonderful than anything Lyddie had ever imagined. More than she'd ever thought possible.

After Nick left today, she would still have memories

of their night to treasure always, through all the long years to come.

The thought was bittersweet.

"I do have to go," she whispered.

He kissed the point of her shoulder again. "I know."

"I'll . . . I'll see you before you leave. Which train are you catching?" It was hard to keep her voice even, but Lyddie managed to smile.

Nick stroked her cheek, his eyes dark with emotion. "I'm not leaving."

Lyddie blinked. Maybe she had just misunderstood. "Hortense said she was supposed to have your bill ready first thing this morning."

"Yes, that's what I told her. But I'm not leaving. This is the end of the month. I'm getting my expenses itemized to mail to my headquarters." He planted quick kisses along her collarbone.

Not leaving. He wasn't leaving. Even as one part of her leapt in joy, a sense of foreboding rose up to tighten her chest. "You aren't leaving. . . ."

"I'll re-register as Nick Bennington. It's time to do away with the pretense. Anyway, I think your grandmother has known for some time." He grinned. "Your sisters and brother will adjust to the fact." He took her hand and pressed a kiss to the sensitive skin on the back of it. "I'm not leaving."

Staring at him in disbelief, she said, "Not leaving?"

"I've found something here, Lyddie, that I want. Something I need. I need you." He frowned. "I get the feeling that doesn't make you happy."

"I . . . I am a married woman. It doesn't matter that my husband is . . . is gone. I'm married in the eyes of the world."

Nick tensed. Cupping her cheek, he forced her to meet his gaze. "Do you still love him?"

"What has that got to do with it?"

"Do you?" The soft words demanded an answer.

"No." Seeing the emotion in his gaze, she couldn't let him think that she was pining for Gerald Seaton. But neither could she let Nick think that what had happened between them meant anything. There was no future for them. "I shouldn't have come here last night."

Abruptly, Lyddie got out of bed, dragging the sheet off Nick. As he sat on the edge of the bed, she snatched her dressing gown from the floor and quickly shrugged into it. "It was wrong," she said while tying the sash. She had wanted to forget, for just a little while. Wanted to know what love should be like.

And, God help her, she had found out.

Suddenly, the years stretched out before her, years alone and lonely, like the last few had been. Memories of the bliss she'd found in Nick's arms wouldn't make them easier to bear, but unbearable.

Nick stood and caught her in his arms. "You don't mean that." He cupped her face, looking deeply into her eyes. "Tell me you regret what we had last night."

She knew the truth was there to see. "I've never experienced anything that was more right," she sighed. "But I'm still married."

"You can file for divorce."

"No, I can't. I can't do that."

"Is there a problem with the laws? If this state doesn't allow a woman to file, there are others where you can. We'll go to Chicago on the next train. I know several good lawyers there. If you can't get a divorce there, we'll go to New York."

"Nick, I'm not going to Chicago or New York. I'm not going to divorce my husband."

Chapter Fourteen

Nick stilled. "Why?"

Looking away, Lyddie blinked moisture from her eyes. "I can't leave the hotel. This place would fall apart without me."

"I'm not talking about leaving your family. I'm talking about going on with your life. You don't have to leave here if you feel you must stay. I'll stay, too. Your husband abandoned you. How any man could, I don't know, but the fact remains that he did. There must be some way to use that to get your marriage annulled." He lifted her chin and smoothed her hair from her face. "Whatever it takes, we'll find it."

"No," Lyddie said, "you don't understand. I don't want you to stay here." If he stayed, it would only be a matter of time before poor Gerald's resting place came to light. Whatever Gram had done, she must have done it to protect herself, or Lyddie. However, there would be no way to prove that.

"Lyddie, you can't mean that." She had been so loving just hours before; what had changed? Shaking his head, Nick tried to wrap her in his arms, but she stepped back.

"I do mean it. I certainly do." She couldn't meet his gaze—she was afraid he'd read how much she needed him in her eyes. She focused on the strong column of his throat. "I wouldn't change a moment of last night. What we had together . . ." She shook her head, at a loss for words to describe the beauty of it. "But I don't want you to stay, and I don't want to divorce my husband." Tugging the sash tighter on her dressing gown, Lyddie turned and left.

Once back in her room, she studied her reflection in the mirror over the washstand. Her eyes were overbright, her hair a wild tangle. Her cheeks looked flushed and her lips were bruised.

She looked like a woman who had been made love to very thoroughly.

Touching her fingers to her lips, thinking of Nick's mouth on hers, tingles of remembered passion coursed through her. What had happened between them had been more powerful than anything she could have imagined. For the first time she understood how her grandfather could have turned his back on wealth and position to marry Gram, the serving maid he'd fallen in love with.

Lyddie even, reluctantly, understood something of how her father must have felt after her mother died. Gram had told her, years after her father left, that her father blamed himself for her mother's death. After Molly was born the doctor had cautioned against more pregnancies.

Love hurt and destroyed more than it healed, she decided.

Shaking her head, Lyddie drew in a ragged breath. She had no other choice; she had to send Nick away.

Not that he would have really stayed anyway. He said he would. He maybe thought he would. But she knew from experience *forever* could be a mighty short time.

Wetting a washcloth in the basin, she pressed it to her bruised lips. Soon they were no longer puffy from Nick's kisses. She sighed, and the image in the mirror sighed back. The bruises on her heart were another matter. No, she couldn't blame Nick for those. They were, she knew, self-inflicted.

She attacked her wild curls with a boar bristle brush. After pinning up her hair, she bathed and dressed. By the time she went down to breakfast it was far later than usual for her, but no one took any notice.

Only the twins and Molly were at the table. Molly had her nose in a large book with drawings of what looked like tangles of sausages.

A steaming bowl of couch-couch, a fried cornmeal porridge, sat in the middle of the table, with a small porcelain coffeepot and milk in a pitcher.

"The show last night was very nice," Lyddie complimented the twins as she sat. "I don't know a lot about such things, but it seemed to entertain everyone who watched." She privately thought that those who had attended might have paid just to see Bobbie June in a dress.

"Why, thank you, Lyddie." Bobbie June beamed, sitting up a little straighter. "I know we got to practice more before we can really call ourselves performers, but I think it went well for a first try."

"Humph." Molly lowered her book. "They wanted me to help them reenact your rescue from the roof!" She arched a disparaging brow at the twins. "I told them they were crazy if they thought I was going to hang off the

roof by a rope and depend on *them* to pull me up."

"It woulda worked. If we coulda just figured out how to get lanterns up there so the scene would be lit up," Billy Fred commented.

Bobbie June said excitedly, "Mr. Elverston says we have potential. If we work hard at it, we could be a headline attraction in music halls in big towns like Chicago and St. Louis in a few years." Her eyes sparkled in a way Lyddie had learned to dread. "After we graduate from school next year, we're to look him up, he said. In the meantime, we can practice."

"Mr. Elverston?" Lyddie poured a little coffee in the bottom of a soup bowl and added sugar, then almost filled the bowl with milk.

"Gus Elverston. He's a friend of Nick's and real rich. Got his own train car—that one on the side track." Billy Fred rose and picked up his bowl and coffee cup. "Gotta go chop wood for the stove." He disappeared into the kitchen.

"I talked to Nick," Lyddie told Bobbie June.

"You did? Guess he had some fancy explaining to do about calling himself 'Brown.' " She tossed her thick braid over her shoulder.

Where had she come up with another red ribbon to tie the end? Lyddie wondered.

"He explained that he had called himself Brown because he hadn't wanted to prejudice us against him and hinder his investigation." She stirred her milk and coffee.

Bobbie June frowned. "He said that? Why would it prejudice his investigation? More likely he's after the gold himself and didn't want us to know."

"He admitted he thought about the gold when he came here. But after seeing how hard we all work, he doesn't think it exists anymore." Lifting her cup, Lyddie took a

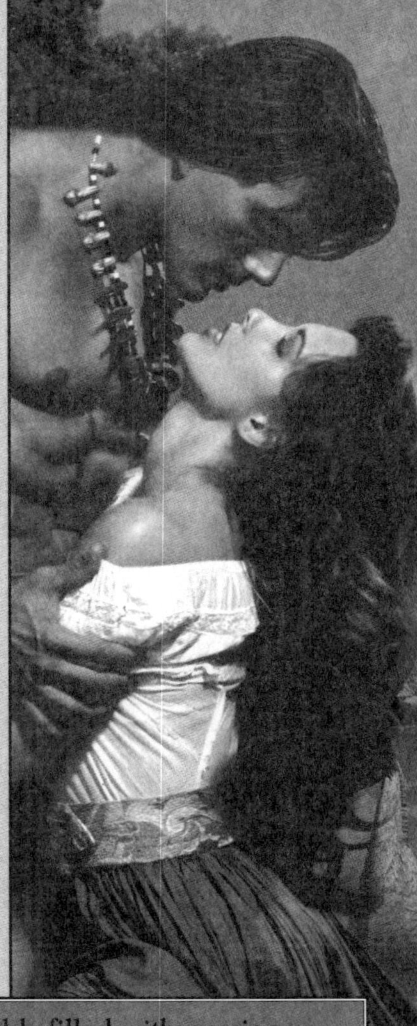

sip of coffee, then aimed a pointed look at Bobbie June. "I think it's time you and Billy Fred told me the truth about what happened at the depot and the rail lines."

Blinking, Molly surfaced from her book again. "Prejudice his investigation? What are you two talking about?"

"You're always two steps behind, Molly. I'll explain later. Just keep reading about your impacted bowels," Bobbie June told her.

To Lyddie, she said, "I don't know what you mean. Nick's been putting suspicions in your mind!" Her bottom lip jutted out, as though her feelings were grievously hurt by Lyddie's implications. "And I don't like Nick. Never did like him. Now I know why—he's a Bennington. It's just plain lucky he'll be leaving today."

"Nick is a *Bennington?* One of *the* Benningtons?" Molly blinked, coming to the surface again.

"Like I said," Bobbie June told her, "he's leaving today, so it don't matter, does it?" She picked up her empty bowl and cup and left the table.

Lyddie sighed and stirred couch-couch into her milk. Trouble was, Nick wasn't leaving today . . . unless she could convince him to go. And he hadn't seemed likely to be convinced.

"Well?" Molly propped her chin in her palm, waiting.

"I don't want to talk about it now," Lyddie said, avoiding her sister's gaze. "If you're through, you might go catch Bobbie June before she disappears somewhere and remind her that we have wash to do today. Otherwise, you and I will be stuck with all the work again, and all those extra sheets from the performance last night."

"If you are going to be like that, I'd just as soon go get her and get started."

Molly left, no doubt, with the intent of finding Bobbie

June and pumping her for information. Maybe Bobbie June would open up to her.

Lyddie added more sugar to her bowl, though a knot had formed in her stomach and she suddenly had little appetite.

What would happen to Bobbie June and Billy Fred if they were charged with the sabotage? They needed to take responsibility for their actions. But how could she see them go to jail? If they survived—which many didn't—their lives would be ruined. What future would they have with the taint of jail ruining their reputations? Billy Fred might live it down, but what of Bobbie June?

"Take care of my babies, Lyddie. . . ."

"I will, Mama. . . ."

If she let the twins go to jail, she would be breaking her promise to her mother. But not making them take responsibility for their actions would be just as wrong.

And who was she to judge? Hadn't hiding Gerald's body been wrong? But how could she have let Gram be arrested and hanged?

Resolutely, Lyddie pushed all her worries out of her mind and took a bite of couch-couch. It was tasteless.

"I don't know why I have to do all the wood chopping," Billy Fred complained, carrying an armload of split red oak wedges down the path to the washpot.

Looking up from their tasks, Lyddie, Molly, and Bobbie June all glared at him. "If you want to take over for me here, I'll chop the wood." Using a laundry paddle, Lyddie gave a hard poke to sheets she was boiling. "I'll be glad to get away from the heat of this fire."

"No, I'll go. He can take over carrying fresh water up the bluff and rinsing the clothes," Molly said, pouring water from the bucket she'd just fetched from the spring into the rinse tub.

"Well, I guess chopping wood is man's work at that. Wouldn't be right to make you girls do it." Billy Fred dumped the wood and was about to beat a retreat.

"Wait." Bobbie June caught the rope handle and lifted one side of a tub of freshly laundered clothes. "Catch a hold of the other side of the tub, Billy Fred, and help me carry it to the clothesline."

"Now I done my part," he complained, reaching for the handle all the while.

"It's everybody's clothes," Bobbie June snapped.

"And more sheets than usual," Molly added, "thanks to our budding music-hall performers." This earned her identical frowns from the twins as they lifted the tub between them. They turned and went up the path, mud squishing between their bare toes as they skirted puddles left by the rain the night before.

After a rain, the twins would usually be wearing their old boots—which now seemed to be missing. Molly told her that Nick had asked the twins about any boots they had, and both denied owning any, inviting him to search their rooms.

Lyddie pounded the boiling clothes with her laundry paddle, pushing this new fact out of her mind, to join all the other things she was trying to ignore.

"Lye-Beth, you're quiet this morning," Molly said as she poured another bucket of water into the rinse tub.

"Am I?" Shrugging, Lyddie continued to poke the clothes.

"I'm worried, too." Molly sighed.

"Dad-blame it!" Billy Fred yelled from somewhere over the crest of the bluff.

"What did you do that for?" Bobbie June's voice demanded. " 'Cause I felt like it—what do you think! Get the dad-blame thing off! *Molly, help!*"

Molly ran up the path, Lyddie on her heels. They found Billy Fred sitting in the wet grass beside the woodshed, his foot stuck up in the air and a piece of board stuck on it. Bobbie June looked pale as she inspected the board and the foot.

"That must hurt." Molly knelt beside the casualty, a frown of professional interest drawing her brows together.

"Naw, it tickles!" Billy Fred snapped. "Of course it hurts!"

Nick came at a run. "What's wrong?" He knelt by the boy and inspected the injury.

"Hold his foot," Molly directed. Nick did as he was told, and she yanked the board off, revealing the rusty nail that had been stuck an inch deep into his arch. Blood seeped from the wound.

"Oh, my." Paling even more, Bobbie June took a wet washcloth from the tub of freshly laundered clothes and wiped her face.

"Give me that." Molly took the cloth and carefully wiped dirt and mud from around the puncture.

"Where are your old boots?" Lyddie asked in exasperation, hands on her hips. A rusty nail puncture was a serious matter. It could lead to a nasty infection, even to lockjaw and death.

"I don't have 'em anymore." Billy Fred shot a petulant glare at Bobbie June.

"Why not? What happened to them?" Lyddie demanded.

"I just don't have 'em!" he snapped. "They was getting old, anyway."

Nick sat back on his heels. "They were, weren't they?"

he agreed lightly. "I think the right one had a crack all the way across the sole."

"That's right. And they were hardly worth half-soling," Billy Fred added, looking squarely at his foot. "You know the Howard's old coon hound totes off everything that ain't tied down. I must a left 'em outside or something."

"Can't find mine, either." Bobbie June looked at her brother's foot and paled again.

"Help me get him inside," Molly said. "We need to wash the wound, then cup it to draw all the rust and dirt out. I have some turpentine to cup it with, but I'll need someone to go to Doc's for some cotton wool to soak."

Molly and Nick helped the invalid into the hotel. Bobbie June stared after them a moment, then turned to the heavy tub of wet clothes and started dragging it toward the clotheslines.

Lyddie caught the rope handle on the other side.

"I can do it," Bobbie June protested.

"I know you can. But we are a family. We help each other."

Bobbie June shrugged, and they lifted the tub between them, carrying it to the clotheslines and putting it down.

"It wasn't my fault," Bobbie June said. After popping a pillowcase to get the wrinkles out, she fished a pin from the bag, which hung on the line.

"What wasn't you fault?" Taking some clothespins from the bag as well, Lyddie moved to the next line and started pinning up clothes.

"Billy Fred stepping on that nail. He didn't wear his old boots when he was supposed to, anyways. Probably wouldn't have had 'em on today, either." Holding a corner of the pillowcase over the line, she stabbed it on with the clothespin.

"What happened to his boots?" Lyddie kept her voice light, without censure.

"I . . ." Bobbie June spotted Nick back outside and frowned. "Like Billy Fred said, could have been the Howards' dog drug 'em off. How am I supposed to know?" She finished hanging a pillowcase and reached for another.

Nick stopped by the clothesline and lifted a bath sheet from the tub. "Bobbie June, Molly wants you to go to the doctor's and get cotton wool. She has Billy Fred soaking his foot in warm saltwater right now. She thinks it will be okay." He fished in the pin bag, then pinned the cotton square by the corners.

Nodding, Bobbie June turned and disappeared around the corner of the house.

Shaking his head, Nick selected another wet bath sheet. "Lyddie, you have to let them take responsibility for their actions, you know."

"I don't know what you are talking about," Lyddie said stiffly. It was difficult to act outraged when she had so recently been thinking the same thing.

"Yes, you do." Nick stabbed pins, on the corners, then grabbed a bed sheet. After neatly folding it in half so it wouldn't drag in the dirt, he began pinning it on the line, too. It was plain he'd hung up clothes before.

"Despite the new red ribbon in her hair today, which I'm guessing came from the mercantile early this morning, the ribbon I showed to the sheriff last night"—he met Lyddie's gaze—"the one found under the platform after holes were knocked into the depot, is Bobbie June's. Molly confirmed as much yesterday afternoon, when I showed it to her and asked who might have lost it. And the twins were seen near the depot the night it was damaged."

Nick paused, as though giving Lyddie time to assimilate what he was saying. He pinned the last corner of the sheet and plucked another from the tub. "The engineer on the train that derailed saw two figures in tan oilskin slickers scampering into the woods just before the accident. The twins have tan slickers hanging on pegs by the kitchen door."

"That's hardly proof of anything." Lyddie felt tears prickle behind her lids. She knew she was only denying the truth to herself. "A lot of people have slickers."

"I have proof: the casts of the boot prints I put in the depot safe. On the larger set, there's a crack across the right one's sole. The smaller set has a run-down heel on the left boot."

Billy Fred had described the larger pair of boots just minutes before.

"And from the way Bobbie June was acting the other day—the day you slid down the roof and needed rescuing—I'm betting I'll find those boots in the old well when I look in it."

Chapter Fifteen

The well. The abandoned well. The well where Gerald's body had been for the past four years. . . .

A bitter taste filled her mouth. Lyddie stared at Nick, dish towel and clothespins forgotten in her hands. "Have you seen . . . looked in the well?" The words seemed to come from a great distance. She wet her lips, certain her face betrayed her guilt, hoping it didn't. Lord, what would she do?

"Not yet." Lines drew a frown between Nick's eagle's wing brows. Obviously, he was wondering at her reaction. "But when I take the evidence I have to Sheriff Wood, I'll ask him to look—"

"Don't!" Lyddie shook her head. *Dear Lord, don't let the sheriff find what's in the well. Don't let Nick . . .*

"Lyddie, it has to be done. You can't protect them in this. You shouldn't try."

"Don't!" she whispered urgently. *"Please."*

"They have to learn responsibility for their actions." His tone was firm, but his expression showed his sympathy. "If you think about it, you'll see I'm right."

Blinking, Lyddie realized he was talking about the twins. She had been so consumed by fear that he'd find Gerald's body, the danger facing the twins had fled her mind.

Dear lord, how had things gotten so tangled?

Could she untangle them and avoid disaster for the twins and Gram? Was there any way out without someone she loved getting hurt?

There didn't seem to be.

She searched Nick's gaze. "Don't look in the well."

Another frown etched itself between his brows. "I have a responsibility to investigate fully."

Turning, she very slowly spread the dish towel onto the line and took great care in pinning it. If she could only draw a deep breath, she thought, she could think more clearly. But with fear squeezing her chest, she could barely breath at all.

"Ah, Lyddie," Nick murmured. Sensing her pain, he turned her around and wrapped her in his arms, and after a moment's resistance, she relaxed against him, pressing her face against his shoulder.

Just for a moment, he told himself. *Only to comfort her. She deserves comfort.*

Tilting her chin up with his finger, Nick sighed and brought his thoughts back to the matter at hand. "As I said, you can't continue to protect them from the consequences of their actions. They have to learn from their mistakes. Lyddie, you have to let them."

"Some consequences are too harsh. I promised my mother I would take care of them and Hortense and

Molly. She knew she was dying. . . ." Lyddie's voice caught.

"You've tried as hard as a person could try. You've been mother and father to them, from what I've seen. You probably never had a childhood yourself."

"It wasn't always this way. Gram was always here for us, after my father left." Still leaning against his warmth, she sniffed and wiped at her wet cheeks with her fists, like a little girl. "Gram was like a mother to us. Took care of us all. I imagined I would die from boredom. All I thought about was leaving this place, traveling. Then I met Gerald and he told such stories about the places he'd been and the great adventures he'd had. . . ."

Lyddie bit back the rest of what she was about to say and pressed her face against Nick's shoulder. She should have realized Gerald only wanted Gentleman John's gold.

Nick held her in the circle of his arms, willing her to say all the things that were troubling her, to share the burdens she carried. "Tell me about Gerald. He hurt you somehow."

She shook her head. She didn't dare tell Nick how Gerald had shown his true colors on their wedding night, demanding she tell him where the gold was and slapping her when she didn't. Then Gram had intervened, and he'd turned on her, drawing back to deliver a punch that would have likely broken the older woman's jaw. Gram had used her heavy walking stick on his hard head a few times and sent him running. She'd told him not to return.

But he had. A couple of hours later, Lyddie found Gerald's body with a bloody gash on the back of his head. She had seen Gram standing at the door to her room, clutching her cane like a club. It had been clear to Lyddie that Gram had whacked him again when he returned. To protect her grandmother, she dumped his body in the old well.

Gram changed after that night. Where once she had taken charge, she just seemed to drift through the days. Lyddie had taken over everything, keeping the family solvent. Sometimes she caught Gram looking at her strangely and wondered if she wanted to confide in her about what happened. But Gram never had.

"She's getting on in years now, I guess." Lyddie wiped her cheeks and drew in a deep breath, then pushed back out of his arms. "Let me talk to the twins. If they did do this damage, I will try to get them to own up."

"Will they?" He touched her cheek.

"I don't know." She caught his hand and pressed her cheek against his palm. It felt so right being in his arms.

And every second Nick stayed would make it harder to lose him. Resolutely, Lyddie pushed the thought away.

Stepping away from him, she turned back to the laundry tub. "I'll try to reason with them. Maybe you could put in a good word for them with the railroad officials?"

"Of course." He didn't tell her, but he already had, suggesting that if damages were paid the railroad not pursue prosecution. They were considering his suggestion.

Nodding, she reached for another dish towel. He took it from her hands and dropped it back into the tub. "Lyddie, what is it? There's something more. I've sensed it almost from the first moment I arrived here."

Lord, was she that easy to read? Swallowing her sudden fear, Lyddie met his gaze. "When you first arrived, you thought I was a chambermaid. That doesn't reveal any great intuitive powers on your part." She raised a sardonic brow. "With the deductive powers you've displayed so far, you might consider a change in profession."

"What brought that on?" he asked gently.

Was the man dense to an insult? Lyddie clenched her fists at her side. "If you will excuse me, I have to get back to the wash."

"No." He caught her in his arms again. "Not until you're honest with yourself, at least. But I'd rather you were honest with me about what's between us."

"There's nothing between us," she said, even as she pressed her body closer to his, giving the lie to her words. "Oh, hell." Fresh tears suddenly blurred her vision.

She still wanted him. That was something, Nick thought. Pulling her against him again, he caught the scent of lavender and buried his nose in her hair. The sweet smell brought back the memory of all they'd shared last night. Having Lyddie in his arms had been magical. The blinding flashes of lightning sizzling through the dark outside, thunder booming right behind, had been powerful and elemental, but no more powerful than the feelings she'd aroused in him.

It had been more powerful than he'd ever imagined loving could be.

Lyddie lifted her head and met his gaze, her tawny eyes dark, her lips parted. As he read her desire, need suddenly thrummed through his veins. They had shared incredible pleasure. He wanted to, again.

There was *something* she wanted from him, at least. It just wasn't a relationship.

He whispered her name against her lips, then kissed her, softly, as though she was fine bone china and would break if he didn't take care. Or perhaps it was the moment that was fragile.

Sweet, rioting sensations flooded through her. Lyddie circled his neck with her arms, pressing nearer still. She felt she could never be close enough. She loved the feel of his hard contours pressing into her softness. Loved the feel of being sheltered by his strength.

Nick deepened the kiss. Sweetness changed to heat with her next heartbeat. Needs satisfied in each other's arms just hours before in the dark, sweet night exploded anew.

"I need you," Nick breathed against her neck, the evidence of his desire a hard bar of male heat pressing into the softness of her stomach.

"I need you, too," Lyddie whispered, blushing to admit such wantonness. Again. Hadn't she shown her lack of control where this man was concerned when she had gone to his room last night, knowing what would happen?

"You don't understand." Nick held her away from him and shook his head. "I need more than to make love with you. I need you in my life. Why won't you tell me what's wrong?"

Tears wet her cheeks. "I can't."

"Ah-hem!"

Lyddie looked up to find Hortense standing on the back steps, her hands on her hips. "So, it's *'Do as I say, not as I do,'* is it, Lyddie?"

Nick held her when she would have pulled out of his arms. "I care deeply about your sister, Hortense. I hope to persuade her to marry me."

Nick felt Lyddie stiffen at his words.

"Marry!" Hortense's expression brightened as she skipped to where they stood. "Really! That's wonderful!" She clasped her hands. "Though I was hoping you'd develop a certain tenderness for me, Nick, I can't begrudge Lyddie's happiness. Have you set a date? Will you have a church wedding?"

Lyddie struggled until Nick released her and glowered

at him, then her sister. "I am not marrying Nick," she told her sister. "In case you've forgotten, I am legally married already."

Nick watched Lyddie disappear down the path to the spring, her steps brisk and her skirts swishing angrily. What was the missing piece to this puzzle—and there was one. His every instinct as an investigator was alive to it.

More than that, his heart told him finding it was the key to his future happiness. What was Lyddie hiding? Was it a wound too painful to expose?

Would she ever trust him enough to share her secrets?

Not bloody likely. Not if he brought out evidence that caused the twins to be arrested.

He sighed and thrust his hands into his pockets. It wasn't that he wanted to see the twins prosecuted. He was certain that they had never meant any harm. Trouble was just a talent with those two. How could he win Lyddie's trust and caring when he was likely to cause her such pain?

Hortense moved up beside him. She patted his arm. "Lyddie has some strange notion of remaining married to that weasel, Gerald Seaton, though from what I heard after they were married, she's well rid of him."

"He left on their wedding night, didn't he?" Nick had learned as much from numerous people. For some reason, knowing he was a Pinkerton agent made people seek him out to talk, telling him any and everything about life in Crossroads.

"Yes. He was drunk and yelling at poor Lyddie."

"What was he saying?"

"Something about Lyddie better tell him where the gold was—Gentleman John's gold—or he would beat her until she did." Hortense shivered. "I never did like him. There was a regular row. It sounded like he chased her down into the lobby and hit her. Lyddie was crying, and she had a black eye the next day."

Nick hadn't heard that before. He looked down at his clenched fists. Cowards beat helpless women. Was her experience with Seaton the reason Lyddie couldn't bring herself to trust him?

"What happened? Why did he leave?" Nick asked.

"I think it was Gram." Hortense smiled. "She used to be a firebrand. Anyway, I heard her shout at Gerald to leave Lyddie alone, and then there was a whacking sound and he yelped like he was hurt bad. He kept yelling for Gram to stop—I think Gram was whacking his shins with her stick." Hortense shook her head. "Served him right."

"Yes," Nick agreed, tucking this information away.

Sighing, Hortense tilted her head coquetishly to the side and batted her lashes. "Anyway, if Lyddie fails to see the light, I hope you'll feel free to call on me."

Making a bow, Nick said, "Any man would be honored, Miss Shea. Now, if you will excuse me . . . ?" Not waiting for her answer, he stared around the hotel. At least there was one thing he could do for Lyddie and her family, he thought, as he headed for the telegraph office. He would find Gus Elverston and suggest that he talk with Mrs. Moreland about the chain of railroad restaurants Gus was selling franchises in. The hotel would offer a perfect location and, given the information Gus had shared with him, it would be bound to prosper, providing security for Lyddie and her siblings.

Nick smiled to himself, imagining how much the twins would like raking in tips for waiting tables.

His smile died as he began mentally composing the reply to the telegraph Lyddie had delivered last night, wherein the president of the railroad had agreed to consider Nick's suggestion to accept payment for damages and not pursue criminal charges. The tone of the telegraph had not been encouraging, however.

Maybe he could get Gus to add his voice to the plea, Nick thought. The financier would have far more influence than a lowly Pinkerton agent. After all, the man had his own private train car.

And if the railroad did drop the investigation, Nick hoped it would convince Lyddie he was not the enemy. Maybe she'd even come to trust him.

Chapter Sixteen

Screwing up his face into pain-filled lines, Billy Fred gingerly moved his bare, bandage-wrapped foot, shifting its position slightly on the tasseled pillow. He, injured foot, and pillow all occupied the swing on the side porch, where he'd been convalescing since Molly finished cleansing, poking, prodding, and tied off the bandage a few hours earlier.

Sighing gustily once the foot was relocated, Billy Fred looked up as Bobbie June approached him with a tall glass of tea. Taking it with a nod, he sipped, smacked, then looked at the glass. "Sure is hot weather. I don't suppose old man Faraday has any ice left in his ice house?"

"Ice?" Frowning, Bobbie June crossed her arms over her chest. "I am not going to old man Faraday's to get a block of ice, which would be half melted by the time I got it back in the wheelbarrow. He probably doesn't even have any left, anyway, being it's the end of June!"

"I understand." Billy Fred nodded, then sucked in his breath through his teeth as he moved his foot again, this time back to where it had originally rested on the pillow. "Just can't seem to get the dang thing comfortable. You know how it is." He added with a touch of worry coloring his voice, "Molly said I gotta be careful. If it gets infected, I could lose my foot and have to have a peg leg."

Eyes flashing, Bobbie June lowered her chin and stared hard at her twin. "William Frederick Shea, wood chopping is your job, and just to show you my heart's in the right place, I've chopped wood for the wash, for cooking dinner, supper, and breakfast, and done all my work besides. And brought you your dinner on a tray! I think I've more than made it up to you for throwing your boo—"

Suddenly aware they were not alone, she whipped around. Nick Bennington was lounging against the porch railing.

He smiled knowingly. "Go on."

Clenching her fists at her sides, she turned back to Billy Fred. "For throwing your balance off and making you step on that ol' board. I said I was sorry four times already," she finished sweetly.

"What are you talking about—" Billy Fred began. "Hey, watch it!" He jumped as Bobbie June bumped his tea, causing it to slosh onto his lap.

"Sorry." She glared warningly at him, then turned to Nick. "What can we possibly do for you, Mr. Bennington?"

"What?" Billy Fred looked over his shoulder and frowned as his gaze landed on Nick. "Yeah, Bobbie June told me who you really are. And to think, I thought you were something special. The big Pinkerton agent," he finished in a mocking tone. "You're just after our gold, is all."

"I'm not special." Nick strolled around the swing to a rocking chair and sat down, stretching his long legs out in front of him. "You two aren't special either. You aren't above the law, you know. And when you've done wrong, you should be honorable enough to own up to your deeds." Propping his elbows on the rocking chair arms, he laced his fingers together, meeting their hostile looks levelly.

"I don't think you two meant any harm. But harm was done. Why don't you tell me all about what happened to the rails by Myers Creek, then about the damage to the depot building, and we'll sort it out with the railroad? The railroad isn't going to pursue criminal charges if you two make restitution for the damages and all expenses incurred because of it." At Nick's request, Gus Elverston had telegraphed the railroad president, requesting leniency for the "perpetrators." He had received a response within the hour.

Bobbie June's eyes widened, then narrowed challengingly. She was getting danged tired of hearing about those railroad tracks and the depot. Lyddie had cornered her a short time earlier and gone on like a revival preacher about the whole business and right and wrong and taking responsibility for it when a body made a mistake. Bobbie June had choked down all she could before telling Lyddie exactly what she thought—that Lyddie should have been on their side, instead of old Pinkerton's!

Looking Nick in the eye, Bobbie June lifted her chin. "How should we know what happened to the rails and the depot building?"

"How much would 'restitution' be?" Billy Fred asked,

ignoring the scalding look his twin threw at him.

"Two hundred dollars and an apology."

"Two hundred." Billy Fred turned a little pale and studied the bandage around his wounded foot. "There's no way a few boards cost the blasted railroad two hundred dollars, and they'd a had to replace 'em anyways, because they was eat up with wood lice. And their own men set that train back up on the rails. That didn't cost 'em nothing."

Narrowing her eyes, Bobbie June wanted to kick him. Did he even know how guilty he sounded?

Shaking his head, Nick said, "They want to be reimbursed for what they've paid the Pinkerton Agency, too. And, remember, the longer it takes me to bring this matter to a conclusion, the higher the total will be." He leaned back in the chair and began rocking slightly. "Nice afternoon. Do you think those clouds will bring us more rain?"

Putting her hands on her hips, Bobbie June asked, "If you're so gall-dang honorable, Mr. Bennington, how come you come here using a phony name and sniffing around trying to find our gold?"

"I'm not interested in the gold." Not anymore, he added to himself. He'd found the gold at Gentleman John's Hotel—Lyddie Shea Seaton. "I did think there was a treasure when I first came here. I don't anymore."

"Why?" both twins asked in unison.

"If any of the gold my grandfather lost still existed, as hard as you two have been looking all these years, you would have found it long ago. You even have what you believe are the real maps to help you."

Bobbie June touched the bib pocket of her overalls, and a loud crumpling sounded. She pursed her lips, irritated with herself for reacting to what Nick said.

Nick went on in mild tones, "Whether or not I came here with the gold in mind has nothing to do with the damage you two did, does it?" Rocking gently, he looked toward the well, certain the boots that would prove his case were at the bottom of it. "My instructions from the railroad were clear: If an apology is received and payment for damages is made within a reasonable time, they won't pursue the matter further. If not, I'm to turn over what I have to the sheriff and let him arrest you."

It would be far better if they would come forward on their own and pay the damages. If he could just make them realize it. Now that he'd planted the idea that they would be held accountable one way or another, maybe they would own up.

"Think about it," Nick suggested, rising. Right on time, he saw Gus Elverston walking down the unpaved street, the silver knob of his cane flashing in the sun. Nick met the older man as he started down the brick walkway to the hotel.

Watching the two until they were out of sight around the corner of the hotel, Bobbie June tapped her fingers on the porch railing. "You mark what I'm telling you, Billy Fred, Nick Bennington's no better than all those other Yankees, who Gram said all come down with their carpetbags after the war, looking for whatever they could cheat people out of."

Billy Fred pointed out, "He didn't carry no carpetbag. He had a valise and a trunk."

Bobbie June glowered at him, but he ignored it. Despite his disappointment that Nick was a Bennington, Billy Fred still saw a lot in him to admire. He wisely didn't tell this to his twin, however.

"What do you reckon Nick is up to with that Chicago man?" Bobbie June asked, changing the subject.

"Something underhanded and lowdown, I'll bet. He ain't a man to trust, for all his fine talk about being honorable. And I think I better find out just what that underhanded something is." Bobbie June threw her braid over her shoulder and headed around the corner, toward the lobby door, where the two men were obviously bound.

"Hey, wait for me!" Billy Fred jumped up from the swing and rushed after her, his injured foot forgotten.

"There's some 'ot brewing in the dining room, Miss Lyddie," Agnes said. Used serving bowls, plates, and silverware stacked high on a tray before her, she maneuvered her plump hips through the door to the kitchen, then let it swing closed behind her and crossed to the worktable with the shifting stack. After setting it down by the dishpan, she wiped her hands on her stained apron. "That Pinkerton man is there, and a fancy fellow with bushy white hair. And the family's all gathered, 'cept for you. Mrs. Moreland said you were to come straightaway."

Lyddie frowned. "I'd better go, then." An unsettled feeling creeping along her spine, she finished washing the plate she held, then dried her hands. She'd known Nick and his friend were discussing something with Gram. She suspected it might be about the twins. . . .

When she reached the dining room, Lyddie found Nick, Hortense, and Molly sat at a long table near the middle of the room. Gram sat on the other side, with the twins standing behind her chair, looking like protective mastiffs. A man Lyddie recognized as Nick's friend from Chicago sat at the end of the table. Both he and Nick rose as she entered.

Tall and handsome and looking at her with a special

light in his dark eyes, Lyddie was totally aware of Nick from the instant she entered the room.

"There's someone I'd like you to meet, Lyddie." Smiling, he moved to her and took her elbow, guiding her forward.

His warm fingers touching her through the sleeve of her old gingham dress drew all her attention. Suppressing a sigh, she realized the new plan she'd worked out as she'd washed dishes wasn't going to work—to just ignore Nick until he finished his investigation and went away was not a viable option.

It had been a good plan, she allowed, except for one fatal flaw—the man was danged nigh impossible to ignore. Especially when he looked at her like he was right now, in that way that warmed her to her toes.

Nodding toward his friend, Nick said, "Lyddie, allow me to introduce you to Gus Elverston."

She forced her attention away from the slight cleft in Nick's chin and met the older man's gaze.

"Gus, this is Mrs. Lyddie Seaton."

"A pleasure, ma'am." Gus nodded amiably as he leaned across the table and shook her hand.

Lyddie nodded. "Likewise, Mr. Elverston."

"Gus, please."

"Gus." Lyddie nodded again, thinking his easy smile was at odds with the shrewd glint in his dark eyes as he took her measure.

The financier, with his flowing white mane and a well-tailored white suit, made her aware of how shabby the dining room had become. No doubt he had noticed that the once red-flocked wallpaper was now faded to a rusty orange and the checkered tablecloths were mended and stained—not that the coarse gingham clothes matched the fancy carved moldings around the ceiling and doors, anyway.

Wondering again just what this was about, Lyddie looked to Gram, but she sat caressing the gnarled top of her walking stick and frowning into space. She'd been especially self-absorbed the last few days.

Bobbie June and Billy Fred hovered behind her chair, looking like they weren't that pleased with whatever was afoot.

"Just what is this all about?" Lyddie directed the question to her grandmother.

"Eh, what Lye-Beth?" Gram blinked as though awakened from a deep sleep.

"Oh, do sit down, Lyddie. You're holding everything up." Hortense crossed her arms on the table and leaned forward, her cleavage spilling forth—which was, no doubt, exactly what she intended. She smiled at Nick, scrunching up her cheeks tightly until she managed to produce a dimple.

Lyddie decided her sister had been practicing in front of the mirror again. "And just what am I holding up?"

"Mr. Elverston has made the most exciting offer, Lye-Beth. Gram wanted us all present before we discussed it," Molly said, eyes bright, a large black tome closed on the table before her.

The closed book increased Lyddie's sense of unease. Little could divert Molly from her study of a medical text once the book was within her reach.

"Here, Lyddie." Nick pulled out a chair for her from a nearby table.

Her attention was snagged by the breadth of Nick's shoulders and the way his muscles played under his crisp white shirt as he slid the chair forward. Sighing, she realized being indifferent to him was far easier when she was looking at stacks of dirty dishes and not the man himself.

How had she expected to stay indifferent to ignore him, when just seeing those shoulders made her remember holding Nick, skin to skin, and exploring those muscles just last night?

Feeling warmth in her cheeks, Lyddie cleared her throat as she took the seat. "Thank you, Nick."

Turning her attention to the financier, she asked, "What is this offer you've made, Mr. Elverston?"

"Gus, here," Hortense cut in before he could answer, "wants us to open the dining room as one of his Birmingham House Restaurants! Just think, Lyddie, our hotel will be known up and down the line. It will be listed on brochures in all the depots!"

"A Birmingham House . . ." Lyddie frowned. "I don't think I heard right. Isn't that a chain of restaurants?"

"Yes! They're known all over the country!" Molly nodded enthusiastically. "We'll finally be able to make money with the hotel, not just survive. That way, I'll have the money to go to medical college. Oh, Lyddie, isn't it wonderful!"

Nick asked, when Lyddie failed to comment, "Aren't you pleased by the offer?"

"Just . . . just taken by surprise," Lyddie managed, trying to sort out what this might mean. The sense of unease she'd had in the kitchen had grown tenfold.

"Lyddie is nobody's fool. She can see that it's not a good idea," Bobbie June declared.

"Oh, Lyddie, of course it's a good idea. It's the answer to my dilemma." Molly caressed the book on the table, running her fingers over the gold-leaf title: *The Treatment and Prevention of Ill-Humors.*

"You ain't been accepted to medical college yet, Molly," Billy Fred pointed out.

Molly's cheeks pinked. "I will be accepted," she said stoutly. "Though I've received several rejections, I've sent letters of application to some of the better institutions."

"You have sent letters of application?" This was news to Lyddie.

The pink turned into full, glorious red. Molly tucked her chin, but her eyes gleamed defiantly. "Yes, I have. I didn't want to say anything until I was accepted. But I will be. It's just a matter of time."

"I think becoming a physician is a noble ambition for a woman," Gus Elverston told Molly.

"Thank you," she blushed. "Not many people do. There's a great deal of prejudice against women physicians."

"And that makes it difficult to get accepted into a medical college," the financier guessed. "I'd like to talk more with you about this quest of yours at a later time. Right now we are all gathered to discuss my favorite subject." He grinned. "Making money." Gus went on, "However, before we reach an agreement, we should discuss the renovations that would be needed to the hotel dining room. Birmingham House Restaurants have to meet certain standards."

Lyddie said, "The twins and Molly told me about the one in Jackson, where they had dinner when they went to see a music hall show last year." She gestured at the room. "We don't have money for damask tablecloths and dainty little chairs with cushioned seats and oil paintings for the walls."

Gus Elverston told her, "Actually, the room will need a bit more than dressing up—it's far too small for the number of diners I would expect to be eating here. And the kitchen will probably need major renovations to handle the numbers I would expect."

Bobbie June's gaze narrowed. "Now that's odd about needing more space, considering there's a danged sight more long straw pine logs carried on those rails through town than there is people. Sometimes we go weeks without a guest at the hotel. What makes you think we'd need to expand the dining area?" She added, "Not that we've agreed to your deal."

The financier smiled, his bushy white mustache spreading. "Young lady, I can see that you are no one's fool, either. I like my business partners to have savvy. Though I hadn't intended to reveal certain facts until we had come to an understanding, I see my hand is forced. However, I must ask that what I am about to tell you be kept in the strictest confidence. Agreed?"

Plainly intrigued, despite their rather hostile attitude, Bobbie June and Billy Fred nodded.

Hortense batted her thin lashes excitedly. "We give you our word!"

Leaning nearer, Molly said, "Of course."

As Gus Elverston stroked his mustache, seeming to weigh his next words, Gram looked up from the contemplation of the top of her walking stick. "What he'd rather not tell us, I suspect, is that the railroad is making the line through Crossroads a main line from Memphis to New Orleans."

Turning to her, Gus's bushy white brows rode upward. "Indeed, that is at the heart of my enterprise, ma'am. But that is also a closely guarded secret. If I might ask, how did you find out about it, Mrs. Moreland?"

Amusement crinkled the corners of her eyes. Gram said, "Eh, I might be old, but I can still see as deep in the rock as the man what pecked the hole."

His brows rose higher. Gus looked at Nick, plainly at a loss to translate the remark.

Gram chuckled heartily and tapped her cane on the floor. "Heard there's a new railroad bridge planned for the Mississippi at Vicksburg, or thereabouts. Turning a train south to New Orleans after it crosses the river just plain makes sense. You're planning to open fancy restaurants along this rail line. It ain't a far leap, Mr. Elverston."

"Gus, please." His smile seemed more genuine. "And that is the plan exactly, Mrs. Moreland."

"How many diners would you expect?" Lyddie asked. This was the answer to her prayers. It would mean enough money to support the family easily.

So why did it feel like a mistake?

"Fifteen to fifty, depending on the season. You can see why renovations will be needed—a larger dining area and more staff, as well as the interior refurbished and the outside painted and spruced up. Though those things could wait until the main line was ready to be dedicated and there was a surety of more customers," Gus Elverston said.

"You expect the legend of Gentleman John's gold to draw people, don't you?" Bobbie June guessed.

Gus grinned. "That I do. Travel and vacationing has become more and more popular with the common man—a trend that can only grow. The legend of the gold and the tales of Gentleman John, himself, will draw people to pause here."

Cold washed through Lyddie. That's why the whole idea felt like a mistake—fifty people a day, poking about, looking for the gold . . . Gerald would never stay quietly resting in the well. Disaster. It could only mean disaster if they entered into a partnership.

"We don't have the money for any renovations." Lyddie put her hand to her throat. "And we don't have the money you require to buy a franchise."

"That's where I would come into this," Nick told her. "Gus told me what he was doing and invited me to invest in one of his restaurants. I thought about scouting for another location. But if Gentleman John's Hotel is to take advantage of this offer and become a Birmingham House, you'll need capital—both for renovations and to buy into the franchise. If the family is agreeable, I would like to put up the money needed."

"Why?" Bobbie June asked suspiciously. "People just don't give other people money."

"No, they don't. It would be an investment," Nick told her. "In return," he looked at Lyddie, "I would own a partnership in your restaurant."

Chapter Seventeen

The soft summer night wrapped a comforting cloak about Lyddie. She leaned on the veranda railing, lifting her face to the faint breeze and listening to the cricket chirps and cicada trills. She willed the peace of the evening to seep into her, soothing away the new set of worries the day had brought her.

Fifteen to fifty diners, Gus has estimated, if the hotel became a Birmingham House and the railroad became a main line. That would mean financial security for the family.

But with fifteen to fifty people tramping about daily, brought there by legends of gold, there would be little hope Gerald Seaton would remain quietly in the well. She just knew he wouldn't.

That was, if Nick didn't find him first. Which he seemed bound and determined to do. If she couldn't get the twins to confess to the damages to the railroad, Nick would get the sheriff to look in the well for the twins' boots as evidence against them.

Maybe, Lyddie mused, she should just get on the next train through and leave town. Then, when the inevitable came about and Gerald came to light, everyone would leap to the conclusion that she was guilty. That would protect Gram.

The night breeze rustling the leaves of the old pecan tree covered Lyddie's sigh. A mockingbird somewhere within its foliage started singing, despite it being past time for it to take its roost for the night.

Listening, Lyddie shook her head. "You're as confused as I am, aren't you?"

"And why are you confused?" said a deep male voice behind her.

A voice she recognized all too well. It washed through her, warming and chilling as it went.

"I didn't hear you come out," she said, avoiding Nick's question.

She sensed exactly where he stopped—close, but not quite touching. The skin on her neck prickled warmly with awareness.

"I hope I'm not disturbing you."

"You aren't." *Liar,* she told him silently. If he didn't want to disturb her, he wouldn't use that dark silk tone and stand so close that she could feel his warmth at her back. Oh, he wanted to disturb her. And he did.

He disturbed her to the soles of her shoes.

"You seemed lost in thought." Nick smoothed an unruly curl at her temple. His light touch sent thrills chasing across her skin. Lyddie stepped away and leaned against a post, pressing her cheek to the cool wood. "I was remembering slipping out here as a child and how the soft summer night would close around me. Music and laughter drifted up from below as my parents entertained their friends." She smiled as she continued, but her tone was bittersweet. "I would sit looking through the railing at the stars, with my feet dangling off the edge of the veranda. When Daddy played on his fiddle, I would kick in time with the music. I couldn't wait until I was old enough to join the fun."

"What happened that makes it a sad memory?" Nick asked gently, moving beside her again.

"It all changed suddenly. One day Mother was showing me how to sew on a button—I remember she kissed the drop of blood from the tip of my finger when I stuck it with the needle. I asked her if I would still be her little girl when God sent the new baby from heaven. She hugged me and told me I would always be her little girl and she would always love me.

"The next day the doctor was here, and my father and Gram and everyone were looking worried. After a long time, they let me see my mother. She was very pale and weak. The twins were in the cradle by her bed. She smiled and told me she loved me and made me promise to take care of the new babies and my sisters.

"A short time later she was gone. People in somber black clothes stood in the parlor talking in whispers. At first, I thought the wooden coffin Mother lay in was a type of cradle and she would wake up. I had never seen anyone dead before."

"And then your father left."

"Yes." Lyddie looked up at the stars.

Nick put his hand on her shoulder, wanting to offer her comfort. "Then you grew up and married Gerald Seaton, and he disappeared, too."

Lyddie stiffened and stepped away from his touch.

Letting her go, Nick wondered again what happened

between Lyddie and Seaton to make her guard her heart so fiercely.

"I'd rather not talk about Gerald." Lyddie twisted her hands in the folds of her skirt, her gaze drawn to the dark shadows tangled in the front corner of the yard, the azaleas and camellias she'd purposefully let grow thick and wild.

"Okay." Nick let the silence mellow between them.

After talking with Hortense that morning, he'd chatted with more people in town about Seaton. He'd formed a picture of a fast talker with a ready smile. It was generally agreed that the man had fooled Lyddie into thinking he was something he wasn't, and that was the only reason she'd married him. One girl who worked in the small saloon on the outskirts of town told Nick that Seaton used to brag about all the money he'd have after Lyddie married him and he got his hands on Gentleman John's gold. The girl also told Nick that Seaton got mean when he was drunk and had once wrenched her arm so badly she had to wear a sling for two weeks.

Everyone Nick had spoken with seemed to quietly agree that it was the best thing all around when Seaton disappeared, though they all felt sorry for Lyddie.

Nick said, "Would you rather talk about my and Gus's offer?"

"It's a nice offer," Lyddie began.

"But you're thinking of turning it down?" Nick guessed. Then shook his head. "I don't know why that surprises me."

"The family hasn't decided yet," Lyddie told him. "But what would happen if we do turn it down? What would Gus do?" She sensed rather than saw Nick shrug. The mockingbird began singing again, as if it, too, found the idea of throwing away the family's chance for real prosperity ludicrous.

Nick moved nearer, his shoulder almost brushing hers. Lyddie felt warm awareness of him down to her toes. How could the man affect her so without even touching her? She would be totally aware of his presence in a pitch-dark cave, she decided.

"I don't want you to feel you have no choice, Lyddie, but I think turning down Gus's offer would be a mistake. If you accept, the hotel will remain wholly the family's, and I'll own a share of the restaurant's profits. Gus wants to locate it here because of its being a logical midway point between others he has planned. If you decide against his offer, he would build one somewhere else in town, or near it. Very likely a hotel, too. Understand, it wouldn't be personal, but Gus is first and foremost a businessman."

"I understand." Which meant she was caught between a rock and a hard place. It would be madness to pass up this opportunity and disaster if they took it.

Crossing her arms, Lyddie stared up at the stars of the Milky Way, scattered across the indigo bowl of sky above the town. The paltry lights on Main Street were no competition at all with the white sparkling diamonds. Once, when she was a little girl, she'd dreamed that she reached and caught a star, but when she opened her hand it had disappeared.

She had to remember that Nick was a dream. He wasn't forever. Not even for a season—having him here for that long would be far too dangerous. As long as she had secrets to protect, he'd be as impossible to hold as those bright points of light in the heavens.

But with him, she had touched those stars, however briefly. Under his tender instruction, she'd learned what loving could be—the echoes of what they experienced still shimmered through her whenever she thought about last night. She would never regret what they'd shared.

Nevertheless, she couldn't hold on to the stars and she couldn't hold on to Nick.

Lyddie said, "Gram hasn't made a decision, but I'm afraid it just wouldn't work out."

Nick asked quietly, "Would being in business with me be so repulsive to you? Lyddie, I can't figure out why you still don't trust me. You're afraid of me—"

"I'm not—" Turning to him, she started to protest.

"Don't deny it," he cut her off. "It's there, now, like a shadow between us. Is it just that I'm a Bennington?"

"Nick—"

"Do you think I still might want revenge for my grandfather's loss, and my offer is somehow a ploy to get it?"

"No. Never. I never imagined you would take my reluctance as a personal slight. I—I . . ." She lost the words she was about to say. Nick stood barefoot, his hair tousled and his shirt open. And he was standing close enough that she only had to wrap her arms about his neck to be against his hard male chest.

Taking a half-step back, Lyddie leaned against the railing. "Why would you think that I don't trust you?"

Thrusting his hands into his pants pockets, he smiled wryly and looked toward the street, where a lone farm wagon creaked along its way out of town in the dark. "Bobbie June thinks my motives are less than honorable. She told me so when she and Billy brought up hot water for my bath."

As the mockingbird sang again, Lyddie was quiet for a moment, her better judgment fighting her need to be in his arms.

Good judgment lost.

She asked, her voice husky to her own ears, "Sir, *are* your intentions less than honorable?"

Why had she done that? Weren't enough disasters looming around her waiting to strike? Another night in Nick's arms could only hurry them along. And it would make it all the harder when he eventually left.

Staring at his chest, the smooth skin inviting her touch, Lyddie bit her lip, feeling her cheeks warm. She needed this man, in so many ways.

Right now, she needed him most as a woman needs a man.

Even if he was only a dream—a star she'd caught that would disappear when she opened her hand—he was a wonderful dream.

Closing the small distance between them, Nick cupped her face. "Completely less than honorable, at the moment." As his mouth met hers, the bird sang out again in the soft dark night. Breaking his kiss, Nick smiled against Lyddie's lips. "Is that a nightingale singing?"

"A mockingbird." Feeling needy, Lyddie pressed her length more closely to his, circling his neck with her arms.

"I didn't know they sang at night." He kissed the tip of her nose, her cheek, her forehead, and the point of her chin. The teasing little kisses only made her press closer still, wanting more.

"Sometimes they do." She caught her breath as his lips traced the line of her throat. "Sometimes they sing all night long," she added breathlessly as she slid her hands under his open shirt and found his hard, muscled chest.

"Why did you say earlier that it was confused?" His eyes gleaming in the half-light, Nick began undoing the front of her dress. As he worked the small buttons, the backs of his fingers lightly brushed the tops of her breasts.

"The mockingbird is singing"—Nick's fingers closed over her taut nipple beneath her camisole—"Oh, yes!" Gasping, she arched against his hand.

" 'Oh yes'?" he chuckled.

"It's singing"—Lyddie found his flat male nipple and gave it her attention, and it was Nick's turn to gasp—"a cardinal's song, instead of its own," she laughed.

Hooking his arm behind her knees, Nick swooped her up. "I think it wants to serenade us."

Carrying her to his room, Nick laid her down on the big four-poster bed.

Lyddie pushed up on her elbows. "I hope you don't think I was waiting for you out there on the veranda. I mean, after last night . . ."

"Of course I do. That's why you were on the opposite side of the hotel from my room, standing in the dark." Light from a single candle splashed his skin golden as Nick stripped off his shirt, then reached for his pants.

Suddenly she no longer cared if Nick thought she had engineered this moment or not. She could do little more than watch the play of light on the muscles of his chest and back, then his thighs. An insistent tingle began deep inside her.

Anticipation, she decided, was a powerful aphrodisiac.

When Nick turned back to her, his manhood fully erect and jutting, her anticipation turned to liquid heat.

"I need you." She lifted her arms, wishing Nick had never come to the hotel, had never made her aware of how beautiful intimacy between a man and woman could be.

Lyddie wet her lips.

"And I need you, Lyddie." He knew he meant the

words in a different way than she did. Maybe she would come to feel the same way.

Maybe.

Nick lay down beside her and kissed her long and deep.

Wiggling against him, she silently begged him for more, for the coming together and glory he'd shown her last night.

Breaking the kiss, he chuckled. "I won't be rushed."

"Won't you?" Lyddie asked, her voice a husky invitation. She wet her lips again.

"No, minx," he growled, then swiftly kissed her before propping up on an elbow. He gave his attention to undoing the rest of the buttons on her dress, down past her waist. He took his time, kissing her flesh as he exposed it. He found the ribbon of her camisole and gently tugged until the bow gave way, freeing her breasts. He then took the frayed end of the satin ribbon and teased it across her nipples.

Watching his movements, Lyddie sucked in her breath, clutching the coverlet. How could such a small action send such thrills chasing all through her? He was only touching her with a tiny bit of cloth!

"Is that necessary?"

"Do you want me to stop?" Nick untied her bloomers and slid his hand beneath. He began stroking her stomach, easing closer to the nest of curls at the apex of her thighs.

"No. Yes."

She moistened her lips, looking delectably confused and aroused.

Chuckling, Nick said, "No? Or yes? You only have to ask and I'll stop what I'm doing." He found her moist center and began to tease the tight nub hidden there.

Clutching his arm, Lyddie was desperate to make him stop, yet afraid that he might. "I'm going to explode!"

"I want you to explode," Nick murmured, watching her face as he thrust his finger deeper. "Repeatedly."

"No." She shook her head. "Not alone." Lyddie grasped his hard shaft, and it jumped in her hand.

He stilled, his features taut. "Lyddie, don't—"

She stroked the length of it, then again, loving the feeling of power it gave her as Nick struggled for control.

"Minx!" Nick hissed on an explosion of breath, seizing her wrist.

She laughed as she released him.

"So, you like having the upper hand, do you?"

"So to speak." Lyddie was delighted at the ease between them. This would be a memory to take out and hold in years to come, long after Nick had returned to his life in Chicago.

"Then I'll give you what you want." Sitting up, he stripped her bloomers off and tossed them aside, then lay back on the bed, pulling her atop him.

"What are you doing?" Her eyes widened, fingers splaying on his hard chest.

"It's what you'll do. Have your way with me," he said, his voice a deep rumble.

"You want me to . . . ?" Intrigued, Lyddie pushed up to look at him questioningly.

Beneath thick lashes, his brown eyes gleamed in the half-light. "I want you to. I want you to very much."

This couldn't be decent, could it? one part of her mind wondered as Nick lifted her and helped her straddle his lean hips. His hard shaft pressed insistently against her sensitive center.

Nick stripped her dress over her head, then her petticoat, leaving her naked in the candlelight. In another moment she was joined with him and half-dizzy from the sensations arcing through her.

No, this had to be decadent.

It was also totally hedonistic, she realized as Nick lay back, eyes half-closed, and waited for her to take control.

He really was giving her her way.

Feeling deliciously filled, she rocked forward and back experimentally. Then again, catching her breath in wonder.

"Yes! Like that!" Cupping her breasts, his fingers and thumbs unerringly going to the taut points, Nick growled encouragement as she found the age-old rhythm of love.

Never had she felt so empowered.

Never had she dreamed such feelings were possible, not even last night, when Nick lifted her to those new and splendid realms she'd never known existed.

Each move of her hips carried them higher. Each response from Nick increased her own pleasure. Striving together, they rose higher and higher, until sensation carried them spiraling through an explosion of stars in a universe where only they existed.

Still joined, Lyddie gently fell back to earth and collapsed on Nick's chest, passion's dying echoes chasing through her.

Perfect.

The word echoed in her mind.

Perfect.

Beneath her, Nick moved, and another wave of sensation convulsed their middles. Shuddering as it passed, Lyddie pressed a kiss to his skin, tasting his salty perspiration.

Yes, this was as perfect as anything had ever been in her life.

Still caught up in the magic, she closed her eyes, resting her cheek against Nick's chest, listening to his heart slowing its rhythm.

Nick whispered, "I love you."

Chapter Eighteen

The wondrous, sparkling place she'd been floating swirled around and turned gray, and Lyddie crashed back to earth.

"I know, we haven't known each other long. But I love you." Frowning, Nick slid his hands over her torso, feeling the tension in her muscles. "Why does that frighten you?"

"It doesn't frighten me." Her fingers splayed on his chest, she pushed upright, needing to put distance between them.

"No?" His look was derisive. "Your whole body went rigid when I said it."

"It doesn't frighten me." Unable to bear intimacy any longer, Lyddie got off Nick and pulled her discarded dress over her body. "Why should it frighten me?"

"You tell me." Watching her closely, Nick took her hand, running his thumb over the soft skin of the back.

A place inside her long shut away tried to open up.

She firmly sealed it up again and pulled her hand away. No. There were no happily ever afters for her. Letting him get too close, become too necessary, was just asking for pain when he left. And he would go.

"It *doesn't* frighten me. I was just surprised, that's all. You said it yourself—we haven't known each other long at all." Pausing, she chose her words carefully, not wanting to wound. "Nick, being with you is the most beautiful, the most perfect thing I've ever known—"

"But the feelings you have are merely physical." He lay back and stared at the ceiling.

"I never asked you to love me." Softly.

"No, that's true. You never lied and claimed you felt more than you do."

His tone held bitterness, though Lyddie sensed it wasn't aimed at her. Playing with a loose button on her dress, she could think of nothing else to say. If, indeed, he did care about her, she was certain it would fade quickly.

"This was a mistake." Lyddie got off the bed and plucked her underpants from the floor.

"Why a mistake?" he asked. "Because we gave into passion, or because I care more than you want me to?"

What did he want her to say? "It just was. It was my mistake." Naked, feeling terribly vulnerable, Lyddie twisted her bloomers this way and that, trying to straighten them out. She had to dress and get out into the fresh air.

"It's Seaton, isn't it?" Nick said on an explosion of breath. He stared at the medallion on which the room's small chandelier was centered, as if the plaster swirls and rosebuds held an answer. How could she still love Seaton when he'd treated her so shabbily?

Remembering his own infatuation with Evelyn, he allowed that there wasn't much logical thought involved in matters of the heart. After his investments started to pay off, he'd thought Evelyn would change, learn to be content while they built a future together. He'd been wrong.

Sighing, Nick sat up and swung his feet over the side of the bed.

"I don't want to talk about it." Feeling tears pricking her eyes, Lyddie jerked on her underpants haphazardly but couldn't get them up over her hips. To her dismay, the string of her bloomers was tied in a knot.

Looking down at it, at a loss, Lyddie couldn't decide what had happened or how to make it right. Tears blurred her vision as she tried to figure it out.

"Here." Nick turned her to him and picked the knot loose, then pulled the bloomers up and retied the string in a bow at her narrow waist.

"I don't know why I'm crying."

"It's okay."

She looked from her camisole and petticoats puddled on the floor to Nick. His expression was stark, but his eyes held an inviting tenderness and caring. After a moment's hesitation, Lyddie circled his waist with her arms and pressed her cheek to his chest, letting her tears flow.

"I'm sorry."

Nick stroked the warm skin of her back soothingly and kissed her wheat-gold curls.

"I know."

Hortense frowned at the mashed potatoes on her fork, then dipped them into the gravy puddled atop the mound on her plate. "Things sure are dull around here. Where's Nick? I thought he and Gus were going to be back today."

"He can stay gone, as far as I'm concerned, and his fancy friend, too," Bobbie June said stoutly, helping herself to more sausages.

Her twin made no comment, but merely forked down his food.

"That young man sure is the spitting image of his grandfather," Gram mused as she helped herself to a spoonful of field peas. "I'm thinking he's got a might more to his character, though."

"The train from Vicksburg is late," Lyddie supplied. Nick had gone with Gus Elverston on down the line, as the financier scouted out more likely locations for his restaurants. Gus had told Gram the family would have a few days to think about his and Nick's offer while he was gone.

Lyddie had been thinking more about Nick. Sighing inwardly, she knew she cared far too much for him. Far more than was wise. And that was her own fault.

He says he cares, too. He loves you, said a little voice inside her.

That didn't matter, Lyddie told herself firmly. Even if she was free, it wouldn't last. Her life was here. If he stayed with her, he would grow tired of Crossroads. Or tired of her. Or something else would happen to take him away. It was just as well she couldn't make commitments that would only lead to heartbreak in the end.

"Gus said when he got back to Crossroads, he might have a surprise for me." Molly glanced up briefly from her beloved copy of *Grey's Anatomy.* Gus had promised to put in a good word for her at one of the medical colleges. Ever since, she'd had her nose firmly pointed at various medical texts, in anticipation of being accepted.

Shaking her head, Hortense patted Molly's hand. "It's

likely Gus was just being polite, Molly. It's likely, too, he's forgotten all about talking for you."

Molly looked mutinous at this. "I think he will do what he said he'd do."

Gram arched a censorious brow at Hortense. "I've not a doubt Mr. Elverston meant what he said about putting in a word for Molly. He seemed a man as good as his word."

Bobbie June declared, "I hope Nick never comes back." Sweeping her siblings with a derisive look, she added, "And we ain't going into any partnership with no Bennington." She seemed to want someone to disagree.

Hortense readily picked up the bait. "You only say that 'cause you got something to hide."

Bobbie June glared. "Do not!"

"Do too!" Hortense snapped. "Everybody knows it. The whole town knows it."

"That's only 'cause Pinkerton has been spreading tales!" Bobbie June said stoutly, her eyes suspiciously moist.

With a sinking feeling, Lyddie noticed that Bobbie June never said the tales weren't true. Billy Fred had his eyes trained on his plate, and he was shoveling in his food like he had a fire to get to.

"Now, you listen to me," Hortense said, fixing her youngest sister with a no-nonsense look. "The railroad officials are going to give you two a chance to pay damages. That's only right and fair."

Shaking her head, Bobbie June declared, "We don't need to go into business with no Bennington!"

"We have to," Hortense said. "We don't have the money to paint and fix up and enlarge the whole dining room, and build and furnish a better kitchen. Gram and I talked with a carpenter, and with his estimates and the cost of the franchise, we'll need near a thousand dollars."

Pointing her fork at the younger girl, Hortense went on, "We'll get the money from Nick in exchange for a share in the restaurant, not the hotel, and we'll *all* have buckets of money when the railroad becomes a main line to New Orleans.

"Would the railroad really blacklist us?" asked Molly, surfacing from her book. "How will I afford medical college if we don't go into business with Nick and Gus?"

"Even if we do, Molly girl, it won't pay off for a year or two, maybe longer. How had you planned to pay until then?" Gram asked.

Molly shrugged and looked dejected. "I have some saved from my teacher's wages. I had hoped the hotel would be making more money by the time that was used up. It seemed like the answer to my prayers when Nick and Gus made their offer."

"We don't need to go in business with a polecat like Nick Bennington!" Bobbie June interrupted.

"He's no polecat," Hortense told her.

Glaring, Bobbie June threw her braid over her shoulder. "He is a polecat! As stinky as the one that fell into the old well that winter and like to stunk us out."

Lyddie's tea glass stilled halfway to her lips. She congratulated herself on not spilling it. She set the glass down before her shaking fingers sloshed it on the tablecloth.

"How do you know it was a polecat in the well?" Gram asked, her gray brows riding up in interest.

No, let it go, Gram! Lyddie pleaded silently. *Let it go!*

"I remember that. It was cold enough to split the hide on a toad frog." Billy Fred nodded. "And it was Jane who said it was a polecat. Said he was up to no good and ended up in the well. She had us put a hundred pounds of quick lime in it for the smell and cover the top of the well with old boards."

Lyddie stared at the peas on her plate as if they held the mysteries of the ages.

"The well is a health hazard and should be filled." Molly opened her book again.

Fill the well? Lyddie blinked. Why had it never occurred to her before? With the well filled, Gerald would be more properly at rest. And there would be little danger of anyone finding him.

"Maybe we should," Lyddie commented.

"What a good idea, and clean out from around it, too, and trim up the camellias. Just look!" Hortense held up a scratched forearm. "There are saw briars everywhere."

"You never go outside. When were you at the old well?" Billy Fred asked as he reached for the bowl of sausages. His hand stilled and his eyebrows road up onto his forehead as Hortense blushed red.

Giving her potatoes new attention, she spluttered, "I just was. That's all. I love to look up at the stars at night and try to pick out the constellations."

Before Billy Fred could comment on his sister's newfound interest in astronomy, Bobbie June said, "Well, I think filling the well is a fine idea. We can get started first thing in the morning, can't we, Billy Fred?"

Everyone at the table looked askance at her, including Gram.

"What did I say?" she asked mutinously.

"Even though I think we should fill in the well, it's not a way out of your trouble with the railroad. Everybody knows that's where your old boots got to, so Nick couldn't match the soles with the casts he made." Wagging her finger at the younger girl, Hortense told her, "Own up and pay up."

"Am not!"

"Are too."

Gram raised her hand, silencing the two. "Honor demands being responsible for whatever you do. My John taught me that. He was an honorable man, and I reckon he'd want his grand young'uns to live that way, too."

Toying with her food, Lyddie wondered if Gram's conscience troubled her over what happened to Gerald. It had to weigh on her.

It certainly weighed on Lyddie.

"Nick talked to us and said the damages would run two hundred dollars," Bobbie June said, head hanging. "How can we get two hundred dollars?"

"It's so much 'cause the railroad wants what it's paid to the Pinkertons back from us. We only have thirteen dollars and three nickels." Billy Fred looked equally downcast. Then he sat up, visibly squaring his shoulders, though his chin trembled. "But a man has to have honor, I reckon." He swallowed hard. "I'll go to jail."

Chapter Nineteen

Gram settled herself more comfortably in the depths of her favorite chair and studied her twin grandchildren. "So, you two finally saw the handwriting on the wall and decided to 'fess up, have you?"

"Yes, ma'am," Bobbie June said as her brother nodded solemnly, tracing the pattern on the carpet with his big toe. "I expect your Grandpa John would be proud of you for doing the right thing." Gram looked up above the cold fireplace at the portrait of a handsome, dark-haired gentleman and a lovely young woman—herself. Smiling, she nodded, as if receiving confirmation from him.

The room, once his study, was permeated with the gambler's presence: Leather-bound volumes he'd treasured lined the floor-to-ceiling shelves on one wall; a massive sandalwood desk was positioned in front of the window; and some of his unfinished correspondence still sat on the blotter, as if awaiting his return. Although

Gram had claimed it as her bedroom when she no longer felt up to climbing the stairs, she kept the room like a shrine to the man she had loved.

As her grandmother continued to stare at the portrait, Bobbie June remembered her grandfather's sketches and touched the bib pocket on her overalls. She'd found the drawings in a book while dusting the bookshelves and had taken them from the room without asking Gram.

It hadn't been wrong exactly to borrow them—Gram had never missed them, after all. Still, it hadn't been exactly right.

When she had a chance, she decided, she'd slip them back into the drawer where she'd found them. No good had come from having them, anyway. Just the opposite, in fact.

As the moments dragged on, Billy Fred nudged his twin and whispered, "Should we remind her we're here?"

Gram's shrewd gaze returned to her miscreant grandchildren. "I know where you are. People my age get to have lapses and people your age just have to stand still till they pass. Particularly people your age who damage railroad lines."

"Yes, ma'am." Both hung their heads.

"Now, I wanted you two in here to tell you two things. First being I'm proud, too. Especially of you, Bobbie June. Nobody would expect you to own up, being a girl."

Darting a glance at his twin, Billy Fred wished Gram hadn't said that. He was having a hard enough time trying to make Bobbie June see sense as it was. "Gram, I tried to tell her to be quiet and let me say I did it all, but she is being pigheaded."

"I won't be treated like some half-wit, not even responsible for her own actions, Billy Fred Shea," his sister said darkly.

Gray brows raised, Gram commented, "You didn't seem in no lather to own up a'fore now, my girl."

Blushing, Bobbie June studied her bare toes. "No, but I ain't going to let Billy Fred own all the guilt, when I did as much as him."

"Gram, tell her to just forget it and let me go to the sheriff on my own."

"Your sister has a right to own up to her own misdeeds."

"But Gram, we ain't got no money to pay for the damages. There's no need in both us gin' to . . . to prison."

"Then let me take the blame by myself," Bobbie June said, her voice not quite as steady as she would have liked.

Billy Fred glowered at her.

"Well, now," Gram said mildly, "I guess you two had a fine reason for doing all that, but what it might have been I can't figure out."

Hanging her head lower, Bobbie June said, "You know we were looking for the gold, Gram."

The gray brows rode higher. "Seems you chose some right odd places to look."

"We had reasons."

"Ah." Gram nodded, just as though this explained it.

Seeing the conversation was taking a hard turn from the problem at hand, Billy Fred said, "But it still won't do for Bobbie June to go to jail. She's a girl. She ought to listen to me for just once and keep quiet."

"I can't vote 'cause I'm a girl," Bobbie June fumed. "When momma died, you inherited her share of the hotel, and even though I was born at the same time, I didn't get anything 'cause I'm a girl. Life just ain't fair when you're a girl, and it ain't right. But I can take my share of responsibility for all this, even if I am a girl—and that's the end of it!"

"That's a right honorable sentiment, too." Gram smiled at her youngest granddaughter. "Women with fire, like you, might just change things, Bobbie June. Now, bring me that roll of gray velvet cloth atop the desk, and let's see if we can figure a way neither of you have to go to jail."

Billy Fred did as he was bid. His grandmother took it and unrolled it, revealing a sparkling amethyst and diamond brooch. He recognized it immediately as the same one she wore in the painting. It had been his grandfather's wedding present to her.

"Now that you owned up, I reckon this should fetch enough to pay the piper," Gram said with satisfaction.

Yawning, Lyddie paused at the foot of the stairs, wishing she had slept better. The first part of the night, she had lain awake wondering how late Nick's train might be and what had delayed it.

Not that she was worried about him, she had told herself, smoothing her hair. She just didn't want him coming in in the small hours and disturbing the whole house.

After she'd heard the train pull into the depot and, later, his firm step on the stairs, she'd rolled over and sought sleep. Only to start imagining Nick getting ready for bed, stripping away his clothing piece by piece. Then he'd get between the fresh sheets she'd put on his bed just that morning. Slipping between those sweet-smelling sheets, not wearing a stitch . . .

For some reason, remembering that he slept nude had made it darned hard for her to go to sleep.

Lyddie yawned again, hoping Nick wasn't there as she opened the door to the family dining room.

It proved a vain hope. Wearing a crisp white shirt, a string tie, and an embroidered vest, Nick sat at the table between Molly and Hortense. The twins sat across from him, barely glancing up as she entered.

"Good morning." Nick rose.

"Morning." Not meeting his gaze, Lyddie took a seat before he could move around the table to pull out a chair for her. There was still no future for them, she reminded herself as she studied the tomato gravy, biscuits, and golden fried salt pork—the smells of which had teased her all the way down the stairs. Suddenly she wasn't at all hungry.

Nick said, "I hope you slept well."

Lyddie met his gaze, which was dark and warm. Did he somehow know how restless she'd been?

"Fine. I slept fine." *Liar, liar, pants on fire!* She took a biscuit from the bowl. "And you?"

"Very poorly." The look in his eyes seemed to say that she was the reason.

Prickles started in her breasts and sank into her abdomen. Feeling a blush warm her cheeks, Lyddie busied herself, giving great attention to cutting her biscuit open with her butter knife. If she could have trusted her voice, or have been sure what words might tumble out of her mouth, she would have answered.

"Oh, Nick, I am sorry to hear that," Hortense declared, snagging his attention and his arm. "You know, if there's anything you need at night"—she tipped her cleavage in his direction as she lay her hand on his sleeve—"I mean, an extra pillow or something, you only have to wake me."

Seeing the expression on Lyddie's face, Hortense told her, "Don't look like you bit a green persimmon, Lydia Elizabeth! You act like you don't want anything to do with Nick, when he's made it plain he wants to marry you! I'd say that pretty well leaves it clear for someone who appreciates him more."

Feeling her face flame under the interested stares of the twins and Molly, Lyddie considered kicking Hortense under the table.

She decided against it. She might miss.

"I wouldn't dream of disturbing your rest, but thank you, Hortense," Nick said smoothly.

Silence settled around the table. Lyddie wondered at the twins. Normally they would have been full of questions or snippy comments on hearing Nick had proposed to her, but neither remarked. Something was definitely wrong, Lyddie decided, as Billy Fred stabbed a piece of fried salt pork with his fork and opened his mouth, only to put the meat back on his plate again without taking a bite.

"I take it that you two had that talk with Nick about the damage to the railroad," Lyddie guessed, pleased they were showing responsibility.

"We did." Bobbie June sighed. "We're going to go to the sheriff with him this morning and straighten everything out. Gram's helping us find money to pay the damages."

"I'll telegraph the railroad officials and tell them, and all should be taken care of within the week," Nick told Lyddie.

"Thank you. I do appreciate all your efforts with the railroad." Lyddie knew that the twins were lucky Nick was understanding. Another investigator might not have been as sympathetic, and might have gone straight for the sheriff and charged them.

On the other hand, another investigator might not have

made her wonder what it would be like if she was really free and not bound by a lie. . . .

Pushing the absurd thought away, she busied herself pouring coffee from the blue clay pot and returned it to the trivet in the center of the table. This was what she needed, some of Jane's good New Orleans–strong coffee. The aroma alone was invigorating. Lifting her cup, Lyddie sipped the rich brew.

Looking up, she met Nick's gaze again, and she felt a heavy thump in the region of her heart. To divert herself, she said to the twins, "It's fortunate that Gram has the money to lend you two."

Putting his fork down, Billy Fred looked completely miserable. "She doesn't. Gram's gonna sell her brooch—the amethyst and diamond one she's wearing in the painting of her and Grandpa John."

Her head drooping, Bobbie June added, "We'll never get enough money to pay her back."

Billy Fred reminded his twin, "Gram said she'll be paid back if we fill in the old well, like Molly said ought to be done."

"She did?" Lyddie asked, her cup halfway to her lips.

Setting her coffeecup down again, she took a moment to collect herself.

"That don't seem a fair trade," Hortense said.

"Well, I'll scythe the grass and trim back the bushes before we start on the well. I might even get the grubbing hoe to the yaupons and pull out the saw briars." Billy Fred thrust out his chin. "It's the best I can do to pay her back."

Hortense shook her head. "You two should be ashamed to take your grandmother's charity. Besides, I was gonna wear Gram's brooch when I get married, for something old and something borrowed."

"Nobody's asked you to get hitched yet," Billy Fred shot back.

"It might not be too far off, Mr. Smart Aleck." A smile played about Hortense's lips.

"How can that be?" Bobbie June demanded. "I saw Frank Worley in town yesterday, and he said that you said you didn't want to see him at all since he almost punched that skinny telegraph operator."

"Keeping Frank Worley at arm's length will only make him want to see me more," Hortense said confidently. "Besides"—her smile was secretive—"he isn't the only eligible man in Crossroads."

Her smile died when no one took her seriously enough to ask what she meant by the remark.

Molly, who had seemed lost in her own thoughts, and even more miserable than the twins, looked up and blinked. "I guess Gram selling her brooch is the only way out."

"I guess." Billy Fred tore off a piece of biscuit and unenthusiastically dragged it through the tomato gravy on his plate. His twin showed much the same lack of appetite.

Watching the two, Lyddie hoped this experience would make them stop and think before acting on their wild schemes. It was just lucky they wouldn't end up in jail. She did owe Nick her thanks for all he'd done.

And Nick had said he loved her, that he wanted to marry her. . . . Her heart was foolish enough that it wanted to believe him.

Nick did seem different from all the other men she'd met. Lyddie remembered that Gerald Seaton and his smooth charm had seemed different, too. Of course, then she'd been pitifully naive.

But even if Nick meant the things he said, it didn't

matter. She wasn't free. And even if she had been, the people she needed and depended on in her life never stayed around.

Sighing inwardly, Lyddie picked up her fork.

Molly threw her napkin across her plate and glowered at the twins. "If you two ever thought about anybody but yourselves, you wouldn't end up in trouble. But you always are in trouble and someone is always helping you out."

"What's wrong, Molly?" Lyddie frowned. This wasn't like her at all.

"The money. I was going to ask Gram to help me find the money to pay my medical school tuition and living expenses for the first year," Molly said, her chin trembling. "But now that these two have made such a mess of things, and she has to sell her brooch to pay them out of trouble, I know she won't have any extra to help me."

"You haven't even been accepted by a school yet," Bobbie June scoffed, but her eyes were suspiciously bright and her chin was tucked guiltily.

"That's where you're wrong," Molly sniffled. "This morning Nick gave me a telegram from the president of the New England Female Medical College in Boston. Gus said he would help me, and he did. But there's no point, is there, without funds."

Tears streaming down her face, Molly hurried from the room.

"I'd better go see about her." Hortense hurried after her sister.

"Will she be okay?" Nick asked, frowning.

"I think so." Lyddie really didn't know what to do or say. She toyed with her food, feeling like she had failed Molly. But she had done the best she could for all the family. What more could she have done?

After Molly and Hortense left, the twins seemed to sink in gloom and soon scuttled away, leaving Lyddie all too aware that she was alone with Nick Bennington. She kept her attention on her plate as she ate.

At length, he said, "I could help with a loan—"

"It's not your responsibility," Lyddie cut in, not meeting his gaze.

"It would be easily tied in with the partnership—"

"No."

Nick put his napkin on the table. "What's wrong?"

"Haven't you done enough to tie yourself to my family?" Lyddie glowered at him.

"Why are you angry?"

Why? She didn't know why, and that fact just made her angrier. Standing, she clenched her fists. "I wish you'd just leave, Nick."

Gram entered the room at that moment and looked from one to the other. "Eh, why do you want him to leave, Lyddie?"

The desk bell dinged imperiously as someone in the lobby demanded attention, and Lyddie brushed past her grandmother without answering.

Fighting tears as she made her way to the desk, Lyddie knew she couldn't have answered. In truth, she just didn't know. There was a bad feeling coiling in the pit of her stomach, growing tighter and tighter whenever she realized how important Nick had become to her.

He *would* eventually go. Like everyone she'd ever depended on had gone. And the longer Nick stayed, the larger chunk of her heart would leave with him when he went.

Chapter Twenty

"You, there!"

As Lyddie approached the desk, a tall blond woman in a fashionable traveling suit rang the bell again, as if to hurry her along. Behind the blonde stood another woman—a maid, Lyddie guessed, from her plain dark dress and gray capelet. A man in a bowler hat with a long-suffering expression on his face gave Lyddie an apologetic smile.

"Good morning. May I help you?" Lyddie asked.

"You certainly took your time. I was beginning to wonder if we were to wait indefinitely," the blond woman complained. To the man at her elbow, she said, "I think dear Nicky exaggerated the quality of this hotel, Charles. I can already tell the service will be deplorable. I can't imagine why he insisted we stay here on our way to Jackson."

"Nick Bennington insisted you stay?" Lyddie frowned.

"He is staying here, isn't he?" The woman brightened. "Or perhaps we have the wrong hotel. Is there perhaps another, more opulent hotel in Crossroads? Surely this isn't Gentleman John's Hotel dear Nicky told me about."

Lyddie tucked *dear Nicky* away for future consideration. "This is the only hotel in Crossroads." Sliding the guest register toward the woman, Lyddie managed to keep her voice even, though she hardly felt up to dealing with difficult people right now. "Though if we aren't up to your usual standards of accommodation, I shall certainly understand if you choose to remain on the train."

Taken aback, the woman's kohl-accented eyes narrowed; then her gaze flicked over Lyddie's much-worn dress and she recovered. She brushed a fleck of train soot from the embroidered lapel of her jacket, as though to emphasize the disparity in their social status. "You are intolerably cheeky, young woman. I shall report you to your superiors. What is your name, girl?"

"This is Lydia Shea Seaton, Elvira. John Moreland's granddaughter," said Nick as he strode out of the hall toward the desk. Lyddie was grateful when he stopped beside her, as if to offer moral support.

"Lyddie, this lady is Elvira Montrose; the 'Songbird of Chicago' is how I believe she styles herself. An old acquaintance Gus and I ran into in New Orleans."

And insisted she follow you to Crossroads, Lyddie added as she nodded in acknowledgment of the introduction. She might have saved the effort. The Songbird of Chicago had eyes only for Nick.

Smiling coyly, the woman came around the desk and hooked her arm through his. "Why, Nicky, when you told me to meet you here, you should have warned me how very rustic this is!" Elvira said over her shoulder, "Charles, do see to signing the register. Gladys, make certain I get the best room in the house, and do be careful with my things." She guided Nick resolutely toward a settee in the corner of the lobby. "Now, Nicky, where did we leave off the other night . . .?"

Billy Fred and Bobbie June had appeared. Lyddie told them, "Go find Hortense and Molly and tell them they're needed." She pushed the register across the desk. The man lifted a pen from the holder and dipped it into the well.

Lyddie didn't wait to see what he wrote. She was soon out the back door and headed for the falls.

Late that afternoon, Lyddie came through the kitchen door, hungry, tired, and no more at peace than when she'd left. Usually, the serenity of the woodland eased her spirit. But today, as she'd buried her feet in the warm sand and watched the rainbow above the frothing falls, she couldn't get thoughts of Nick from her mind.

"Leave the door open, please," Jane told her. "It's hot as Hades in July in here."

"You mean this isn't Hades in July?" Lyddie propped the door with an old iron used for that purpose and a slight breeze wafted the kitchen curtains, stirring scents she couldn't quite name, scents which steamed from the large black pot simmering on the stove. "Why is the kitchen so hot?"

"Her highness wanted a hot bath—not just a hip bath, but had the twins drag that big old brass tub into her room. So the stove has been blazing most all afternoon." Jane arched a brow and motioned with a long-bladed knife at a brass bell on a spring high in the corner. "That bell has dingled more today than in all the twenty-odd years I've been cooking here put together." Her mouth a thin line, she cleft a large head of cabbage into two pieces with one brisk motion. "That woman better watch herself."

"What are you cooking?" Lyddie asked as she pulled out a ladder-backed chair. She used it to climb onto the worktable, then unhooked the bell from the spring.

Jane's black eyes glinted. "I'm fixing *la pied de cochon avec chou.*"

"Pig's feet with cabbage?" Lyddie laughed. "I like it myself, but not everyone does. Why are you fixing that?"

" 'Cause nobody had any chitterlings to sell me. Seems my marinated pork stew didn't meet with her highness's approval at noon, so we'll see if she likes this better."

"Well, that explains the scent." Laughing, Lyddie climbed down and dropped the bell onto the worktable. "I hope you never take me in dislike, Jane."

The cook smiled and began cutting the cabbage into smaller pieces. "Girl, you know I never would. Her highness is a gimme, gimme. You'd never be like that. You're a giver, not thinking about yourself so much as others, even when you ought. You hold this place together."

"Then why can't I be happy?" Lyddie hadn't meant to voice the question aloud, but it had popped out.

Frowning, Jane chopped in silence for a second. "Could be sometimes we get so used to disappointment, we figure that must be all we deserve."

"It's not that simple, Jane."

"It's not as simple as binding up your heart and taking a chance?"

"When her highness showed up, I knew it was a good thing I hadn't," Lyddie said.

"Nick got her to come here just to try to make you jealous, so you'd see the light."

"Why do you say that?" Lyddie asked.

Jane merely gave her a sardonic look, then put down

the knife and took a crockery bowl from the back of the stove. "Here, I saved this for you."

Her stomach grumbling hungrily, Lyddie took it and sat down at the worktable and tasted the savory pork stew. "Thank you. This is delicious."

"Glad you like it." Jane picked up her knife and attacked a new head of cabbage. "Nick and the twins talked with the sheriff and got everything sorted out. Right now, Nick and your grandmother have gone to meet with that Elverston man to get the final deal worked out." Shaking her head, Jane added, "But whenever Nick left her side, which seemed like every chance he got, that woman would start ringing and demanding. The twins ain't got nothing done as far as filling in the old well. They been too busy molly-coddling her."

At the mention of the well, Lyddie gave her attention to the stew, which didn't taste quite as good as it had before. She didn't know how Jane knew about Gerald, but the cook had always seemed to know everything.

After she finished her food, she reluctantly left the sanctuary of the kitchen. She'd barely gained the lobby when Molly spotted her.

"There you are!" Molly rushed down the stairs like Lyddie had been gone a month instead of a few hours. "Where have you been? You've been missing all day!"

Sighing, Lyddie paused by the desk. "What's the problem?"

"More like, what isn't?" Molly thrust out her bottom lip, looking askance at her sister's callous absence.

When Lyddie didn't ask what she meant, she said, "We didn't get the wash done. That woman has kept everyone running all day." Her eyes narrowed. "She calls me, 'You, girl.' "

"We've had difficult guests before." Lyddie got a dust

cloth from under the counter and started cleaning the walnut top, which was still littered with candle flies from the night before.

"Well, you should have been here to help." Molly propped herself on her elbows at the end of the desk and watched Lyddie work.

"I'm sure you handled it."

From her sour expression, Lyddie judged that this wasn't what her sister wanted to hear.

Abruptly, Molly changed the subject. "I didn't notice at breakfast, but Hortense has a bunch of scratches on her arms. Looks like she's been wallowing in a briar patch."

"Oh? Where did she get them?"

"How should I know?" Molly shrugged.

"You could ask."

Frowning, Molly let that remark pass. "And you better find out what the twins are up to, now."

"The twins?" Why did she have to be the one to find out? Lyddie wondered. "Didn't they go with Nick to talk with the sheriff?"

"That was this morning. This afternoon I saw them hunched over some paper, and when I asked them what they were looking at, Bobbie June near about jumped out of her skin and said it was none of my business—which means they're up to something again, and it must be bad."

Sighing, Lyddie got the feather duster from beneath the desk and started dusting the pigeonholes.

"Well, what are you going to do about it?" Molly demanded.

"I'm not going to do anything. I'm tired of trying to keep this family in line. It's like trying to herd marbles uphill." As soon as the words left her mouth, she heard her mother's voice: *"Take care of my little ones, Lyddie. . . .*

Guilt pricked her conscience. Blinking, she turned her back to Molly and stretched to reach the topmost section as she tried to regain her composure. What was wrong with her? Since Nick Bennington had come to Crossroads, she'd lost all emotional control.

At the sound of the front door opening, she sighed, knowing when she turned around, she'd see Nick. Think of the devil and he'll appear. . . .

Looking over her shoulder, she saw he escorted her grandmother, who looked resplendent in a dark silk blouse, adorned with the amethyst and diamond brooch, and a dark skirt. Gram removed her wide-brimmed hat as she entered, and her silver hair was braided in a coronet, which seemed to wreath her head in light. With the regal tilt to her chin, she still bore traces of the beauty she'd once been.

"Well, we got it done," Gram said, a sparkle in her eyes. She released Nick's arm and caned her way toward the desk. "Worked out terms for a partnership with this young whippersnapper here, and both of us teamed up on Gus and wrangled a good deal for a franchise in his fancy restaurant chain." She chuckled.

Lyddie was drawn to smile. Obviously, Gram had hugely enjoyed the wrangling.

Nick cocked a rueful brow. "I don't know how your grandmother managed it. I wanted a quarter interest in the restaurant for my investment in expanding the hotel dining room and kitchen. I somehow seem to have agreed to just three percent for every thousand I invest," he told Lyddie and Molly. "What she did to Gus wasn't pretty, either. I don't doubt he's still reading the terms to which he agreed and shaking his head."

"Eh, business is business. When me and my John traveled about, he always had me handle his business dealings. He drew up the plans for the hotel but left it up to me to see to the practical side of getting it built." She nodded. "Now that we're in partnership, Bennington, I'll teach you a thing or two 'bout negotiation."

Nick smiled. Then his gaze found Lyddie and his smile faded.

Don't you dare look disappointed in me! What do you expect? Lyddie wanted to ask.

Gram went on, "I'll send for my lawyer and he should have the papers drawn up in a day or so, for everybody to sign." As her grandmother paused by the desk, she was still chuckling, but Lyddie noticed she leaned heavily on her cane.

"I tell you, m'girls, wonders will never cease."

"What do you mean, Gram?" Molly asked.

"Who'd ever a' thought the Moreland-Sheas would be in a partnership with a Bennington, and all of us on our way to owning a fancy restaurant." She paused for a minute, as though catching her breath, then added, "Now when I turn up my toes, I'll know you young'uns will be taken care of."

"Gram, don't talk like that!" Lyddie protested. "We'll need you around for a long time to come."

"Eh, you havn't needed me in years. You've been the lynchpin of this bunch, Lyddie," her grandmother said. "More the shame to me, I let you bear the burdens all alone."

"How can you say that, Gram? We all help out," Molly protested, indignantly.

"Aye, that you do somewhat, but Lyddie bears the load of worry, and that gives you time to study your fine medical books or prepare your lessons when you're teaching school."

Molly looked stricken. "You don't feel burdened, do you, Lyddie?"

"I've never thought about it," Lyddie answered, then realized that wasn't true. She had felt overburdened at times as she tried to hold the family together and keep the hotel running. But, at the same time, somehow she'd thought it was supposed to be that way.

Shaking her head, Gram went on, "I'm not taking you to task, mind you, Molly girl. Lyddie has had the choice of making the rest of you tote your share of the burden, but she's bent her own back to it."

Her gray brows arched, Gram's shrewd gaze found Lyddie. "Or that's the way of it up till now. And now, Lyddie, I 'spect it's time you gave more thought to your own concerns." She slanted a meaningful glance in Nick's direction, then started down the hall toward her bedroom, leaning heavily on her cane as she went.

Pausing, Gram told Molly, "Don't give up on that fancy medical school just yet. If things work out, I might have a surprise for you. We'll see after tonight." Gram shrugged her thin shoulders. "If it don't work out, we'll have the money in a few years, after we get the restaurant up and running when the main line comes through. You can reapply then.

"Now, I need a rest a'fore supper. I'll be dining with our guest and Gus Elverston." Gram arched a brow at Nick. "I trust you'll join us, like we discussed?"

"Of course." Nick nodded.

"Not an appetizing thought, eh?" Gram chuckled and went on down the hall.

As Gram closed the door to her room, Molly said, "Is it just me, or is she suddenly looking old?"

Twisting the dust cloth, Lyddie was quiet, unable to deny that Gram was fading in some ways. The thought put a knot in her stomach.

"Lyddie"—Nick took her elbow, compelling her to look at him—"we need to talk."

"We do?"

"Yes, we do."

"Oh." Lyddie swallowed, wondering how she could have thought all day about this man and not have gained control of her feelings at all. A riot of butterflies still sprang to life in her stomach at his touch. Warmth radiated outward from where his fingers rested on her sleeve.

A crash and raised voices from the guest rooms upstairs interrupted her thoughts.

"Sounds like her highness is at it again," Molly murmured. "She might be your friend, Nick, but I swear, that is the most annoying woman I've ever met."

"Jane said you told her to come here just to make me jealous," Lyddie mused.

"Jane is far too astute. I did hope to make you jealous." Nick hung his head in mock contrition. "It was a silly thing to do. I was sorry the instant she showed up. I hadn't seen her in years before Gus and I bumped into her in New Orleans. We grew up on the same street in Chicago. She used to be shy and quiet. . . ." Nick shrugged and looked up as a noise drew his attention. "She's changed since she became a chanteuse," he finished apologetically.

Sobbing, the maid, Gladys, appeared at the top of the stairs and rushed down them at a heedless pace. As her foot found the rag rug at the bottom, it shot out from under her.

"Oh!"

Only her grasp on the newel post kept her from falling.

She looked at Lyddie and Nick in surprise and sat on the bottom riser, rubbing her arm.

"Are you all right?" Nick rushed to help.

"Aye." Testing her arm, the maid sniffled the last of her tears. She nodded at the offending rug. "That's right slippery, ain't it?"

"I'm sorry. Here, let me see if you have a sprain." Molly took the girl's arm and turned it gently. "I have to say, this braided rug isn't as slippery as the fancy Persian rug we used to have down there. I don't know what happened to that one, but I'm glad it's gone." She turned the arm in the other direction. "Does that hurt?"

The maid winced. "It does a bit."

"I have some liniment that will help. Come with me."

As Molly led her down the hall, Gladys said, "I'll be catching the next train back to New Orleans. I've only been working for the woman for two weeks, but I'll be bound, I'll not stay another minute in her employ."

"Lucky she wasn't hurt." Nick straightened the rug in front of the stairs. " "Maybe I can find a hammer and tack it down, so it won't slip."

"I'll get you one." Lyddie turned to go.

"You don't have to do it right now."

"I don't?" She stilled. "I just don't want anyone else hurt." All too aware of how hollow the excuse sounded, Lyddie saw the glint in his eyes and realized they both knew that she just didn't want to be alone with him.

As Nick moved closer, she picked up the dust cloth and started polishing the counter again, fighting back a strong urge to bolt.

"Have you decided what you are afraid of, Lyddie?"

Chapter Twenty-one

Lyddie glared at Nick. "What do you mean? I am not afraid," she said, enunciating each word carefully, as though saying them clearly would make them true.

Nick said nothing. He didn't have to. The look in his eyes spoke eloquently.

"Stop looking at me like that. I'm not afraid. What reason would I have to be afraid?"

Lyddie brushed an annoying curl back from her cheek and glared at him. But it was something of a shock to her to realize she wasn't afraid—not of all the things she'd had to fear for so long. There had been many reasons to keep Nick at arm's length—to protect the twins, to protect Gram—and those reasons were rapidly disappearing.

After the well was filled she would have no real reason to fear having him near.

Except the best reason of all—that she liked having

him around far too much. He was becoming too important to her.

And nothing good could come of that.

"Think what you will." Turning her back to him dismissively, Lyddie lifted the globe from the lamp and started to wipe the soot from the inside with her dust cloth.

Moving closer, Nick took the cloth and the globe from her and set both down. He turned her around and wound his fingers through hers. The look in his eyes said she would not avoid an honest discussion. Not this time.

"Tell me you're happy I'll be a business partner with your family."

Lyddie looked down at his strong, tanned fingers twined through her slender paler ones. *Oh, unfair!* It felt so right when he held her hands. She felt safe and cared for.

Feelings and reality were two different things. Her mother had made her feel safe and cared for, as had her father. Hurtful, hurtful lessons she needed to remember.

Choosing her words carefully, Lyddie said, "If you didn't provide the money for improvements and to buy into the franchise, we couldn't take advantage of the opportunity Gus is offering. A partnership with you is the best thing."

Nick sighed. "That's not what I asked."

"What do you want from me?" she snapped.

"That you trust me."

Trust him? Eyes wide, Lyddie shook her head. "I don't mistrust you."

"Don't you?"

"No."

"But you don't trust me." Nick held her tawny gaze, willing her to be honest, at least with herself. But he could see the wariness in her eyes. He wanted to ignore it but couldn't. Reading people had always been his strong suit as a detective. He'd seen the same look when interviewing bank robbers and murder suspects. "I keep trying to figure you out, Lyddie, but every time I think I know you, something happens that makes me realize I don't understand you at all. What the hell are you hiding?"

The question caught her off guard. Feeling her knees quiver with the urge to flee, she stood ramrod straight. "I'm not hard to understand."

It wasn't an answer to the question he'd asked, but, to her relief, he didn't seem to notice.

"Not hard to understand? I know your husband beat you on your wedding night, then disappeared. But you refuse to try to seek your freedom. What reason you could have to act that way is a mystery."

Lyddie pulled her hands free of his grasp and moved away. She couldn't breath properly with him so close. "That's my business and has nothing to do with you."

"Doesn't it? I have the feeling it has everything to do with me. Is the fact that you made a mistake once what keeps you from risking your trust again?"

"That's my business. And it has nothing to do with anything!"

"Doesn't it?" Nick moved to her again, determined to get answers. But when he drew close, he caught the scent of lilacs emanating from her wet hair. "You bathed at the falls," he murmured as he realized why her hair was wet. He imagined her waist deep in the clean, cool water as she lathered her hair, her arms upraised and her perfect breasts uptilted. Desire hot and hard slammed into him. He reached out and lifted a wheat-gold strand, testing its weight.

Lyddie watched his eyes darken as he bent and brushed the damp strand against his cheek. He brought the tress to his lips and kissed it, all the while his eyes holding hers. Unexpected heat flooded her breasts and pooled in her lower stomach.

"Your hair needs brushing," Nick murmured, releasing the strand.

His words broke the spell, which had started to envelop her. Her cheeks warming, Lyddie said, "If you have finished commenting on my grooming—"

"Gerald Seaton hurt you. Betrayed your trust in the most despicable way. And now you won't risk your heart again. Is that it, Lyddie?"

"He lied to me, but he just told me what I wanted to hear—that we could go to these exotic places he told me about and come back here often enough to make sure everything was all right. I should never have listened. I wanted to leave here. I thought I was so unhappy, I just wanted to experience new things. I was thinking only of myself."

"That wasn't wrong, Lyddie. You deserve a life of your own and dreams of your own." Nick wanted to fold her into his arms, but she stood trembling like a fawn. He sensed she would bolt for the door if he tried.

Slowly, he took another of the golden ropes of hair and spread it in his fingers. Why did he need this woman so much? Was it simply because she didn't need him? Was he one of those men who was fascinated by the unobtainable?

Lyddie said, "If I had left, my family would have suffered. It would have fallen apart. It takes all my energy now just to hold everything together."

"Without you to depend on, they would have learned to get by on their own."

"At what price? Something terrible would happen without me here. I think that's why my father told me what he did."

"And what did he tell you?" Nick asked gently.

She was quiet so long, he thought she wouldn't answer. When she did speak, her words were soft. "When I saw my father walking toward the front gate, his best hat and coat on and carrying a carpetbag, I got the strangest feeling he would just disappear if I blinked. So I ran after him and begged to go with him, but he told me no. I was only ten, but I knew he was leaving for good, and I told him he'd disappear forever if I let him out of my sight. I knew he would.

"He smiled and said I was being silly, and then he made me promise to take care of my brother and sisters. I knew he was going away, but I made myself believe that he'd come back if I promised to take care of everyone." Lyddie blinked but couldn't prevent tears from spilling onto her cheeks.

She hadn't taken these memories out for a very long time and had never told anyone else about them. Tears spiked her thick lashes as she looked up at Nick, seeking understanding. She saw in his eyes that she had it.

Nick wrapped her in his arms then, and stroked her back, aching for the child Lyddie had been.

With her cheek pressed against his chest, Lyddie felt secure and safe, as if she'd found a place she'd been seeking all her life. A fallacy, she knew. But surely it couldn't hurt to enjoy the feelings, just for a moment or two.

Sniffling, she said, "I think Father left because he missed Mother so much, he couldn't bear to stay here where everything reminded him of her."

"You missed her, too. You needed your father here to take care of you and your family."

"We did fine without him."

Nick said softly, "Then why is there anger in your voice when you say that?"

She stilled. "I'm not angry with my father."

"You have a right to be." Nick kissed her hair, wanting to soothe the hurt child he sensed within her.

Abruptly, Lyddie pushed out of his arms. "I'm not angry with my father. I'm not angry with my mother. I'm not even angry with Gerald—not anymore." She glared at Nick. "I want you to just leave me alone. No, to just leave! Leave Crossroads—that would make me happy!"

Lyddie smoothed her crisp white apron, then picked up Jane's sweet potato pie and inhaled its warm, cinnamon scent. "This smells wonderful." Her stomach rumbled, reminding her of her own supper waiting on the stove.

"If that woman says anything about my pie, you dump that right on her head." Jane arched a brow as she rasped a knife against a style, honing the blade.

"I'd never waste one of your pies, Jane." Frowning, Lyddie paused, her derriere against the swinging door. "Why are you still here? Your children will be wondering where you are."

"My children are almost grown. Anyway, I'm going." The cook stood the sharpened knife beside others in a crockery jar on a shelf beside the stove. "Just making sure everything's ready to cook breakfast in the morning."

"My eye." Agnes chuckled as she rinsed a pot in the porcelain dishpan. The round-faced Irishwoman then handed the pot to Molly.

Tearing her gaze away from the medical text she had

propped on the windowsill, Molly took the pot and started to dry it off. "You just wanted to hear how loud Miss Songbird would sing when she found out about the exquisite Creole dish she was eating," Molly told Jane.

Blinking innocently, Jane said, "Why, I just went in and asked if everything was to her satisfaction, and when she said it was only passable, I apologized for my failure. I explained to her that *la pied de cochon avec chou* was my second choice. I couldn't find no chitterlings to cook her." Her dark eyes gleamed.

"I think that's when she hit 'high *C*,' " Molly said.

"She hit high *C*? I thought somebody stepped on a cat." Jane wrapped her shawl about her shoulders with a victorious flourish and started for the backdoor. "Coffee's ready on the stove."

"See you tomorrow, Jane," Agnes called, handing Molly another cookpot.

"Good night, Jane." Lyddie pushed backward through the door and into the hall. She couldn't say she was sorry for Jane's actions. Though it wasn't haute cuisine, the main dish was good, hearty fare. And it couldn't have affected Elvira Montrose's supposed delicate constitution too adversely. Not the way she'd been hanging on Nick's every word and gesture all through dinner—except for that one shriek of distress.

Entering the dining room, Lyddie saw that the songstress was at that instant grasping Nick's forearm, making cow eyes at him as he told about a burglary he'd solved, wherein a valuable amethyst pendant had been taken. Raising her eyebrows as she set the pie on the sideboard, Lyddie met Gram's gaze and understanding dawned.

Well, so that's what Gram had in mind to save the twins, Lyddie thought, trying to hide her smile as she sliced the pie and placed it onto saucers.

"Yes, I think I shall try a slice of pie." Elvira grandly signaled Lyddie to serve her.

"So, the amethyst pendant was returned to its owner?" Gus asked, meeting Lyddie's gaze with a twinkle. "Amethysts are the preferred stones of royalty, you know."

Lyddie bit the inside of her cheek, forcing the smile from her lips.

"Yes. This pendant was quite valuable, too." Nick looked at Gram's brooch and said, "Though I have to say, it wasn't nearly as striking a piece as that one, Mrs. Moreland."

"Eh?" Raising innocent brows, Gram looked down at her brooch.

Elvira's interest was immediately taken by the piece. "It is lovely, isn't it?"

Smiling conspiratorially, Lyddie slid a saucer of pie before Gus.

The older man winked surreptitiously. "Thank you kindly, young lady."

Gram fussed with the brooch, straightening it on her blouse. "Oh, this here bauble isn't all that valuable, I suppose."

The singer's interest visibly waned at her words, until Gram added, "It has more sentimental value, being as it were my dead husband's great-aunt Honoria's—she was the Duchess of Talbot, you know."

"Oh, really?" Elvira leaned forward for a better look at the glittering jewels.

"The amethyst pendant I recovered was valued at eight hundred dollars," Nick said, to no one in particular. His eyes sparkled like sherry wine as he looked at Lyddie. "I'd like a slice of pie, too, please."

When Lyddie returned to the kitchen, Molly was still

reading the medical book she had propped open on the windowsill as she absently dried a pot.

Agnes dunked another pot in the pan of rinse water, then held it out with a grin. "Here. You are falling behind, m'girl. You're sure to make a fine doctor, 'cause you've no future as a dishwasher, that's for sure!"

Molly blinked and finished her task, then reached for the next pot. "I guess it's a good thing I have my teaching certificate then, 'cause I hate washing dishes, and it's certain I'll never get to medical school."

Yawning, Hortense pushed through the door from the family dining room and set a stack of plates by the washpan. Carrying the serving dishes, Bobbie June and Billy Fred were close on her heels. "You two can finish clearing the table. I'm going to bed," Hortense told the twins.

"When is the last time she wanted to go to bed before midnight?" Billy Fred said wonderingly as she disappeared up the backstairs.

"Maybe she's taking ill," Molly said. "Summer complaint is going around. Think I should check on her?"

"She's up to something, more like," Bobbie June said, putting a stack of bowls down where Agnes indicated.

"By the way, young'un, I brung you that carbide lamp you asked about yesterday," Agnes said as she scrubbed another pot. "I doan know why my husband keeps the thing, now that he ain't working in that Virginie coal mine."

"Thanks, Agnes." Bobbie June busied herself scraping scraps from the bowls into the slop bucket in the corner. "Sure was a pretty day, today."

"What on earth are you going to use a carbide lamp for?" Molly asked, undistracted by the weather.

"I'll get the rest of the dishes." Looking decidedly

guilty, Billy Fred ducked back through the dining room door.

Considering Billy Fred's guilty look and Bobbie June's bland expression, Lyddie felt a rock form in the pit of her stomach. What were they up to now?

"You know that momma cat has her litter somewhere under the hotel. I want to move 'em to the woodshed, before we get eat up with fleas, only it's dark under there and likely full of spiders. Remember, we were talking about fleas the day Lyddie slid down the roof."

Molly raised a suspicious brow.

Hands on her hips, Lyddie said, "Bobbie June, will you never learn?"

"But, Lyddie—"

"Don't!" Untying her apron as she went, Lyddie headed for the backstairs. "Whatever you have in your head, just don't!"

Lyddie rolled onto her back, her gaze probing the dark, picking out the familiar shapes of her dresser and chair and the slight movement of the curtains as a stray bit of breeze found its way through the open French window. The hotel had been quiet for hours. No doubt everyone else had long been asleep.

Those with a clearer conscience.

She had told Nick to go away. That that would make her happy. When had she become such an awful liar?

Drawing in a deep breath, Lyddie let it out on a sigh. What she'd said had been wrong and hateful and it had hurt him. She saw in his eyes that it had hurt him. He deserved better than to have his profession of love flung back in his face like that. It wasn't his fault that if she let herself care for someone, they left.

It had been the way he made her feel. She couldn't

control her emotions when he was near, and that scared her. And he deserved to hear the truth.

Making a decision, Lyddie swung her legs off the bed and got her wrapper from a hook behind the door. She owed Nick better than that.

On the balcony outside Nick's room, Lyddie wiped her damp palms on her flannel wrapper and hesitated. Maybe she should have waited?

Chapter Twenty-two

The lace curtains on the French windows were pulled gently inward on the sweet night air entering Nick's bedroom, as if beckoning Lyddie to follow.

Feeling drawn as inexorably as the curtains, Lyddie went quietly inside. Blinking against the dark, she could see little, but the faint smell of a cheroot cigar lingered, as did the even fainter smell of bay rum, and another scent she couldn't identify. Nick's essence filled her senses, conjuring up images of him as he had been, gloriously naked and male, when they'd made love.

Suddenly she wasn't at all certain this had been a good idea. Taking a step backward, she decided to leave before he awoke.

"Do you want me to light a candle?" he asked from somewhere in the dark, startling her. So, he was awake, and, no doubt, he had been watching her as she lingered on the veranda outside his room.

"No, no candle." Since he was awake there was no reason not to tell him what she'd come there to say. "I have something to tell you. It won't take long." And maybe it would be easier to say what she wanted to if she didn't have to look into his eyes.

Carefully, Lyddie moved toward where his voice had come from and bumped into the bed.

Nick reached out and caught her arm, steadying her. "Here. Sit by me. Tell me, to what do I owe this pleasure?" he asked, a slightly sardonic edge to his voice.

Her mouth suddenly went dry. As Lyddie perched on the edge of the bed, she remembered Nick slept in the nude. She sat so close to him, she could feel his thigh touching hers through her nightclothes. Was it bare? It was certainly warm. It was too dark to tell.

She hoped he wasn't nude—what an awful thing to remember when she had something important to tell him!

Drawing in a deep breath as she steadied her resolve, Lyddie identified the other smell in the room. It was the sweet scent of whiskey on his breath. "You're drinking!"

"Only the best Kentucky bourbon."

"I'd better go." She started to rise.

"No." He caught her arm. "Stay. I'm not drunk—more's the pity."

She sat back down, ripples of sensation coursing through her as his fingers lingered on her arm. No, this had not been a good idea at all. And she still wasn't certain that he wasn't nude.

"I'm just pondering the vagaries of life, Lyddie, and I think being intoxicated might be very helpful in understanding them."

"You *are* drunk."

"I'm not drunk at all. Confused, yes. Drunk, no. I tell a woman I love her and she turns to stone. I tell her I want to be here forever and she tells me to go away and, I assume, never return. I do think being drunk would be better than being confused, but I have just begun to imbibe my third drink, so only time will bear out that assumption. Do you want a glass?"

"No. Do you always talk like a medicine showman when you drink?"

"Do I?"

"I asked you first." As her eyes adjusted to the dark room, Lyddie saw a faint light slash, his teeth flashing in a smile in the darker shadow of his face. And, judging by the shadow from his waist down, he did, indeed, have on trousers. That was a relief, she told herself firmly.

"You did ask first. I hadn't noticed, but now that you mention it, I do seem loquacious, don't I? It may prove the key to a future career—I did tell you this is my last assignment for the Pinkertons, didn't I? I will get a wagon and tout Dr. Nick's Patented Painkiller, it soothes aches, it cures meat, it greases your wagon—"

Lyddie laughed aloud, popping her hand over her mouth to smother it.

"Was that so hard?" Nick asked her softly when her laughter subsided. "Why is it that you so seldom laugh or smile?"

"I guess I seldom feel like it."

Reaching out, he touched her cheek, and Lyddie caught her breath as rippling pleasure cascaded through her. "I didn't come here to . . . to . . ."

"Make love?" His lips followed the trail his fingers had left.

"Nick!" Lyddie gasped as he moved to nibble her jaw line, while tugging the string tying her wrapper.

"What?" The word was a husky invitation for her to ask for more. And, lord, she wanted to.

"I came here to say I'm sorry," she blurted out.

Ceasing his assault, Nick lifted his head. "What?"

"It's not you. It's me." Lyddie laced her fingers together tightly. "When you told me you loved me, it did scare me. It scares me still to think about it. It scares me because I care about you, a lot more than I want to."

"Lyddie—"

"I don't want to count on you, to need you the way I do. It scares me because everyone I count on goes away. Can you understand? Everyone!"

"If you'll let me into your life, I won't go—"

"Yes, you will!" She stood up, unable to bear his nearness a second longer. Nick stood, too, and she took a step backward, putting distance between them. "I know you don't think you would, but you would go," she said earnestly. "It might not be your choice. You might die, like my mother. Or, or another war could break out—or a plague could come."

"I won't go willingly if you'll just trust me."

"Don't tell me that! I know you mean it, but you don't know that for certain. And there are other things, things you still don't know. Things I can never tell you!"

She put her hand over her mouth. Why had she said that? She hadn't meant to say that.

Nick was quiet for a moment, waiting for Lyddie to go on. When she didn't, he said, "Okay. I won't tell you that I'll be here always. I won't tell you I love you more than my next breath." Untying the sash to her wrapper, he murmured, "I'll never talk about being with you forever. Forever would be far too short, anyway." He cupped her cheek, then slowly smoothed his hand down her neck and over her shoulder, pushing her wrapper off as he did. "We will live minute to minute. Never thinking about tomorrow."

Lyddie sucked in her breath as he slipped her wrapper off her other shoulder. It slid down and caught on her arms. All she had to do was straighten her arms and it would fall to the floor, signaling her acceptance of him, but on her conditions. Could she really have Nick? Moment to moment, not expecting forever?

The vision of Gerald's body, blood covering his head, swam before her eyes. What price would her bid for happiness cost this time?

Nick sensed Lyddie drawing away before she ever moved to shrug her wrapper back onto her shoulders. He'd lost, then, he thought, as she stopped by the open windows.

"I just came to tell you that it isn't you, Nick. It's me. But I guess you knew that." She turned to go, a wraith in the half-light, ephemeral, impossible to hold on to.

"Lyddie . . ." He had one more card to play.

She turned back to him. "Yes?"

"What if there's a child?" Nick asked softly. He could see her face pale, even in the dim light of the stars shining through the French windows. So, she hadn't thought of that.

"No. I . . ." Something caught Lyddie's attention, and she glanced back outside. Beyond the veranda railing, a strange spot of light danced down the front walk and flashed on the gateposts—not a wide, flickering glow, like a lamp or a lantern, but one spot that was strangely bright and steady.

"Nick, come here," she whispered urgently. "There's something strange out there. What is it?"

Even as she asked the question she realized what it was—a miner's carbide light.

* * *

"Got everything?" Bobbie June asked once they were safely behind the corner of the depot building. "More carbide? The skeleton key for the lock on the storage shed?"

"Yeah, I got everything. You asked me twice already." Billy Fred knew that showed how nervous she was. Not that he blamed her. He was nervous himself.

Waving his hand, Billy Fred shooed a moth away from the light, which he'd strapped to his head with a leather thong. The carbide lantern was sure a strange contraption. The reflector dish looked like a miniature washbasin, from the center of which a bright flame hissed, fueled by gas from the reaction of carbide nuggets and water in the little metal jar beneath. It stunk like the burned powder had when that Chinese firecracker blew up in Robert Hasting's hand last Fourth of July.

"You sure this is a good idea?" Billy Fred asked, eyeing the depot with trepidation. Looming upward into the night, when his light struck the windows the building seemed to be watching them menacingly.

"Good idea?" Bobbie June's stomach roiled with doubt, but she would never admit it. "You saw the map." Touching the bib pocket of her overalls, she went on in awed tones. "The real map this time. Why else would it have been hid behind a drawer in Grandpa John's desk? I didn't even see it until I pulled the drawer all the way out by accident."

"Yeah, it's gotta be the real map." There was no question in his mind it was—that was the only way Bobbie June had convinced him to come along. But even though it was the real map, something told him that this still might not be a good idea. Lately, their luck had been just plain bad.

Bobbie June said, "You get the railroad jack out of the

storage shed. I'll start dragging boards under the platform. . . ."

"I can't see anything, now. Where could they have gone?" Standing in front of the telegraph office, which adjoined the depot building, Lyddie looked around in consternation, trying to peer into the shadows. Bright stars and a fingernail of moon offered the only light.

"I'll look on the other side of the building," Nick said, still buttoning his hastily donned shirt.

As she looked around the area, Lyddie tugged her shawl more tightly about her, glad she'd taken time to run back to her room and put on a dress. Rounding the corner, her attention was caught by an odd noise and then a flurry of hissed conversation. She couldn't decide just where it came from.

"Where is that?" Lyddie whispered as Nick drew near.

Nick put his finger to his lips, then pointed at the high platform, where a sliver of light shone from underneath. Bumps and thumps and a series of whacks, interspersed with shrieks, erupted. The light leapt and grew brighter, then brighter still.

Blinking, Lyddie realized the whole platform was tilted at a strange angle. Then she smelled smoke.

Squatting, she peered underneath the building and saw a cross beam afire. "Oh, my God!" Lyddie cried, as Nick scrambled beneath the depot.

The twins frantically beat at the flames with boards, which just seemed to fan them. The fire rapidly spread along the beam. Nearby, a railroad jack sitting atop a haphazard stack of boards held the building up. And the jack was in danger of being bumped as the twins fought to put the fire out.

"Throw dirt," Nick ordered, scooping his hands full of

the powdery earth from between his knees and flinging it on the flames.

Billy Fred followed suit, scooping and flinging as fast as he could. "I knowed it was a mistake to listen to you, Bobbie June! I knowed it!"

"I didn't tell you to touch that dad-blamed light against a pine-pitch sill and—*help!*" she cried as her sleeve caught fire.

"Hold still!" Nick caught her arm and beat out the small flame, then returned to fighting the blaze.

Tears streaking the soot on her face, Bobbie June crawfished backward out of the man's way.

The fire grew smaller with each handful of dirt scooped up and tossed on it. After several long moments it was out, but for a few red embers glowing eerily in the dark and the smoke, which stung Lyddie's eyes.

"Will it be okay now?" she asked, then coughed as smoke clogged her throat.

"I think so." Nick coughed, then said, "Billy Fred, get some water. All this wood is full of pitch. We'll douse the sill to be certain."

"Okay. I'll find a bucket somewhere."

In the dark, Lyddie sensed Billy Fred scrambling out, then his shadowy form passing by her. As his hurried footsteps retreated, all was quiet, except for small snuffling sounds and occasional coughs.

Nick said, "We caught the fire before there was any real harm done, Bobbie June. When we're certain it's out, we'll jack down the building and then get back to the hotel."

A scraping sounded and a Lucifer match flared. Tears made trails in the grime on Bobbie June's face as she held up the flame. "But I never got to get the gold out."

"The what?" Nick asked, dismay written on his soot-streaked face.

"The gold! Grandpa's map says it's in the corner-stone!" Holding the fast-burning match above her head, Bobbie June scuttled toward the brick cornerstone. In her haste, she brushed against the jack atop the unstable stack of wood.

Her hand over her mouth, Lyddie stifled a scream. *God, no!*

"Be careful!" His heart beating in his throat, Nick watched as the railroad jack leaned farther and farther sideways, helpless to stop it. The building's timbers groaned as it started to fall. Diving, Nick caught Bobbie June's waist before it crashed down on her, hauling her backward. As her match went out, he rolled, using his momentum to haul her with him. As the groans of the timbers became shrieks, Nick, summoning all his strength, threw the girl away from him, toward the edge of the platform, and scrambled after her. "Get out of here, now!"

A darker blur among shadows, a body came rolling out from under the depot. Catching her sister's braid, Lyddie realized it was Bobbie June and helped her get away into the open, just as wood splintered and groaned in a horrific crash.

"Nick?" Lyddie looked back, her gaze trying to pierce the half-light to be certain he was safe.

She couldn't see him.

"Nick!"

Chapter Twenty-three

"Nick!"

There was no answer. Lyddie fell to her knees in the dark. "No, God!" Dust kicked up by the falling building threatened to take her breath. Coughing, she covered her mouth with her skirt, straining her eyes to peer under the building.

"He has to be all right!" Bobbie June cried. "He has to!"

Lyddie coughed, then called again, "Nick!"

Again there was only silence, except for the pounding beat of her own heart. If she had made love with him tonight, this would never have happened.

"What was that infernal noise?" Lantern held high as he squinted into the night, the stationmaster, Hal Williams, rushed out of his house, next door to the depot. "Good Lord!" Nightshirt flapping about his calves, he ran to where Lyddie knelt. "What happened here?"

"Nick!" Lyddie clawed at the narrow opening left under the platform. "Nick's under there!"

The stationmaster knelt down beside her and held his lantern where it shone under the narrow gap. The light showed only a fog of dust. "I can't see him if he's under there."

"He is!" Shaking her head, Lyddie said, "I can't see anything."

"Neither can I." He looked back at more lanterns bobbing on the street as people rushed to the scene. "But here comes help. We'll get him out."

Drawn from all over town by the crash, people gathered quickly, murmuring in lowered tones. Lanterns and candles lit the scene eerily.

"Where is he exactly?" Hal Williams asked Lyddie.

Lyddie sobbed, "I think he's about ten feet straight under here."

"Don't worry. We'll get him." The stationmaster started issuing orders, organizing the men to start shoveling beneath the building, to get Nick out.

Paying little attention to what was happening around her, Lyddie continued to dig at the earth, trying to make a passage wide enough to squeeze underneath the depot.

"Bobbie June, what's happened?" Carrying a bucket of water, Billy Fred pushed through the crowd to his sister, the unlit carbide light still strapped to his head.

"Nick's trapped. He . . . he might be dead. He hasn't said anything, and Lyddie's called and called." Wiping her cheeks, Bobbie June sniffed.

Billy Fred stared in horror at the skewed building. "Oh, no."

Eyeing the unlit carbide light, his twin clutched his arm and swiped at her cheeks. "I still have the carbide nuggets in my pocket. Now that you brought water, let's get that light going again and go around and see if there's anywhere high enough for us to crawl under. We're smaller than most everybody else."

"Good idea." Still carrying the bucket, he followed close on her heels.

"Lyddie, are you all right?" Wearing a wrapper over her nightgown, Molly knelt by her sister. "What's happened? Someone said Nick is under there."

"Yes. I have to get to him." She had to tell him how she felt. She should have done it when she had the chance. Lyddie stared in frustration at the narrow gap beneath the building. Her frantic digging had done little but scratch the dirt and break her nails. Finding a stick to gouge with, she started to dig at the earth again.

"No, Lyddie," Molly said, pulling her arm, trying to make her stop. "You aren't helping."

"There's nothing that you can do." Gus Elverston appeared on her other side. "Come away." Taking Lyddie's other arm, he urged her to stand.

"No! You don't understand!" Lyddie tried to pull away from both of them. She succeeded in breaking Molly's hold, but the financier held her firmly.

The look in his eyes was kind. "Yes, I do understand. But you can't help Nick like that. Come away and let the men get there. They're bringing out tools to dig with."

Reluctantly, she let herself be led a short distance away. A few moments later, Lyddie was seated on an empty crate Molly had found somewhere, watching and praying as the men used adzes and shovels to dig. She heard Hal Williams explained to Gus that they couldn't take a chance on jacking the building up before Nick was brought out. If the building shifted again, Nick could be crushed.

If he was still alive . . .

God, grant that he was!

"How on earth did this happen?" Mrs. Graves, whose husband owned the mercantile, demanded of Lyddie. Other women flanked her, frowning, asking questions of their own.

"I'm not sure. . . ." Shaking her head, at a loss, Lyddie didn't know what to say.

"Can't you see my sister is in shock? Leave her alone. There'll be time for answers when we have Nick out." Molly made shooing motions at the curious women. Reluctantly, they moved away.

Watching the crowd around the men working, Lyddie stood abruptly as she noticed that Bobbie June and Billy Fred were nowhere to be seen. "Where are the twins?" she asked, catching Molly's sleeve. "Are they all right?"

Looking around, Molly shrugged. "I don't know."

"We have to find them."

"Lyddie . . ." Molly began, but held her peace as Lyddie hurried into the crowd.

When she didn't see them, Lyddie went around to the side of the depot by the rails, where the boarding platform was. Two small boys dressed in their nightshirts were squatted on the railroad tracks, peering underneath the depot.

"What do you see?" Lyddie asked, kneeling by them.

"Billy Fred's sure got a fancy lantern strapped to his head," one of the children said enthusiastically.

"Sure does!" the other boy chimed in.

Lying down, pressing her cheek to a rough cross tie, Lyddie saw her brother worming his way beneath the building, going in from the backside, opposite where the men were digging. The carbide light he wore threw a swath of illumination before him. Between the tumbled pillars and broken bricks, that light fell on Nick. He lay on his back, still and unmoving, in the narrow cavity left between the sills and the ground where the building had fallen atop broken brick pillars. A bloody gash on his head stood out in the stark flashes of light.

Sucking in a sharp breath, Lyddie crammed her knuckles against her mouth.

"What's that? Where's that danged light coming from?" The digging stopped as men peered under the building, their faces eerily catching the stray light flashes.

"Can you get to him?" Hal Williams called.

"It's danged tight," Billy Fred huffed, "but I think so."

He crawled on toward Nick. Quiet blanketed the crowd. Everyone seemed to hold their collective breath.

"What's going on?" Molly found Lyddie and knelt on the tracks beside her, looking under the depot. "Oh, my goodness! I hope he's not pinned."

A cheer went up as Billy Fred made it to Nick. Lyddie clutched Molly's arm as she prayed for a miracle. But Nick was so still, the blood on his head so stark.

After pausing to shine his light all around Nick as he examined the situation, Billy Fred called, "It's kind of close, but it don't seem like the building is mashing him anywhere. I see a little gap between him and the floor joists."

"Is he breathing?" Lyddie called. A roaring filled her ears. Her heart beat hard and painfully as she waited for what seemed a lifetime for her brother to answer. Then Billy Fred shook him, and Nick moaned.

"Yep, he sure is!" Billy Fred shouted.

A cheer burst out, dying just as quickly as it erupted. The men started talking among themselves about how best to get Nick out.

"I found a rope in the supply shed," Bobbie June called. As Billy Fred looked back, the light flashed on her, rapidly crawling under the building, playing out a rope coiled around her shoulder as she did.

"Come on!" Lyddie grabbed Molly's sleeve, and they ran around and took hold of the end. In a few moments, the twins had it tied around Nick's chest.

"Pull easy and we'll help him along." The light bobbled as Billy Fred called to Lyddie and Molly.

As Lyddie and Molly pulled, Nick moaned. Within seconds, other hands took hold of the rope as the crowd and the men who'd been digging came around to help.

Nick groaned louder as they dragged him along. "Just let the depot finish falling on me," he complained, then coughed. "It would hurt less."

"Just hang on, Nick, we'll have you outta here in three shakes of a goat's tail." Billy Fred and Bobbie June scuttled along beside Nick, throwing chunks of wood and clods of dirt out of the way as Nick was dragged out.

Lyddie and Molly heaved as the twins' faces appeared under the building's edge. Another tug and Nick, coated in dust, face streaked in blood, appeared between them under the edge of the depot.

"Pull him on out." Billy Fred edged out of the way as the men gently pulled Nick the rest of the way into the open.

"Nick?" Lyddie knelt by him and brushed at the dust caked on his face. "Nick, I'm so sorry. . . ." She couldn't go on for a moment as tears closed her throat.

Molly, on his other side, had produced a wet handkerchief from somewhere and gave it to Lyddie. Gently, she wiped Nick's face, and his eyes opened.

"You scared me to death!" she said, her tears flowing freely.

"Careful; I'll think you care." Nick smiled, then groaned.

"I do." Sniffling, Lyddie cupped his cheek. "Don't you know I've come to depend on you?"

"Ah, Lyddie!" Nick grinned, then coughed, rolling onto his side, his face etched in pain.

"Let me through." Doc Wilkins pushed between the onlookers and set his bag beside Lyddie. "Let me examine him, young lady. Might have a broken rib or two, in addition to that knot on his head."

Lyddie moved back as Doc, Molly at his elbow, went to work checking Nick out.

Nick was alive! She felt like laughing and crying at the same time.

Doc straightened, pronouncing Nick okay, except for bruised ribs and a concussion. Looking at Molly, he added, "Take him to the hotel and make sure he recuperates well. You know what to do."

"Here, let me help." Frank Worley stepped forward. The burly timberman would have scooped him up and set him on his feet, but Nick held up a hand, warding him off.

"Thanks, but if you just lend me a hand, I can make it." Nick shook his head as if to clear it, then groaned.

Grinning, Frank did as he was asked, and a small cheer went up as Nick gained his feet. He swayed unsteadily, looking at Lyddie, his eyes the only bright spots in his dirt-smeared face. "Lyddie, I might need you to support me on the way to the hotel."

She smiled. "I think I can commit to that." Moving to him, she helped him wind his arm around her shoulders.

"Just a minute." Sheriff Woods stepped in front of them. "No one has explained what happened here. And I'm thinkin' it's goin' to need a lot of explainin'." He looked over the wrecked station.

"Yes. What happened?" Still in his nightshirt, Hal Williams moved up beside the sheriff.

Lyddie looked around, half expecting the twins to have disappeared.

Bobbie June pushed through the onlookers, a broad smear of dust and grime on her cheek and cobwebs caught in her hair. "I did it," she admitted, hanging her head.

"We both did, sir." Billy Fred joined her.

Shaking his head, the sheriff looked at the pair incredulously. "I thought after our talk and the railroad lettin' the pair of you off, you two would have learned your lesson." The twins said nothing. He went on, "I have to ask, just what in heck did you two hooligans think you were doin'?"

Bobbie June answered, still looking down. "You know we were looking for the gold."

A sudden murmur rippled through the crowd, with the word *gold* repeated again and again. People pressed closer.

The sheriff gave the crowd an uneasy look, then pushed his hat back and stared at the twins. "Again?"

He turned and glowered at Nick. "I have to say, I'm danged sure surprised that you're involved, Bennington."

Bobbie June shook her head. "Oh, no. Nick and Lyddie were trying to stop us. But the big sill under the depot caught on fire, and Nick helped us as we put it out. Then I bumped into the railroad jack—"

"Hold it! Hold it!" The sheriff held up his hand, the deep furrows on his brow deepening more in the lantern light. "Start at the beginning—why did you have the depot jacked up?"

Bobbie June pulled a crumpled paper out of the bib pocket of her overalls. "We found a map to the gold. Grandpa John's map. . . ."

Chapter Twenty-four

The next morning at the breakfast table, Gram eyed her twin grandchildren with a look of mild disbelief. "You're telling me that you two hellions set the whole rail station off its foundations—and after that you set it afire?"

"Yes, Gram," Bobbie June sighed.

Gram shook her head. "I'll own, that's some'ot over the top, even for you two."

"We didn't do it on purpose, Gram." Bobbie June swirled a spoon through her bowl of steaming grits. Hot biscuits, ham, and pear preserves were on the table, but neither Bobbie June nor Billy Fred had shown their usual enthusiasm for food.

" 'Course not a'purpose," her grandmother commented.

"It just kinda . . . happened," Billy Fred offered, and received quelling looks from Molly and Lyddie. "And we sure didn't mean for Nick to get hurt!"

But Nick had been hurt. Lyddie lifted her coffee but set it down without taking a sip as her stomach clenched. He could have died. She might have lost him . . . not that he was ever really hers. But that wasn't because he hadn't made his feelings for her clear.

And if she had lost him, it would have hurt beyond bearing.

"What do you have to say to all this, Lye-Beth?" Cocking a gray brow, Gram looked at her oldest grandchild.

Lyddie drew in a deep breath and expelled it slowly, reminding herself that the twins were indeed far past the age to own responsibility. She had to let them reap what they had sown.

But, goodness, it was hard. She kept remembering the promise she'd made to her mother to take care of them. . . . How could she bear to see them hauled off to prison?

Gathering her resolve, she said, "Like I told the sheriff, these two are old enough to take responsibility for their actions, I guess. Ask them."

"You're right, a' course," Gram agreed. "They can't be headed nor heeled, so they ought to bear the consequences." Bending her gaze upon the two miscreants again, she commented, "Seems like a lot a things just happen when you two are looking for gold. And you say you had the real map this time. I'd sure be interested in seeing it."

"Yes, Gram." Going around the table to where her grandmother sat, Bobbie June pulled a dirty, crumpled paper out of her overall's pocket. She spread the paper out on the table.

"Does seem to be John's handwriting," Gram allowed, her gray brow riding higher. "Tell me how you come by it."

Bobbie June cleared her throat. "I . . ." Her eyes grew bright with unshed tears and she hung her head. "I took it from Grandpa John's desk without asking, Gram, and I shouldn't have."

Lyddie silently applauded, hardly daring to believe her sister's straightforwardness. Perhaps, Bobbie June had learned her lesson.

"When I showed it to the sheriff, he said he thought it was real, too," Bobbie June added, a telltale edge of excitement in her voice. "So did everybody else. They wanted to tear into the depot right then and there and find our gold!" She frowned. "But Mr. Hal said they weren't doing no such thing, 'cause the building wasn't so bad off that some of it couldn't be saved."

"Wise man, the sheriff." Gram nodded.

Molly said, "There wouldn't have been two boards left nailed together this morning if he hadn't posted a guard. Frank Worley had to stand watch with a shotgun."

"I hope Frank was able to keep people from making off with our gold," Bobbie June said.

"Bobbie June!" So her sister wasn't completely cured, Lyddie thought, pushing her half-eaten breakfast aside.

"What?" Bobbie June glowered at Lyddie, a spark of her old belligerence showing.

"Well, I hate to disabuse you two young'uns of the notion, but this ain't a map." Gram made the pronouncement with the certainty of someone who knew. "It's a missing page of a letter John was writing to his brother but never got finished and sent. He was aiming to get him to go into partnership with him and build this cotton gin sketched here." Gram pointed out a square drawn on the map by Myer's Creek, a building that didn't exist in reality. "And the same for these factories, there and there"—she pointed to two more spots—"though what all he planned to man-u-factor, I forget now."

"A letter?" Billy Fred asked incredulously. "It can't be just a letter! But it says in plain talk, *'gold to be had in Crossroads'* and it has *'depot cornerstone.'* Doesn't it?"

"Oh, that it does—almost. John's handwriting was so bad, he couldn't even read it once it got cold." Gram chuckled, bending over the sheet. "It says among the splotches and ink blots that the 'depot is *the* cornerstone.' He had a plan to make this town thrive, but it all depended on the railroad." She pointed to the top of the page. "See how the sentence at the top of the page is carried on from somewheres else. I got the other two sheets of this letter in the bottom drawer, but I knew this one's been missing for quite awhile. Where'd you find it?" Gram looked at Bobbie June, who seemed to shrink.

"I put some drawings back that I had borrowed and the drawer fell out. This was stuck in behind it, like it had been hid there." Studying her bare toes, Bobbie June added, "I took the drawings without asking, too."

Lyddie smiled. "I think you're growing up." She nodded at Billy Fred. "Both of you." Maybe everything would be okay—*if* they survived the current crises.

Bobbie June looked at her in complete surprise. "You do?"

Billy Fred shot a baleful glare at his twin. "Well, you won't get to be grown up for long. The *real map!*" He shook his head in disgust. "I seen wagonloads of people coming into town since early. No doubt about it, word got out and they're aiming to have at the pillars under the depot and will likely lynch us when they find out that there's no dad-blamed gold!

He pushed away from the table. "Come on, Bobbie June." To his grandmother, he explained, "We told the sheriff we'd be back to the depot by nine, so he could arrest us."

Gram nodded. "Seems like you two being safe in jail for the time being might be a good idea."

Billy Fred agreed. "Yeah. You might be right, Gram."

"I'm coming. Let me finish my breakfast." Bobbie June went back to her seat and spooned in her grits.

"What's going on?" Hortense paused and yawned just inside the door. "Who's going to jail?"

"What are you doing down here?" Molly said. "I asked you to sit with Nick while I ate breakfast." She had, of course, taken his care upon herself, refusing to let Lyddie sit with him the whole night.

"He woke up." Yawning again, Hortense shrugged. "I offered to help him put his clothes on, but he didn't want any assistance."

"Hortense, Molly said you weren't in your bed when she was awakened last night by the crash. Where were you?" Lyddie asked.

Hortense's gaze skittered away to a potted fern in the corner. "I couldn't sleep, so I went out for a walk to look at the stars. Then I heard the crash and saw all those people rushing to the station. Though, I never did understand why it fell. And just how did Nick get hurt?"

"A walk, eh?" Gram sipped her coffee.

"Yes." Red tinted Hortense's cheeks as she pulled out a chair and sat down. Diverting everyone's attention, she said, "Nick wants to see you, Lyddie. He said for me to ask you to go talk to him." Then added, as she spooned hot grits into her bowl, "Maybe, he's gonna ask you to marry him again. Better say yes before he comes to his senses and changes his mind."

"I'll . . . I'll go make certain he's all right." Lyddie left the family dining room and bounced up the stairs.

Though she'd peeked in at him this morning as he'd slept, she was anxious to speak with him, to assure herself that he was healthy. Both the doctor and Molly had cautioned that a concussion was a serious thing.

Before she reached Nick's door, Elvira Montrose cornered Lyddie on the second-floor gallery, stepping in front of her when Lyddie would have darted past.

The singer frowned. "I swear, I've never had such a horrible stay anywhere. First my maid ran away, abandoning me! The food—if one can call it that—is indigestible. Then there was that horrible noise in the middle of the night. What was that awful racket?" As she spoke, Elvira rearranged her shawl about her shoulders so that the amethyst and diamond brooch she wore pinned to her bosom was prominently displayed.

"I'm sorry—"

Before Lyddie could say more, the singer went on irately, "And this morning wagon after wagon has rolled down that dirt rut that passes for a street—is it market day? And doesn't anyone in this fly speck of a town know how to grease their wheels? I have an engagement in Jackson tomorrow evening and I just know I shall have dark circles beneath my eyes from lack of rest!"

Straightening, her shoulders, Lyddie said, "I am sorry for any inconvenience you might have suffered. I shall certainly understand if you refuse to stay here in the future."

"Well, I never!" Elvira flushed, the ruddy color clashing madly with her brassy blond hair. "You and Nick Bennington deserve one another. You are two of the rudest people it has been my misfortune to know. Nicky, after practically begging me to join him here, had the nerve to tell me he could never think of me as more than a . . . friend." Elvira said the word in the same tone Jane might have said *caca* or *merde*.

"Excuse me," Lyddie said, biting her lip to keep from smiling as she brushed past the outraged singer. "Lovely brooch," she threw over her shoulder.

Reaching Nick's door, she knocked lightly, her heart suddenly beating faster. Nick had put himself in harm's way to save Bobbie June. He might have died.

The future was uncertain. There were no guarantees. But Nick Bennington was noble and good. He was a man she could trust. . . .

Why did the thought scare her so much?

A scarier thought was what would happen if she didn't tell him she loved him. She could lose him forever.

"Come in," Nick called, his voice firm, relieving some of her fears. After getting him cleaned up as best they could, Lyddie had sat with him most of the night, watching him sleep. Around daylight, Molly insisted on taking her place, and she'd reluctantly gone to her own room to wash up and change clothes.

Lyddie swung the door open and stepped inside. The bed was empty, the covers rumpled and dusty where Molly and Lyddie had insisted Nick go to bed, dirt and all. The doors to the balcony stood open, the white curtain blowing inward gently. "Nick, where are you? Are you feeling all right? I want to talk to—oh!"

The last as Nick, standing out of sight behind the door, surprised her by grasping her wrist and pulling her farther inside and into his arms. He was shirtless, dressed only in his underwear. As her breasts flattened against his hard chest, she was acutely aware of the warmth of his skin through the thin camisole and the fabric of her dress.

"Good morning," he whispered, looking down into her upturned face. Her hair was pulled back in its usual practical bun, but springy curls had escaped at her temples. Her tawny eyes were wide and luminous. "Ah, Lyddie." Nick kissed the soft curls and the tender skin beneath, inhaling the scent of lilacs that always seemed to cling to her. "I feel much better. Now." He lowered his lips to hers.

This feels so right, Lyddie thought, twining her arms around Nick's neck as she melted into his kiss. Awareness sizzled through her, followed closely by need.

Triumph surged through him as he realized that she wanted him as much as he wanted her. Groaning, Nick deepened the kiss, his tongue delving into the sweet recesses of Lyddie's mouth. Reality whirled away as almost unbearable need slammed into his groin. Breaking contact with her lips, he kissed her throat. "I want you."

Lyddie shuddered in response, warmth pooling deep within her. This was what she wanted, she realized. This man. To be with this man. Always. She only had to claim what he offered. "Nick, I—"

"I need you." He nibbled her ear, his hands stroking her warm back, pressing her closer to his growing erection.

"Nick!" Lyddie pushed away while she still had a shred of control. "You're obviously no worse for wear after being hit on the head with a whole building!"

"I do have a headache." He grinned ruefully and plucked his trousers off the chair. "But if you tried, you might make me forget about my head."

Her cheeks warming, Lyddie turned away as he dressed. Moving to the open French windows, she looked down the street at the gathering crowd of people. Women holding babies or parasols stood in small knots talking among themselves while men pressed closer to the depot itself. Laughing children ran through the crowd or dodged through the remarkable number of buggies, wagons, and horses blocking Main Street. "I think everyone in the county is at the depot this morning."

"I'm sorry, Lyddie." Nick moved up beside her as he fastened the buttons on his once white shirt. "I can't do anything to save the twins this time."

"I know." She did know. But that didn't ease her sense of failure.

"I will do whatever I can."

"I know that, too. You're a good man, Nick Bennington, for all that you came here just to find Gentleman John's gold."

"I've found the only gold worth having in Crossroads." He touched her cheek.

She pressed her cheek into his palm. Somewhere outside the open French doors, a mockingbird burst into full-throated song—no doubt the same bird that had been serenading the hotel for the last few weeks.

Stepping away from Nick, Lyddie moved farther onto the balcony in the cool morning air. She spotted the gray bird perched on the edge of the old well, its tail bobbing up and down as it sang.

Obviously Billy Fred and Bobbie June had gotten started on their chore of filling in the well. Some of the bushes had been cut back from around it and a wheelbarrow full of rusting tin cans and broken crockery stood beside it. Half the boards covering it had been thrown off the top, and the exposed hole looked like a macabrely smiling mouth.

Gazing at the open well, Lyddie realized that it didn't matter if she trusted Nick or not. It didn't matter if she loved him more than she'd ever known it was possible to love someone. She'd made her choice when she put Gerald's body in the well.

She would always be bound to Gerald Seaton. And it was a bond she couldn't break.

With a stone where her heart had thumped happily just a few moments before, Lyddie blinked back tears as the mockingbird continued to sing.

Nick came up behind her and placed his hand on her shoulder. "What is it about the well, Lyddie?"

"Nothing!" Caught by surprise, she knew she'd overreacted. Turning, she schooled her features into a smile and said, "You startled me."

Nick frowned, searching her face. Lyddie kept the smile on her lips, though it felt wavery. "There's nothing particular about the well. I was just noticing that the twins must have started to fill it in like Gram asked. Molly says it's a health hazard." She knew she was babbling but couldn't stop.

There was more to it than that, Nick guessed as he watched her twist her fingers together as she spoke.

"Why are you being evasive?" he asked gently, determined not to have secrets between them. Secrets, he knew from bitter experience, were only for those with secret agendas. He'd ignored his wife's evasiveness for too long.

"I'm not being evasive!" Lyddie turned back to the railing.

"What are you afraid of? You have to trust me."

"I'm not afraid of anything."

A knot of doubt started to coil in his stomach. "You aren't good at half-truths, Lyddie."

"Why are you questioning me like this? Is this one of your investigations?" she demanded.

Nick stilled as his wife's voice came to him from the past: "I won't be interrogated like one of your suspects!" He'd had reason to doubt her, but he'd let it go, even though his instincts urged him to confront her, to learn the truth then and there.

Now Lyddie was playing the same kind of game.

He'd thought he'd found the one woman he could trust completely. But she wasn't trustworthy, after all.

Looking at the crowd down by the depot, Nick thrust his hands into his pockets. "You'd better go."

Feeling she had failed him somehow, Lyddie said, "Nick, there are things I can't tell you!"

"Why?" he asked softly, his eyes stark with pain. "What do you have to hide?"

A chill crept through her. Moments before she had been happy and hopeful for a brighter future, a future with this man. She'd thought she could count on him, no matter what. And she could, to a point. He would dive beneath falling buildings to save her sister; he would use his influence with the railroad to try and save the twins.

But he wanted her unconditional trust, and he didn't offer his own in return.

"I think I'd better go." Her feet feeling leaden, Lyddie left the room.

Nick stared at the door long after she'd closed it, willing her to come back and explain, to dispel the dark feeling that had settled in his soul—the feeling that he couldn't trust her after all.

Well, wasn't it better he'd found out now?

Chapter Twenty-five

Billy Fred thrust his hands into his pockets and kicked at a dirt clod. Hundreds of footprints were stamped into the dust of Main Street. Young, old, well-to-do looking and downright poor, men and women, people flocked around the depot three deep. He reckoned everybody in the county had found out about the gold somehow and had showed up for a part of it. People were going to be mighty disappointed, he thought.

Now that he saw it in the light of day, the depot itself was a sorry sight. Although the twenty-by-forty building was intact, it sat at an odd angle, one end resting practically on the ground, the other a foot or so off—the end where Billy Fred had crawled beneath to rescue Nick last night. The whole building, besides being lowered by four to five feet, was about five feet from where it had originally sat, with the platform for people to get on and off the trains.

The wires, which had been ripped away from the telegraph office at one end of the depot building, had been tied around a hitching post. One of the horses tethered there nibbled curiously at them.

"So, you two made it." Sheriff Wood nodded his approval.

"We said we would." Bobbie June moved up beside Billy Fred, as though uncertain of what to expect and looking for the support of her twin.

" 'Sides," Billy Fred added, "Gram says that wasn't a map and there ain't no gold under the depot, so it'll be safer for us if you lock us up."

"No gold, eh?" A look of disappointment wreathing his craggy features, the sheriff looked over the eager crowd. "I expect your grandmother is likely to know if anybody does. But there's no hurry about locking you two up. We'll stay here for now, so I can watch the goin's on. You young'uns might be some help when they start raising the depot up again—you've sure had experience with working a railroad jack."

"Raising the depot?" Billy Fred asked, looking back at the building.

"Yep. Can't get to those pillars until the building is raised again, so me and Hal Williams decided to just see it set back in place while everyone was willing to lend a hand to get it up." The sheriff nodded toward several thick blocks of longleaf pine. Some were positioned alongside the building; others were being rolled into place by several men. "Frank Worley has had his crew busy with their crosscut saws since first light. They ain't brick pillars, but maybe no knot-headed young'uns will take it into their heads that there's gold inside 'em." He hooked his thumbs in his suspenders and spat a stream of tobacco toward the street, putting the feet of passersby in danger.

Several hours later, Billy Fred and Bobbie June sat on Hal Williams's porch, munching ham and biscuits Jane had sent to them by Hortense. Nick leaned against a leg of the water tower, which serviced the steam engines of the trains, and watched the odd proceedings winding down. It had been a long process, but the building had been returned to its original position. This had been done by the rather ingenious method of having all the hundred or so present, who wanted a chance to look under it for hidden gold, catch hold under the edge of the building and walk it over the four feet or so to where it belonged. There, railroad jacks were placed beneath it and it was raised up to the right height; then the new pine pillars were worked underneath.

Nick would not have believed it possible, but the result was a depot that was almost as good as new, except for missing a few shingles and the stovepipe hanging at an odd angle.

A soft breeze blew away the dust kicked up by a departing wagon and ruffled the boughs of tall pines, which surrounded the town like green sentinels. The tangy smell of pine pitch from the sawdust where logs had been cut for the new pillars scented the air.

Children and dogs ran up and down the street, their exuberance undiminished by a mere lack of gold, even as their parents drifted away. Some people had shoulders slumped with disappointment. Other laughed and joked, taking their failure to locate Gentleman John's gold in stride.

Nick pushed his fingers through his hair and resettled his hat onto the back of his head. He would miss this town.

Removing his cigar, Gus Elverston tipped his hat to Lyddie's grandmother as he passed her. She inclined her head regally and continued on her way back to the hotel. Smiling, the financier made his way on to Nick. "Well, Bennington, the excitement's over and there's no gold. What do you think happened to your grandfather's money?"

"I'm inclined to believe it was spent long ago." Nick looked toward the hotel, rising like a grand dame above the small town. "The hotel was built the year after my grandfather lost to Gentleman John."

"And I'm inclined to agree with you." Gus considered the tip of his cigar for a moment. "Though let's keep it our secret. The legend of the gold and of Gentleman John, himself, once we publicize it, will be our draw. The ambiance of the hotel and the charm of the town will insure they go home and tell their friends, who will come in turn. You're making a wise investment, son, with your money," he added with a twinkle, "and with your heart. Lyddie is a special woman."

Nick straightened. "With my money, maybe. When the business is settled and the renovations to the dining room underway, I'll be heading back to Chicago." The sooner the better, now that he knew there was no future for him here. He wanted to be away as soon as possible.

"Eh?" Gus frowned, his bushy white eyebrows drawing together above his nose. "I thought you were planning to marry the girl, after you worked out the small problem of her current wedded state."

"I was." Nick looked at the westering clouds, gold-rimmed as the sun hid behind them. Would he never learn? "It didn't work out."

"What's brought this on?" Gus asked.

The urge to confide in his friend was at odds with his

desire to nurse his disappointment in private. The need to talk won out. "I thought I could trust her completely."

"And you can't," Gus prompted.

"There something she's hiding. I don't know what it is. She won't tell me. After Evelyn, you must understand how I feel. I can't trust Lyddie if she has to keep secrets from me." He couldn't go through that again.

"I see." The financier tapped the ashes off his cigar, then rolled it between his fingers. "A shame, that. Lyddie is a looker, and she has a backbone of steel. But I understand. After Evelyn, you just can't let someone with secrets be an important part of your life."

Nick straightened, not liking his friend's condescending tone. "Gus—"

"You remember that information I gave you about Homestead Steel's plan to crush its competition?" the older man went on thoughtfully. "You wanted to know my source, but I wouldn't tell you. Did you take that against me?"

"Of course not. I understood that your source was confidential." Nick scowled. "And I realize what you're doing. It isn't the same thing at all."

"It's not?" White brows rode high on the older man's forehead. "Well, I guess you're right. There are lots of reasons for secrets. I don't know what Lyddie's secrets are. I'm sure she has her reasons for them." Gus went on, "If I were you, I'd put my trust in someone who cared so much, she fell down on her knees in the dirt and scratched at the hard earth, scratched until her nails were broken and bleeding. Then, ignoring her pain, she kept on digging with her bare hands. She was frightened for you. And so determined to get you out alive, I had to force her to come away so men could dig there with shovels."

Thrusting his cigar into his mouth, Gus strode away.

Watching him go, Nick realized he'd noticed Lyddie's damaged nails that morning. Never had it occurred to him how she'd hurt her hands.

Suddenly the truth hit him as hard as the depot had last night—he'd asked her to trust him, but he had never given her his trust in return. Far from it, he'd demanded, pried, and probed, guarding a part of his heart as he waited for her to prove he could trust her.

He'd sensed from the first that Lyddie was a woman of honor, a woman he could love and put his faith in. But he'd let his past experience make him doubt.

What a fool he'd been.

Stretching onto her tiptoes, Lyddie plucked the last of the clothespins off the rope line and caught the freshly laundered sheet as it dropped, letting it fall atop the sweet-smelling stack in her arms. The sun was dipping beyond the tops of the tall trees, casting long shadows over the grass. She was getting the last of the clothes in just in time. Soon the dew would be falling, casting damp over everything.

" 'Ere, let me take those inside with these 'ere and I'll fold the lot." Agnes's younger sister, Mabel, already had an armful of clothes, but she deftly caught Lyddie's stack, combining it with her own.

"Thank you. I won't argue." Lyddie smiled gratefully, putting her hands to the small of her back and stretching to relieve the tightness there. She'd hired both of Agnes's sisters to help out for the day, so she could catch up on the laundry.

It had proved a wise decision, as both Molly and Hortense had disappeared shortly after breakfast. They'd been caught up by the excitement of the crowd looking for gold, ignoring what Gram had said about the twins' so-called map. Poor Molly saw a windfall as her only hope of ever getting to go to medical school. Sadly, Lyddie suspected she might be right.

Though she wished things were different, she couldn't protect Molly from disappointment. Maybe, after the main line came to town and the hotel became a Birmingham House, there would be the extra money to fund Molly's dream.

A black swallowtail flitted among the wildflowers as Lyddie walked tiredly back to the washpot to put out what was left of the fire underneath it. Watching the butterfly, Lyddie wished she had the ability to dream. When had she lost it? When her mother died? When her father walked away from the family? Or was it when Gerald Seaton had made her believe in his empty promises?

None of that compared with the fresh pain Nick had dealt her that morning. He'd made her feel that she had found her other half. She'd been ready to take a chance. Damn him, he'd made her believe she could count on him, depend on him to be there, no matter what. And she had believed him. When would she ever learn to guard her heart?

Angry at herself, Lyddie raked the still-glowing coals from beneath the huge cast-iron pot with a stick, then dipped water from the pot with a bucket and doused the embers. Steam rose, scented with the acrid smell of lye from the wash water.

It had been a long day, filled with bending over the rub board, then poking and churning the boiling clothes with a long stick to get them clean, before rinsing and wringing and hanging them up to dry, but the hard work had kept her pain at bay. For as long as she'd kept busy.

Impatiently, Lyddie wiped her eyes with her apron, then picked up the bucket.

"I'm sorry," said a deep voice behind her, a voice she recognized all too well.

Spinning around, she found Nick standing on the path. "Why are you always coming up behind me? Go away."

"I'm sorry I made you cry. I trust you, Lyddie. I trust you." His eyes were dark with pain, his chiseled features set in harsh lines. She could almost believe he was sincere.

Not that it mattered.

"That isn't what you said this morning." She dashed tears from her cheeks and doused the coals again. "And I'm not crying. It's the smoke from the fire. That's all. Go away."

Moving to her, he caught her hand, holding it firmly and examining it when she would have pulled away. A lump formed in his throat as he saw the nails were ragged and broken, some into the quick. Her fingers were red and raw.

"We need to talk." He raised her bruised and raw fingertips to his mouth and gently kissed each one.

"I don't think so," Lyddie said, trying to stem the mad, shimmery feelings that coursed up her arm at the touch of his lips to her fingers. It was followed closely by tears, which pricked her eyes and made her vision swim. The argument they'd had that morning had hurt. It still hurt. "I can't think of anything you'd have to say that I want to hear."

Nick grimaced. He deserved that, and more. Looking into her tawny eyes, he silently begged her to listen.

"Not even that I was wrong?"

Chapter Twenty-six

"What?" Lyddie stared at Nick in disbelief. "You can't be saying this. You can't expect me to listen to you after what you said this morning."

"I was wrong. Forgive me." His voice vibrated with sincerity that made her listen in spite of her hurt.

Nick touched her cheek, searching her gaze. The warm breeze set the springy curls around her temples to dancing, and he smoothed one behind her ear. Then he dropped his hand as bitter memories of broken trust flooded his mind. If she was to forgive him, he knew he had to tell her all, even though it meant taking out and examining things he'd long shut away.

Lyddie was waiting, listening. That was something, at least. Drawing in a deep breath, he expelled it slowly and wondered where to begin.

"My wife betrayed me," he said at length. The words were softly spoken, flat and emotionless. His tone revealed more than if he'd ranted and raged. "She ran away with a man I thought was a friend—a man who happened to be rich enough to buy and sell me," Nick added in the same flat tone, his face a bland mask. "She was four months' pregnant—"

The mask cracked. Pain darkened his eyes as he looked somewhere beyond her, into the forest. "I have no idea if the child was mine."

"Oh, Nick." Lyddie clasped his hand between her own, her heart going out to him. She knew how it had hurt to be betrayed after one night of marriage. How much more he must have suffered!

"Both my wife and her lover were killed in a carriage accident as she was leaving me." Nick drew in a deep breath and shook his head, his gaze finding hers again. "I thought I'd never trust again, Lyddie."

"I'm sorry." Lyddie kissed his hand and cradled it to her chest. "How you felt is understandable. But I know," she stated with certainty, "you're past the bitterness now."

"Because I met you, Lyddie. Life has dealt you just as harsh a hand as it did me, harsher in many ways. But you don't complain. You aren't bitter. You're giving and empathetic. You simply go on from day to day, doing whatever you have to do to keep the hotel running. But I didn't quite believe you were truly all you seemed, even though I wanted to. You see, mistrust had been etched into my soul. And right from the start, I sensed you had secrets. Shadows that kept falling between us.

"I thought before I could give you my trust, I had to see every inch of your soul, to know everything about you, including your secrets. But that isn't the way it works, is it? Trust is taking someone, or something, on faith. And I do have trust in you, Lyddie. I love you so much it's frightening."

Need to believe him quivered through her. Followed closely by fear. If he pulled away again, it would hurt more than she could bear. "And what will happen if you decide you can't trust me after all?" Lyddie wiped at her cheeks.

"That won't happen." Nick pulled her against him, tucking her head under his chin.

"Won't it? You were pretty certain this morning that you never would believe in me. Now you say you do. You could change your mind again." And there was so much he still didn't know. So much she couldn't tell him. "I have secrets, remember?" A sob caught in her throat as her vision blurred. "So just go away, now," she croaked, wrapping her arms about his waist and holding on to him as tightly as she could. "Go away. . . ."

As she cried, she pressed her cheek against his chest. Nick stroked her tense shoulders and back. "So many people in your life have left you, haven't they? Your mother and father. Even the man you trusted with your heart. Then I made you feel you couldn't count on me to be here, either. But I promise, Lyddie, I'll never give you reason to doubt me again."

As the storm of emotion passed, Lyddie's sobs became quiet sniffles. Nick smoothed the wheat-gold waves of her hair, then bent and kissed them.

"Your hair smells like lye soap."

"What?" Lyddie's head snapped up.

"It smells like—"

"I heard you. I just couldn't believe you'd say that." Her tawny eyes were red-rimmed from her tears, but they flashed with angry golden lights. "Oh!" She tried to push out of his arms.

Grinning, Nick held her firmly. "Don't worry. I find I'm starting to like it. You smelled of lye that first night, when I sat by you in the swing, remember?"

"You said it smelled like we were painting the porch!"

His grin widened. "I had to make you angry. Otherwise"—he pulled her close again, his eyes darkening with intent—"I would have lost control and kissed you right then and there. A practical stranger."

Lyddie stilled, her fingers splayed against his warm chest. Her tear splotches stained his white shirt; the sight was oddly endearing. "I don't know how 'practical' I was. I wanted you to kiss me."

"With iron control, I managed to deny indulging myself until the next day, by the falls," he said, his voice deep and resonating. It vibrated through her from where her chest pressed his. "You looked like some pagan goddess resting on the sand, your wonderful hair haloed around you. I could never have resisted claiming that kiss."

Nick pulled the pins from Lyddie's bun as he spoke, then tucked them into his pocket and combed his fingers through her hair, spreading it over her shoulders in a wild, wheat-gold mane.

"I fancied you were Poseidon, rising from the water," she murmured.

"Sorry to disappoint you. I'm only flesh and bone." Slowly, Nick lowered his head, his lips gently touching hers. Then he kissed her again.

Lyddie shivered as warm sensation rushed through her. Rising on her tiptoes, she kissed him back—quick, light, teasing, tantalizing kisses.

Nick growled with frustration as he tried to deepen the contact, only to have her pull away again and again, like a butterfly that couldn't quite decide where to settle. He caught her about the waist and pulled her against him.

Her eyes widened as she felt his growing arousal. Prompted by some impish impulse, she pressed her lower body more tightly against it. "Oh, but I'm not disappointed that you are flesh and bone. Not at all."

"Minx!"

"Me?" Enjoying her power over him, she moved against his erection, laughing as he sucked in his breath sharply.

"Come." He caught her hand and led her into the woods and down the path to the Roaring Falls.

The roar of falling water grew steadily louder, until Nick pushed through the last huckleberry bushes and stepped onto the coarse white sand of the creek bank. Dusk was deepening the shadows under the trees. The last rays of the sun were pried like fingers between the tops of the tall pines, edging the green boughs in gold. It lighted the mist rising above the falls with a rainbow of hues.

Still holding Nick's hand, Lyddie kicked off her shoes and walked out onto the still-warm sand. The air, always cooler near the creek, was sweet with the scent of swamp cyrillas.

Turning to Nick, she fell on her knees in the sand and tugged his hand, inviting him to join her. He needed no further invitation. Dropping to his knees, he caught her face between his palms and kissed her, rekindling the flame of desire.

Lyddie melted against him, opening her mouth, inviting more intimacy.

Hot need slammed into him as he deepened the kiss, probing the soft, sweet recesses of her mouth with his tongue, feeling her tremble in response. The spark had become a raging inferno within a few moments, fuelled by no more than a kiss. Slipping his hands between them, he found her breasts. As he stroked them, Lyddie arched back helplessly, her nipples drawing into hard buds under the fabric of her dress.

"We have too many clothes on," he rasped.

"I know." Leaning away from him, she unbuttoned the row of buttons along the front of her dress, making slow progress, as Nick quickly stripped away his own clothes.

"Let me help you."

Lyddie looked up. Nick stood before her, completely, gloriously naked. His wide shoulders and torso tapered into slim hips. Fully erect, his shaft jutted from a thatch of rusty curls at the apex of his heavily muscled thighs.

"Keep looking at me like that and you'll make me blush," Nick teased. Going down on one knee, he tackled the buttons. Her clothes joined his, and Lyddie went into his arms.

As Nick kissed her, all thought spun away, leaving only sensation—warm skin against warm skin, hard male muscles against her feminine softness, the taste of his mouth, his warm male scent. Hunger and heat filled her.

Brushing aside her fall of silken hair, Nick kissed the side of her neck, then the point of her shoulder, then moved on down her chest to the firm swell of her breast. When he sucked the taut pink tip into his mouth, she moaned, twining her fingers through his curls and pulling him closer, begging for more. Begging him to come together with her.

Laying her back onto her discarded dress, he moved over her and into her, joining with her fully. As he filled her, the woodland around them faded and blurred, the roaring of the falls grew distant and indistinct. All that existed was Nick, over her, moving inside her, until it seemed their souls merged and exploded, scattering on the breeze into the rainbow mist above the falls. Then Nick held her tenderly, whispering love words as they settled back to earth together.

Sometime later, Lyddie woke up, startled by the roar of the falls. Night had fallen. Her cheek was pressed to Nick's bare shoulder. Propping up on her elbow, she found that they had been lying on her dress, and Nick must have pulled her petticoat over their middles. Where her bare legs and shoulder were exposed to the air, her skin felt damp and cold and she shivered.

"You're awake." Nick smiled, a flash of white in the half-light as he sat up. A quarter moon sat above the western trees, casting a faint light over the scene.

"It's late!" Spotting her camisole, she grabbed it. "Hurry. Get dressed!"

She stilled as Nick cupped her breast. Her nipple was still sensitive from his earlier attentions, and pleasure arced through her anew. With an effort of will, she pulled away. "Nick! We have to get back."

"Why? We're already late. May as well be hanged for sheep as for lamb."

"I've never understood what that meant," she complained, still trying to sort out her clothes and shake them free of sand.

He made it more difficult by nibbling her neck, his hand slipping to her abdomen as he imagined their loving bearing fruit.

Circling her with his arms, he pulled her back against his warm chest. She felt safe and sheltered and cherished and loved. All the things she'd longed for, without even knowing it, she had found in this man's arms.

"I want to marry you." He breathed the words against the back of her neck and they shivered down her spine, shattering her fragile illusions.

Nick knew he'd said the wrong thing again as Lyddie stiffened beneath his hands.

"But right now I want to go for a swim in the starlight." He stood, grabbing her hand and pulling her up.

"A swim?" She pulled back, digging in her heels. "You're daft! The water is freezing at midday."

"Then it can't be any colder at night." He held on to her hand when she would have pulled free, dragging her along with him. "Besides," he laughed, "your hair still smells of lye."

"Lye!" Laughing, she suddenly stopped resisting and lurched toward him, throwing him off balance and pushing him into the water.

Holding on to her hand, he pulled her in with him.

Lyddie held her finger to her lips. "Sssh-sh-sh—"

"Are you imitating a snake?" Nick whispered.

Pressing her hand to her mouth, she dissolved into giggles and leaned against the old pecan tree at the side of the hotel as she tried to control them. "Hush!" she finally got out. "We have to be quiet!"

"You're the one making all the noise," Nick murmured.

"You're making me!" she whispered back.

"I never made you imitate a snake." His tone was aggrieved. "In fact, I prefer you don't. I've been afraid I might trod on one in the dark."

"Nick!" Lyddie buried her face against the damp fabric of his shirt as a new fit of giggles took her. She couldn't remember the last time she had felt so happy, so alive.

Moving closer, he pressed her against the huge bole of the tree, running his hands up and down her torso. "I'd much rather we imitate Apollo and Daphne."

"You're, you're . . . you're terrible!" she whispered, and laughed as she remembered the myth.

"You skewer my ego. I thought my lovemaking was at least passable. Actually"—he leaned close to her ear—"I thought it my greatest talent."

As she dissolved into muffled laughter, he nuzzled her ear, loving the sound. He wanted to hold her and tell her how much he loved her, and how much he wanted to wed her, that he would be there always. But that wasn't what she wanted to hear.

Nick resisted the urge to ask probing questions that would spoil the moment. She would tell him when she was ready. If not, then he would trust her.

"Hold still while I empty my shoes," Lyddie whispered. Catching his shoulder for balance as Nick held on to her waist, she shook the creek sand out of first one shoe, then the other. "There. I—"

"Hush." Nick touched his fingers to her lips, cutting off the rest of what she would have said.

As Lyddie listened, a muffled voice came to her out of the dark. A man's voice. "I hear it," she breathed, barely daring to whisper. "It must be some treasure hunters, probably digging up the yard."

"Come on." Nick took the lead, moving quietly.

Keeping her hand on his shoulder as he led, Lyddie followed closely through the dark. With the setting of the moon, the night was lit only by the brilliant stars.

Nick stopped. Lyddie realized there was a man's and a woman's voice, coming from somewhere near the old well. As she listened, she recognized one of them. No, it couldn't be. . . .

Easing around Nick, she blinked, focusing on the two shadowy figures sitting on the boards atop the well, pointing up at the sky.

"Now, when will we be able to see Sirius, the Dog Star? It should be appearing this week, shouldn't it?" the woman purred.

The voice was unmistakable.

"Hortense!" Lyddie marched forward, ready to send her sister back inside the hotel with a flea in her ear.

In the dark, Lyddie ran into the wheelbarrow the twins had left beside the well, sending it crashing over. The broken crockery pieces and old tin cans made a terrible racket as they tumbled out onto the ground.

"Ouch!" She hopped, rubbing her aching shin.

"Who's there?" Hortense cried. "Stay away, you—*oh! Help!"* The cry ended in a scream. She disappeared, followed by a distant splash.

Chapter Twenty-seven

"I tried to hold on to her. I really did," Willard Turlow croaked.

Pushing the telegraph operator out of her way, Lyddie bent over the well. "Hortense! Are you all right?"

"Of course I'm not all right! Get me out of here!" Hortense's disembodied voice rose an octave. "Please hurry! There's something down here—it has teeth! Get me out!" The plea ended in sobs.

"She doesn't seem to be injured," Nick told Lyddie, squeezing her fingers. "And the water must not be very deep. She'll be okay until we can get her out."

"Thank God," Lyddie breathed. Then the full impact of what this meant hit her. Cold washed through her veins, and her stomach clenched.

It was all over.

The beautiful dream she'd only just dared to let herself dream was over. . . .

Drawing in a deep breath, she told herself she'd think about that later. First she'd worry about getting Hortense out of the well. Then she would face whatever consequences came.

Nick told Lyddie, "Get some lanterns and wake the others. Then we'll figure out what to do."

As Lyddie ran toward the hotel, Nick tossed the rest of the boards off the top of the well, to assure none were accidentally knocked in on the hapless girl. He called down the well, "We'll get you out. Try to stay calm."

"Calm!" she shrieked, then sobbed louder. "There's something down here, I tell you!"

A short time later, Lyddie had brought out lanterns and fetched Molly and the twins. Nick dispatched Billy Fred to get a rope, and told Bobbie June to fuel the carbide light she'd brought outside with her. Willard Turlow had vanished, she noticed.

As Nick talked to Hortense, telling her how they planned to get her out, a strange calm took hold of Lyddie. Feeling as though she was watching herself from a distance, she righted the overturned wheelbarrow and started picking up the old cans and other trash that had spilled, to make certain it was out of the way when they pulled her sister out.

Gerald would be found. Any moment now.

It was as if time slowed as she waited for it to happen. Picking up half a broken crockery bowl, she held it, at a loss for a moment as to why she held it.

Nick took it away from her and tossed it into the wheelbarrow, then he caught her hands. "Your fingers are like ice." He searched her face in the lantern light, his concern written in his eyes. Then he kissed her fingers and folded her hands between his warm palms. "Don't worry, Lyddie. We'll get her out. I promise."

Lifting her gaze to his face, she studied the lean planes and angles, harshly lit by the lantern. There was strength. Determination. Caring. She wasn't sorry that she had known him, no matter that the dream would all be over soon. "I love you."

Nick stilled. Closing his eyes, he savored the words he'd waited to hear, trying to ignore the feeling of alarm they raised in him. There was a hopelessness in her voice he couldn't figure out.

No. He'd just waited so long to hear this, he was afraid it wasn't real, he told himself. "I love you, too." He kissed her fingers again. "When this is all over, we'll talk about the future."

As he spoke, Lyddie shook her head. "Just know that I love you. I do love you."

Unease grew and shimmied down his spine. "Lyddie, what is it?"

The look in her eyes held infinite regret. Blinking, she glanced at where Molly was lifting a lantern above the well. Hortense's sobs grew louder. "You'd better go."

Molly said, "This lantern isn't much good. I can just make out Hortense huddled to one side."

"Lemme see." The carbide light hissed to life as Bobbie June touched a Lucifer match to it. Scrambling to her feet, she shook out the match and shined the light into the well. And a scream came out of the well.

"What's that?" Bobbie June shrieked.

"What?" Molly peered into the well, then gasped, "Oh, my God!"

"What is it?" Nick caught Bobbie June as she sprang backward in fright and steadied her on her feet. Inside the well, Hortense screamed again and again.

Looking pale, Bobbie June handed him the light.

Flashing it in the well, he spotted Hortense, wailing as

she huddled against one side. On the opposite side sat a grinning skeleton, the black water lapping at its naked bones.

"It was awful. Just awful." Hortense sat wrapped in a blanket, a hot cup of coffee cradled in her hands. With Molly's help, she had cleaned up and put on dry clothes, but she was still badly shaken. "I thought that rope would cut me in two and I'd fall back on that . . . that thing!"

"We had to get you out." Molly took a seat at the table. "You'll need medical treatment after being in that water—very fouled after flesh rotted in it."

"Molly!" Hortense paled.

"You'll likely take the ague if not thoroughly purged. I'll check my books on how best to proceed," Molly said enthusiastically, ignoring Hortense's negative shakes of her head. "But first I want some coffee." She poured herself a cup from the clay pot on the table.

Hortense's voice held a wild note. "You're not purging me! I've been through enough! I'll likely get nervous prostration as it is!"

In a show of sisterly affection, Bobbie June hugged her blanket-wrapped shoulders. "It's over now, 'Tense. Put it out of your mind."

"But it was grinning at me!" The coffeecup trembled in Hortense's hands, and she set it down.

"It was not grinning." Molly sipped her coffee, then added, "Skeletons just look that way. It's the lack of flesh." Turning to Nick, who stood at the window looking out, she asked, "Do you think it will be long before we can pull it out? I've never gotten to look at a human skeleton before."

Nick looked away from the sunrise he'd been contemplating while waiting for Lyddie, who had gone upstairs to change clothes and freshen up. "When Billy Fred gets back with the sheriff, we'll turn things over to him. He'll probably get in touch with the coroner before acting."

"The sheriff is the county coroner," Bobbie June supplied. "Which is pretty convenient."

"I wonder how he or she died." Molly sipped her coffee thoughtfully.

"How who died?" Gram asked, leaning heavily on her cane as she entered the room.

"Good morning, Mrs. Moreland. You missed the excitement last night," Nick told her.

"Eh?" Arching a gray brow, she met his gaze levelly. "I heard ever'body making a racket, right enough. But if there's one thing I learned after all these years, most things are just as exciting in the morning, after a good night's sleep. I figured somebody would fetch me if I was needed."

Nick pulled out a chair for her. With a gracious nod of her head, she sat down. "So, what happened?" she asked of her grandchildren, leaning the cane on the edge of the table.

"Hortense fell into the well," Bobbie June said, her eyes gleaming.

"Eh? Well, how'd you manage that?" Her grandmother looked askance at Hortense. "And in the middle of the night?"

Bobbie June rushed on. "Gram, that wasn't the exciting part. When we went to pull her out, we found a skeleton!"

The older lady digested this news with interest, but not the total shock Nick might have expected.

But then again, it could be that she was just made of strong stuff—the same strong fiber that she'd passed on to Lyddie.

As if summoned by his thoughts, Lyddie entered the dining room, tucking a pin into the bun atop her head. She had changed her clothes and now looked her usual neatly dressed, practical self. However, the look in her eyes chilled Nick. Flat and unemotional, it was the look of one who had no hope.

"Who could it be?" Molly asked. "The body, I mean."

"Gerald Seaton," Nick supplied, watching Lyddie carefully. His gut clenched as she gazed at him with something akin to relief.

"Eh?" Gram stared at him in mild surprise.

Moving to Lyddie, Nick squeezed her shoulder, wanting to reassure her that, whatever happened, he would be there for her. "I think we need to talk."

She covered his hand with her own for an instant, then shook her head. "There's nothing to say." Turning away, she moved to the kitchen door. "Excuse me. I have things to take care of."

Nick followed her into the kitchen. "Lyddie?"

"Jane, please tell Agnes we'll need her sisters to help out indefinitely, if she's interested," Lyddie said, barely glancing at Nick. The cook was in the process of cutting up a duck. "And you'll have to take charge of shopping for the kitchen from now on."

Jane paused, shaking her head. "Don't talk like that."

A sense of foreboding gripped him. "You knew your husband's body was in the well." Clenching his fists, Nick silently railed at Lyddie to deny it.

"She hasn't done nothing that wasn't right." Her black eyes flashing, Jane brought the cleaver down sharply, splitting the duck in half.

"Jane, I want to help her, but she has to talk to me."

"I have nothing to say to you." Lyddie shook her head. "Go away."

"I have something to say to you, and I'm not going away. Ever." Catching Lyddie's arm, he led her out to the swing on the side porch, where he could talk to her privately, hoping she would open up.

As she sat down, that flat hopelessness was still in her eyes. Nick sat beside her and took her hand, wrapping her cold fingers in his own. "Let me help."

Sighing, she shook her head. "Just leave, Nick. It was a nice fantasy, wasn't it? But I always knew it would end. That was the secret I couldn't tell you. I knew once it came out . . ." She shook her head. "Just go."

"I'm not going anywhere," he said, angry that she was shutting him out when she needed him. "We have a future to build together. And I don't just mean the restaurant."

"There's not any future for us! Don't you understand? You'd be a fool to honor the partnership. Under the circumstances, Gram will probably bow out of the agreement herself."

"Lyddie—"

"This is my problem. Stay out of it. Go back to Chicago," she snapped. She couldn't let him stay and get involved. He was a good investigator. He might find out the truth.

As her tawny eyes flashed, Nick felt a small measure of relief. Her anger was infinitely better than the hopelessness she'd shown before.

"You knew Seaton's body was in the well," he said again.

Her mask fell into place again as she tried to shut him out. Having none of it, he went on, "But you didn't kill him."

Turning away, she looked out at the new morning. "Yes, I did."

Fear closed Nick's throat, making it hard to breathe as he examined the flat statement for truth. "How?"

Lyddie looked annoyed. "I . . . , ah . . ." She clenched her hands into the folds of her skirt. "He was walking away from me. I grabbed that heavy brass candlestick that sits on the desk and hit him, as hard as I could, and he fell on the floor and died."

"This was in the hotel lobby?" Nick asked.

"Yes. Almost at the foot of the stairs."

"What are you saying?" Lyddie's grandmother stood in the open French window, a look of shock on her delicately lined features.

Nick remembered she had shown a strange reaction to the news that there was a body in the well. She had been more surprised that Nick had guessed the identity than the notion that it was Gerald Seaton.

The older lady regained her composure rapidly, lifting her chin. "If you go believing that, you're not as bright as I take you for, young man. I did the sculpin in myself. I 'spect that Hortense told you I had took my cane to him one time and sent him out the door. When he come back, I knew there was no help for it, so I took my cane to him again."

"No, Gram." Shaking her head, Lyddie looked truly frightened. "Don't say such things!"

"Be sensible, child. I'm old. You have your whole life before you." Her grandmother caned her way to them. "And this nice young man, who loves you."

Nick stood as she drew near. "Your granddaughter wants to protect you, Mrs. Moreland."

"Aye. She's got a right fine sense of duty." She looked at Lyddie with pride. "But I'll own this deed, m'girl."

"Don't listen to her," Lyddie said to Nick, catching his sleeve. "I told you, I did it."

"One thing is certain," Nick said in a no-nonsense tone, "we need to sort out the truth of this. Then we can decide what to do. And we should do it before the sheriff arrives."

"But—" Lyddie began.

"No 'buts,' " Nick told her firmly. "We'll get to the truth. Now, show me where it happened."

Both women looked at him mutinously.

"Look, have you ever thought of the possibility that neither of you killed him?"

Lyddie and her grandmother looked at each other. Nick's instincts said both were lying to protect the other.

And if that was the case, then who had really killed Gerald Seaton?

Chapter Twenty-eight

"It was right here." Lyddie pointed to a spot about ten feet from the foot of the stairs, halfway into the hall, at the end of which was her grandmother's room.

"It was night. Was it dark in the lobby?" Nick asked.

"We'd left oil lights burning that we'd used to decorate for the wedding." Lyddie drew in a deep breath, pushing away the bitter emotions the memories evoked. "It was well lit. When Gerald came down the stairs, I hit him behind the head with that candlestick there on the front desk, and—"

"Please"—Nick held up his hand—"no fairy tales."

"But, Nick—"

"Here comes your grandmother. We'll see what she has to say."

Lyddie thought Gram had aged ten years as she caned her way down the hall from the family dining room. The observation made Lyddie more determined than ever to protect her.

"I sent Bobbie June to the general store to fetch me some arthritis liniment, and told Molly to take 'Tense and put her to bed, doctoring her however she thought best." Gram chuckled. "Molly was praising the purgative powers of mineral salts for warding off ill humors when she hauled her sister toward the backstairs. So"—the tiny woman crossed her hands atop her cane—"now we can get this tangle straight without lots a ears."

She looked up at Nick. "You want to see where I did it, eh?" She tapped her cane on the floor, at the same spot where Lyddie had pointed. "He fell right there, after I whacked him a good one upside the head with my cudgel, here." She tapped the stout cane again. "Heard his neck snap. A terrible sound." The older lady seemed quite pleased with the gruesomeness of her confession.

"But it was the back of his head that was bloodied. He was lying facedown and there was a big gash on it. Blood was everywhere. The rug was soaked." Lyddie put her hand to her throat, feeling ill at the memory. It had been a horrible scene. "I used it to drag him out to the well and threw it in after him."

"So that's what happened to my Persian rug!" Her grandmother scowled. Then she realized she'd given her innocence away. "I mean, I was so mad, I didn't remember I whacked him on the back of the head, instead of beside it. Or that the rug was ruined."

"Mrs. Moreland, you didn't kill him," Nick told her.

"She didn't!" Lyddie realized suddenly. All this time, she'd thought her grandmother had laid into Gerald in a fit of rage, as she had earlier that evening. But had that been the case, Gram would have known where his injury was and that he was lying on her prized rug. When Lyddie saw her standing in the door of her bedroom, that must have been as close as her grandmother got to the scene.

Suddenly, Lyddie felt like a stone had been lifted from her heart. "You didn't kill him, Gram."

"If I say that's how it was, you can't prove I didn't," her grandmother said stubbornly.

"You don't need to protect Lyddie, Mrs. Moreland. She didn't kill him either," Nick said thoughtfully.

"Eh? Then who did?" the older lady demanded. "Someone had to do the sculpin in!"

"That's what we need to figure out." Nick frowned as he imagined the scene.

"Lyddie and me were the only ones here, 'sides Hortense, who was in her room. And it wasn't her—she was just a young'un of fourteen. After the sculpin cut up ugly at the wedding supper, I had sent Molly and the twins to spend the night at Jane's house. I had a feeling there might be trouble."

"You said Seaton was drunk. How drunk?"

Lyddie said, "He'd broke out his whiskey samples at our wedding supper. He'd been drinking a few hours, I guess, when he died."

"He was still spry enough to catch Lyddie when she run downstairs to get away from 'em. He caught her in the middle of the lobby and threw her to the floor, demanding she tell him where the gold was or he'd beat it outta her." Gram seethed. "I never been so mad in my life, and I would have killed him then and there, if he'd not caught a hold a my cane."

"He would have hit Gram with it, but I had run behind the front desk and pulled my father's old army pistol out. I cocked it and told him to leave and never come back."

"He left?" Nick asked.

She nodded.

"How long was it before he returned?" He resisted the urge to take her in his arms and erase the shadows from her eyes. If Gerald Seaton hadn't been dead, he would have been tempted to kill him himself.

"A couple of hours. He did sound like he was stumbling more, by that time. Bumping against the walls as he went up the stairs," Gram said. "Then I heard him upstairs, bellowing for Lyddie to let him in and rattling her door."

"Lyddie, you had locked your door so he couldn't get in. Did you keep your father's gun with you?" Nick asked.

"I had left it downstairs." She sighed. "Gerald came back when he remembered my father's old pistol won't fire. It's just a keepsake."

"What happened then?" Nick prompted.

"He said he was going to get an ax and he bloody well would open the door. That I didn't have any right to throw him out, 'cause he was my husband. Then I heard him going toward the stairs." Tears welled in Lyddie's eyes. "I never loved Gerald, but I had liked him. I thought he was a good man." She blinked back tears. "How could I have been so wrong about him?"

Nick folded her in his arms, unable to resist. "It's over now," he murmured.

"Aye, 'cause I took my cudgel 'ere—"

"Gram, please!"

"Mrs. Moreland!"

Nick and Lyddie spoke at once, both looking askance at her.

Sighing, the older lady shrugged. "Well, you tell me what happened, then, Pinkerton."

"I will." Kissing Lyddie on the forehead, he released

her and went halfway up the stairs, then turned around. "Lyddie, you could hear Seaton as he made his way down. Maybe bumping the wall"—he demonstrated, falling against the wall, then the banister—"like this."

"Yes. I think. It's been a long time, but I remember he was making a lot of noise."

"He must have been very drunk, then. Did he talk to anyone? Were there other voices?" As Nick came down the stairs, the hooked rug caught his notice. Someone had tacked it down, so it wouldn't slide on the polished heart-of-pine floor.

"Just his voice. He was cursing and shouting all the while, and his speech was slurred. Then—" she hesitated and looked to her grandmother, uncertain. What if it had been Gram?

"Trust me," Nick said, drawing her gaze back to him as he rejoined her. The look in his eyes implored her to have faith.

She did trust him, Lyddie realized. With her life. More than that, with her heart. He would protect Gram.

Drawing in a deep breath, she went on. "There was a heavy thud, and he was quiet for a while. I listened, wondering if I should come to see what had happened, but I was afraid he was just trying to lure me down. Just as I did start to come down, there was a groan, and he cursed. Then there was another big thud. After that last time he was quiet again. That time he stayed quiet."

"Two heavy thuds?" Nick looked surprised. "How long between them?"

"I don't know. It couldn't have been long. But it did seem forever."

"I heard the same thing," Gram confirmed. "Maybe a half minute passed betwixt the two."

"After you heard the second 'thump' you waited a long

time before coming downstairs," Nick surmised. "And you waited before opening your door, Mrs. Moreland."

"Oh, do call me 'Gram.' I 'spect you'll be my grandson-in-law sooner than later."

"Gram." Nick grinned.

"I waited quite a spell," Gram said. "When I did bind up my heart and get courage to open my door, I seen Lyddie bending over him with that brass candlestick."

Nick surmised, "And she saw you clutching your cudgel."

"Aye." Gram nodded. "I guess she did. She told me to go to bed, that she'd take care of him." To Lyddie, she said, "I never doubted you did what you had to do. I just never imagined you were trying to protect me." Arching a gray brow, she asked, "But if you didn't do it, who was the culprit?"

"Your Persian rug, Mrs. More—Gram." Nick surveyed the distance to the base of the stairs, a little more than a body length. "He slipped on it and hit his head."

"It's not possible," Lyddie said. "How could Gerald have slipped on it? He was lying facedown on top of it."

"The rug was normally at the foot of the stairs, but it was out of place. It was finely made, wasn't it?"

"That it was," Gram said.

"And that meant it was well knotted on a good backing, making it stiff and more prone to slide than to wrinkle." Going to the stairs, Nick stood on the last stair and turned around to face them. "Seaton was drunk. When he stumbled off the last step, the rug shot out from beneath his foot and he fell, hitting his head on the edge of the last riser. It was a very hard lick, knocking him out and probably cracking his skull.

"When he came to a short time later, he was already dead—figuratively speaking. He just didn't know it. He staggered to his feet, then fell forward atop the rug, where he lost a great deal of blood as he died." Nick met Lyddie's gaze.

"There was so much." Lyddie shivered. "After I dragged him out to the well, I cleaned it all up, I thought. But the next day I found a large spot on the bottom stair and wondered how it had gotten there. I thought I might have carried it on my shoe."

"Here's just one problem with the whole thing, as far as I can see," Gram said emphatically. "Everybody, including the sheriff, knows the polecat got drunk and mean at the wedding supper and after, showing his true stripes. And him coming up missing like that kinda sealed it in ever'body's heads. The sheriff ain't likely to believe the sculpin was kind enough to slip and kill hisself—nor would a jury, come to that. Not after Lyddie hid him in the well." Shaking her head, she added, "People plain like to believe the worst."

"I hear the sheriff and Billy Fred now," Lyddie said. Looking through the lobby and out of the front door, she added, "They're at the gate. What should we say?"

Gram clutched her cane in a menacing posture. "That I did the polecat in—"

She shrugged as Lyddie glared at her in exasperation.

"I think both of you should say as little as possible. Let me do the talking." Moving to Lyddie, Nick caught her hand, giving it a reassuring squeeze. "Don't worry. We will think of something." He grinned. "Now that I know you're a widow, I have plans for us. And they don't included getting married to a woman in jail."

Gram chuckled.

Lyddie blinked, at a loss as to why being happy made her want to cry. As Nick met the sheriff at the door, she was surprised to find she wasn't really anxious. Now that she knew what really happened, she didn't need to protect her grandmother. Though just how Nick was going to convince the sheriff that there was a perfectly logical reason Gerald was in the old well and quite dead, she had no idea.

Sheriff Woods paused in the doorway, pulled off his battered hat, and nodded at Nick, then to Gram. "Mornin', Mrs. Moreland. Lyddie." He replaced his hat. "I can't say I was surprised to have Billy Fred here beatin' on my door first light. Gettin' where I see him right often."

"But this time it ain't got anything to do with Bobbie June and me," Billy Fred said, sounding pleased by the fact. He stood on the front walk, a long ladder beside him and a coil of rope on his shoulder. "We wouldn't a been so long, but we went down to the railroad depot and borrowed these. Guess they'll come in handy."

"Guess they will." Nick nodded.

"Word has a way of spreadin'," Sheriff Woods said. "If you don't mind lending a hand in this, Nick, let's get on down to it, a'fore we have people ten-deep gettin' in the way."

After they'd gone to the well, the men positioned the ladder inside the well, and Lyddie watched, Gram at her side. She could scarcely believe it would all soon be over.

Bobbie June appeared, clutching a stoppered bottle, which she thrust into her grandmother's hands. "I had to wait for Mr. Graves to have breakfast before he'd open the store," she said, aggrieved. "I almost missed everything!"

Hortense and Molly were right behind her. "A ladder!" Hortense glared at her brother. "Why didn't you use a ladder last night? Being pulled up by that rope near about cut me in two!"

"It wasn't too easy on us, neither!" Billy Fred shot back. "If Nick hadn't been as strong as he is, we'd never have hauled you out."

Sheriff Woods cocked a curious brow. "Billy Fred never did explain just how you ended up in the well and found what you did. Last night, did you say?"

Blushing furiously, Hortense mumbled something about Orion's Belt and the Big Dipper, then stammered further into incoherence.

Lyddie took pity on her sister. "Sheriff, if you don't mind, you could ask Hortense all this later. I'm anxious to get on with this, and, well . . ."

Patting her arm in a fatherly fashion, Sheriff Woods nodded. "I'm sure you are, Lyddie. Billy Fred said Nick here thinks it is likely Seaton down there."

"It would explain what happened to him," Nick said, meeting Lyddie's gaze reassuringly.

"That it would," Sheriff Woods agreed.

As Nick and the sheriff discussed the best course of action, Lyddie heard Bobbie June quietly tell Hortense that she would come up with a story for her that would leave the older girl smelling like a rose—in return for a favor.

"I don't want to lie," Hortense whispered.

"You don't have to," Bobbie June said confidently, "if you just tell the truth right."

As Hortense agreed, Lyddie sighed inwardly. She had hoped her youngest sister would have learned her lesson. . . .

Because of the sheriff's age and Nick's investigative experience, Nick climbed down the ladder, while the sheriff and Billy Fred steadied it at the top. Lyddie found herself holding her breath as the sheriff and Billy Fred leaned over the lip of the well and carefully hauled up the rope. Hortense shrieked, putting her hands over her eyes, and Molly rushed to get a closer look as they lifted out the gruesome prize.

Lyddie caught a camellia bush and held on as her legs threatened to give way.

Choosing a clear place on the ground, the men carefully laid out the skeleton. It still wore boots, some scraps of fabric, and a leather belt hung from the hip bone. A rotting rope was still tied about the chest.

"That must be what happened to the old well rope," Billy Fred said, prodding the rotted hemp around the rib bones with his bare toe. He looked at the crossbar above the well. "It used to be tied up there. It's been missing a good while."

"It's hard to tell, but that end looks like it broke. Which might explain how he got down there. Question now is why would he have been lettin' hisself down in a well in the middle of winter and at night?" The sheriff scratched his head, then replaced his battered hat.

He looked at Lyddie. Obviously waiting for an answer. She couldn't speak at the moment. Standing was taking all her will.

From the depths of the well, Nick called out for them to untie the rope from the body and to throw it back down. Looking curious, the sheriff and Billy Fred did as he asked, then held the ladder again as Nick climbed out.

"It's going to be all right," Nick told Lyddie enigmatically.

To the sheriff, he said, "I found something else interesting while I was down there. I think it'll answer some questions." He passed the rope over the old crossbar as he spoke, then tugged it, testing the strength. "If you'll give me a hand, we'll pull it out."

Moments later, after a difficult time pulling whatever

it was, the men heaved one final time, raising an old crockery churn out of the well. It spun at the end of the rope, and the crossbar creaked ominously.

Billy Fred grabbed it and guided it over the well wall, then on down as Nick and the sheriff lowered it slowly. The instant it touched the ground, Bobbie June thrust her hand into it and pulled out several wet, shining gold coins.

"Well, I'll be. So that's where John put it," Gram murmured.

Chapter Twenty-nine

"Doesn't Gram look nice? I think having a male friend agrees with her," Lyddie said, leaning back against Nick. They stood on the veranda outside Gentleman John's room, enjoying the summer afternoon. As she watched, Gram laughed at something Gus Elverston said as they strolled down the brick walkway. They made a handsome pair, with Gus dressed in his usual dapper white and Gram in her dark silk blouse and skirt, her newly reacquired diamond and amethyst brooch winking in the sun. Gus was laughing at whatever Gram retorted as they disappeared from sight beneath the edge of the veranda.

Lyddie smiled. Her grandmother seemed happier and more relaxed than she had in a long time. "It was very good of Gus to help her buy back her brooch. Though I do wonder just how he managed. Elvira seemed quite taken with it."

"Gus owns a share in the St. Louise Opera House,"

Nick said. "He offered Elvira an extended engagement." He paused to kiss Lyddie's temple, where springy little curls were blowing in the breeze, then added, "It was really good business on Gus's part. Elvira does have tremendous talent."

"I'll take your word for it," Lyddie said dryly.

"Jealous?"

Lyddie snorted. "Hardly!"

Nick chuckled. "If you say so." Deciding it was best to change the subject, he said, "I'm glad the sheriff decided that Seaton was after the gold when his rope broke, dropping him into the well. 'Death by misadventure' seems an appropriate ruling."

"It's all behind us now. Let's not talk about it," Lyddie said. "It's too lovely a day." Cottony clouds dotted the bright blue sky, beneath which puffs of black smoke boiled as a train chugged, leaving the depot. A farm wagon rumbled along the street, and two small boys chased it, a dog yapping energetically at their heels. The legendary gold had at last been found, but nothing had changed in sleepy Crossroads.

Giving proof to her thoughts, a large, rather dilapidated tent had been erected in the corner of the yard, completely hiding the old well from view. A queue of people stood outside the closed flap, ready to pay a nickel for a peek.

"I can't believe Bobbie June and Billy Fred found a way to turn a profit from it all." As Lyddie watched, Billy Fred collected money from those in line before Bobbie June guided them inside. As the people exited, Billy Fred sold them pieces of broken crockery from the old wheelbarrow.

Nick laughed. "I find that easy to believe—it's been a full week since they knocked the depot off its foundations. It was time for them to come up with some scheme—especially considering that they only got enough money from the gold to pay the railroad for damages. The amazing thing to me is how they find the time."

The railroad had agreed not to prosecute the twins for either the derailment or the vandalism of the depot in return for full reimbursement, as well as six months of free labor. Hal Williams had them whitewashing the depot, as well as sawing down and chopping up oak to replenish the wood boxes of the steam engines that stopped in Crossroads. Hal's theory was, if they were tired enough, the twins wouldn't have energy to derail any trains.

Nick thought Hal had underestimated the pair. "And how long do you think they'll get away with selling those chunks of old bowls and crockery for authentic souvenir pieces from the gold churn?"

"Until someone spots them digging through the town dump and realizes what they're about." She sighed, refusing to worry about it. "Well, I *am* glad Molly has all the money she could possibly need for medical school. The money that would have been left over from Gram's brooch, after the railroad was repaid, would not even have been enough to get her started."

Nick nodded toward a couple strolling down the brick walkway. "Frank Worley told me he and Hortense have set a date."

"Hortense told me." Lyddie smiled. "I am glad for her."

Shaking his head, Nick said, "I'm not certain how she convinced him that she was only stargazing when she fell into the well."

"But she *was* only stargazing," Lyddie protested. "Although I think she has Bobbie June to thank for convincing Frank she was alone at the time—I'm not certain how."

"Bobbie June has a talent. But I wonder why she would do that for Hortense."

"Sisterly affection?" Lyddie grinned as Nick chuckled. "Actually, Bobbie June had to patch things up between 'Tense and Frank, so Frank would lend her his old tent when 'Tense asked him to. He has a new one the logging crew uses.

"But, Nick," Lyddie added, feeling compelled to defend her sister, "you have to have guessed, for all that she's an awful flirt, 'Tense isn't given to easy virtue."

"She's not." Nick bent and nuzzled Lyddie's neck in a most suggestive way. "But I'm glad her older sister is more flexible."

"Oh, you!" Lyddie gasped, then giggled as he whispered an intriguing suggestion as to a way they might test the flexibility of her virtue. "In the middle of the afternoon, Mr. Bennington?" she asked, turning to face him, obviously intrigued.

"Indeed, Mrs. Bennington." He kissed her on her lips, a sweet, tantalizing promise. Lifting his head, he searched her face, finding no shadows or secrets, only love shining in her tawny eyes. It had been one of his wisest decisions to convince Lyddie to skip a prolonged engagement and to marry him as soon as he could get a preacher to perform the ceremony.

She pressed closer, smiling as she felt his growing hardness against her abdomen. "After five days of wedded bliss, I'd have thought you would be showing signs of fatigue!"

"You underestimate me." He kissed her, then again, deepening the contact as she wound her arms about his neck and pressed closer.

Lifting his head at length, Nick said hoarsely, "I think I'd better escort you inside, Mrs. Bennington, before we give the twins another event they might charge an audience to view."

CONNIE MASON

Down and out, his face on wanted posters across the West, Sam Gentry needs a job. And the foreman of the B & G ranch is hiring cowhands. But who is the behind-the-scenes owner the ramrod mentioned? Surely this Lacey isn't the same one who has haunted his dreams for the last five years. This Texas rancher can't possibly be the dyed-in-the-wool Yankee whose betrayal sent him to a Northern prison camp. Most unlikely of all, this widowed mother simply cannot be the hot-blooded wife who once warmed his bed. Yet one look in her emerald eyes tells him the impossible has happened. How can he take a paycheck from the golden-haired beauty when what he really wants to do is take her back in his arms?

___4865-5 $5.99 US/$6.99 CAN

Dorchester Publishing Co., Inc.
P.O. Box 6640
Wayne, PA 19087-8640

Please add $1.75 for shipping and handling for the first book and $.50 for each book thereafter. NY, NYC, and PA residents, please add appropriate sales tax. No cash, stamps, or C.O.D.s. All orders shipped within 6 weeks via postal service book rate. Canadian orders require $2.00 extra postage and must be paid in U.S. dollars through a U.S. banking facility.

Name____
Address______________________________________
City____________________State______Zip_________
I have enclosed $________ in payment for the checked book(s).
Payment <u>must</u> accompany all orders. ☐ Please send a free catalog.
CHECK OUT OUR WEBSITE! www.dorchesterpub.com

Coming in June 2001
from **Leisure Books . . .**